THE GUILD IN THE GRANARY

ഇൻ

A Granary Guild Novel

Alma Lynn Thompson

McDiggs Publishing

THE GUILD IN THE GRANARY

McDiggs Publishing

The publisher acknowledges the copyright holder of the individual work as follows:
Copyright © 2008 by Alma Lynn Thompson

McDiggs Publishing
4817 Heycross Drive
Grove City, Ohio 43123

visit: www.McDiggsPublishing.com

ISBN: 978-0-9820964-0-6
Printed and bound in the United States of America

Dedications

Janis Biggs – Dedicated to the women who nurtured my creative side. My maternal grandmother, Alma Oksness; my mother, June Hintz; my mother-in-law; Martha Biggs. My husband who has endured the writing process. And last but not least, my dear writing buddies Mary and Diana.

Diana Forrester - To all the folks who carried on and saved me a place at the quilting frame while I was off doing other things for years and years. Thank you.

Mary Clark - Dedicated to the special women in my life that have inspired me to reach for the stars, to never give up, even through the worst of times, and most of all they shared with me their Belief In ME! Mom, Jorgy, Carol, Terry, Sue, Bert, A & L, Mailey, Kristen, Diana, Aggie, the list goes on and on!

Acknowledgements

The learning curve for writing this book has been steep. Thanks to members of the Monday Morning Book Club at Always in Stitches who helped with character development and served as early readers. They are still furiously reading: Rosemary Cline, Charlene Hayes, Wilma Rogers, Earlene Sanborn, Kathy Stumpf, Judy Phillips, Sheryll Hatfield and Terry Crosier.

Also special thanks to all the people who advised us on technical aspects of law enforcement, building maintenance and autopsy results: Franklin County Coroner, Brad Lewis, Steve Jenkins, Shawn Hannon and Jason Rafeld.

Also those who helped us with actual production and publication of the book: Audrey Cox, Nancy Schlagheck, Linda Teufel and Pat Hatem.

Also thanks to those people who leant us parts of their names to combine into one for a nom de plum. Alma Oksness, Jan Biggs' maternal grandmother; Kyleigh Lynn Hannon, Diana Forrester's grand daughter; and Dallas Thompson, Mary Clark's maternal grandmother.

Love multiplies as it is expressed. Thanks to all.

About the Authors

Janis Biggs brought the precision of her career in accounting to the art of quilting. Her love of the craft grew slowly as the logic of taking big pieces of fabric, cutting them into little pieces then sewing them back together again eluded her. When she spent time with her mother-in-law in Pennsylvania making a Cathedral Window pillow, she came to appreciate the art of quilting.

The desire to write had been simmering deep inside Jan since grammar school. She always thought, secretly, that she had stories to tell. Her passion for quilting merged with her desire to write when she joined the Monday Morning Book Club. Her new passion is to speak from the heart with the written word.

She has been married for twenty-nine years and enjoys her stepdaughter and grandson.

∞

Diana Forrester is a relatively new quilter, who took it up to give her hands something to do when she quit smoking six years ago. She is still learning many things from members of the Monday Morning Book Club.

Her first grandchild is the love of her life. Her second love is writing and she has published many short stories in the United States and Europe. This is her first quilting book.

She has been married thirty years and has four grown children.

∞

Mary Clark was born with a needle between her fingers and has been sewing ever since. She modeled her first machine-sewn dress at the age of eight. Mary currently owns Always In Stitches where there is a party going on every day. She loves fabric, quilting, pressing and the camaraderie with her fellow quilters and guild members.

The quilt shop is the realization of a dream and many of the problems Caroline experiences in starting up her shop in the Guild in the Granary actually happened but we won't tell you which ones.

When she's not quilting, Mary enjoys reading, the outdoors, and spending time with her daughter Jordann, her husband Jeff, and other members of a big extended family.

THE GUILD
IN THE
GRANARY
ഌൟ

Chapter 1

Life turns on a dime. It happened to Caroline Clarkson the day Butch Talbert and Carmen Stilotto decided to rob the Third National Bank in Buckeye Grove, Ohio, where Caroline had worked security for the previous eight years. Before it was over Carmen had escaped in a souped-up, partially restored 1965 Pontiac GTO; Butch was in police custody and Caroline was in Our Lady of Hope Emergency room with her devoted husband Charles, her best friend Olyria and an emergency room doctor, who looked like a teenager, leaning over her.

"She's going to be sore tomorrow," the doctor said. "Luckily, the bullet just grazed the bone and missed all the major blood vessels."

Olyria held Caroline's hand and massaged her shoulder while Charles stomped and yelled his anxiety into the room. "That's it," he said. "No more bank guard work. You could have been killed. What would the girls and I do without you?" He ran stiff fingers through his tousled hair and sucked air out of the emergency cubicle the way only a frightened man can.

The doctor wrote a prescription for antibiotics and pain pills. "Stay off your leg for at least two weeks and, in the meantime, see your family doctor. Take the antibiotics till they're gone and the pain pills as needed."

"I'll see she does it," Charles said. He was still pacing, but the yelling had stopped after a nurse told him he'd be asked to leave if he didn't "put a lid on it." It was as if someone had let the air out of him. Charles was a good-looking man with dark brown, almost-black, hair. His six-foot, one-inch frame seemed to have shrunk and his middle had rounded as his shoulders sagged. Both the brown of his eyes and his hair had dulled and he had gained a few additional streaks of grey hair as if an evil spell had been cast on him. He'd had a very long day.

Olyria left them at their car and Charles got Caroline home and settled into her bed before their girls arrived. Budd, who was fourteen, got home first. Her cocoa-brown hair was pulled into a ponytail that bounced as she hurried into the room. "Is she going to be okay?" She was holding back tears that threatened to spill from her dark blue eyes.

Before Charles could answer, he heard the back door slam and Jamie came running up the stairs. "I came as quickly as I could," she gasped. Jamie was petite and blonde, fine featured and delicate looking, not athletic like her younger sister. She'd driven home from Bowling Green State University where she was a freshman studying to be a teacher.

Charles shushed the girls and led them to the kitchen, where he made omelets and reassured them their mother was going to be fine. It was clear how much they all depended on Caroline and how they would have missed her if Butch Talbert had aimed a foot or so higher. Budd carried her mother's omelet upstairs on a tray.

Caroline was awake and greeted the girls with love and reassurance. "I'm going to be fine."

"Does it hurt?" Budd asked. Budd had a perfect rosebud-shaped mouth, which caused her parents to nickname her Rosebud while she was still a baby. When she was six, she stood with her fisted hands at her waist like the Jolly Green Giant and insisted it be shortened to Budd, which had stuck.

"It doesn't hurt now," Caroline said.

"Did they catch the guys?" Jamie asked. "I just hate when criminals mess up regular people's lives this way." Tears rolled out of her eyes and she hugged her mother fiercely. Jamie believed in truth, justice and the American way as if it were her passage to heaven.

"I'm sure they'll catch them," Caroline said. She returned her daughter's hug, but gingerly. "The bank will have the entire episode on surveillance tape. On the other hand, they were wearing ski masks."

Caroline nibbled at the omelet and toast until her head sank back onto the pillow.

"Your Mom's tired," Charles said. The girls kissed Caroline, and Charles gathered up the tray with the half-eaten omelet and they all left the room.

⌘

Caroline passed her two weeks' recovery time visiting with friends who dropped in and by stitching quilt blocks together, her favorite hobby. She'd been frightened by the shooting and dreaded going back to the bank, but they needed the money she earned with Jamie in college and Budd not far behind.

Olyria stopped often on her way to the Buckeye Grove Day Spa where she was a manicurist. She carried an armload of flowers and bundles.

"You are my absolute favorite," Caroline said.

Olyria's face lit up each time she saw Caroline, like someone had just turned on the sun. "We nearly lost you, Caroline. I can't even think of life without you as my friend and confidant." Olyria was tall and thin with thick auburn hair she wore spiked on top with flat little spit curls at her ears. The spit curls accentuated her high cheekbones and deep-set eyes. She was striking without being beautiful.

"I'm fine," Caroline said. "Not exactly dancing in the street, yet, but I'm fine."

Caroline was still using a cane to get around the house. She grabbed it and poked it into the air.

Olyria giggled. She was one of the few grown women in Buckeye Grove who could get away with a giggle, but she carried it off just like she carried off the red print broom-straw skirt and the gathered gypsy blouse she wore. There had never been anything ordinary about Olyria and that was just one of the things Caroline loved about her. She had recently taken up palmistry as an adjunct to her long-standing fascination with hands that had led her to become a manicurist.

Olyria's bracelets tinkled as she dumped her bundles on the end of the couch and arranged the flowers on a table. Caroline smelled the flowers and gave Olyria a hug. "I've brought something to keep your mind occupied till you go back to work, which is when?"

"Another week," Caroline said. She opened the package Olyria had set in her lap. Olyria watched the smile that came to Caroline's face as she felt the fabric. It was an experience in Braille. Olyria and Caroline had traipsed across the Ohio countryside on Shop Hops together, and Olyria knew Caroline would especially enjoy the 30's feed-sack reproductions she'd brought today.

"Thanks so much. These are beautiful," Caroline sighed. "I love them. I'm just about finished with this lap quilt. These colors are perfect for the dining room. I think I'll make a table runner to remind me of you."

"Good plan," Olyria said. She pulled two lattes from her

carryall, handed one to Caroline and settled down on the couch. "Now," she said, "Tell me everything, we didn't have time to talk about it at the hospital."

Caroline gave her all the details of the shooting and laughed as Olyria compared her to Wyatt Earp, the infamous law officer. Caroline had been a rock for Olyria three years earlier when her husband was killed in an automobile accident. Olyria swore Caroline kept her from going over grief's edge when she saw no other direction. The laughter faded; Olyria reached for Caroline's hand and held it. Her eyes turned serious. "You must've been scared to death. I know how it is to have your life ripped out from under you. You have to search for a new normal, and sometimes it's very hard to find."

The women sipped their lattes and chatted until Olyria headed back out into the world.

⌘

By the end of two weeks Charles was carrying in dinner each evening from some place along his route home, and Budd had taken to eating in her room to avoid the conversation about her mother's return to work.

Caroline picked at chicken chimichangas from 'The Raging Bull' Mexican restaurant.

"I have to go back to work," she said. "We need the money."

"Jamie could transfer to Ohio State. She could live at home." Charles was forking refried beans smothered in gooey cheese into his mouth as he talked.

"I'm not even going to respond to that," Caroline said. "She's settled. She loves her new friends, she loves Bowling Green." Caroline dropped her fork onto the plastic plate the chimichangas were on. "It's out of the question."

"I could get a second job," Charles said. "Jamie could get a job."

"Charles, be reasonable. Eight years I've worked security at the bank. ONCE, ONE LITTLE TIME, I got shot."

"Once is enough," Charles said. He shoved another forkful of beans and cheese into his mouth.

"That food is going to kill you faster than the bank is going to kill me," Caroline said. Charles began eating faster and fell into the frustrated silence that had been coming between them more and more often the past two weeks.

⌘

Olyria had scheduled Caroline for a manicure on Saturday before she was to return to work. Her hair was stiffly spiked and she was wearing a blue paisley granny dress with sandals, and one of her little spit curls was sticking out as if it had also been spiked. Caroline felt better, just looking at her. Life had taken some hits at her and she had survived. Caroline could, too.

"Did you bring your lap quilt or your table runner to show me?" Olyria asked. She studied Caroline and could see the stress in the set of her jaw. "You need some extra pampering today?"

"I didn't bring anything," Caroline said. "And, yes, I could use some pampering."

Olyria took her hands and turned them over to inspect both sides. "We have our work cut out for us, my friend."

"I've been quilting a lot and have stuck myself several times. Look, I've developed a callus. I'm not as steady as I was before the shooting."

Olyria patted the back of Caroline's hand like a mother might and went about soaking them, trimming the cuticles and massaging them gently, talking all the while.

"Are you really ready to go back to work?" Olyria asked.

"Being shot by a perfect stranger makes you evaluate what

you're doing with your life. But still no message from the great beyond telling me what to do."

Olyria nodded and examined Caroline's palm closely. "Your life line is long," she said. "You don't have to worry about dying soon."

"That's what I keep telling Charles, but he's nagging me worse than a medieval harpy about quitting my job," Caroline said. "I wouldn't mind a change, but . . ."

"Your palm shows strong entrepreneurial interest," Olyria said. "Your head line tilts up at the end, which means you would be successful in business. Have you considered opening a shop of some kind? A place where you could work for yourself? Kind of like what I do?"

Caroline cocked her head, looking across her hands to Olyria. "No," she said. "With Jamie in college and Budd not far behind, we need my reliable salary to make that happen."

Olyria shrugged. "It's possible to be too practical in life. Sometimes we all need to take a flying leap . . . throw caution to the wind." Caroline smiled. Olyria was a great risk taker as well as being very responsible. Her father died in Viet Nam and her mother had devoted her life to trying to make up for it. She also lost her husband at an early age, which reinforced her ability to let life flow around her without losing her balance. It also made her susceptible to picking up strays of all descriptions. It was another one of the things Caroline loved about her.

"You've always been better at that than I am."

"Could be your time is here," Olyria said. "If you could do anything you wanted, what would it be?"

A shiver ran up Caroline's spine. "I've thought of opening a quilt shop," she said. "I love everything about quilting. I love cutting fabric and sewing it back together to make something beautiful.

When I go into a quilt shop I feel like a kid in a candy store."

"It's all there, written in the creases of your palm," Olyria said. The smile on Caroline's face showed her resolve. "Well that's it," Olyria said with a smile of her own.

In that moment a plan formed from the turmoil of the past few weeks, and Caroline knew what she wanted to do with the rest of her life.

⌘

Charles brought home gourmet cheeseburgers for supper. Caroline poured them both wine and they sat at the dining room table. Budd was out with friends. Caroline cleared her throat. "I think you're right, Charles. I should get out of the security business."

Charles' eyebrows went up. "It's about time you saw it my way. What are you thinking of doing?"

"Well, you know how I love quilting. I have to confess that I've always loved quilt shops, too, and today Olyria and I were talking while she did my manicure." Caroline sipped her wine. "I think that's what I should do."

"What?" Charles said. "What should you do?"

"Open a quilt shop." Caroline watched Charles closely for his reaction.

He sipped his wine, rubbed his chin. "Hmmm, what do you think it would take to open a shop? What is the market like? How much competition is out there?" Charles peppered Caroline with so many questions she almost wanted to give the idea up. Almost.

"Seems I have some homework to do." Caroline cleared the table and put the dishes in the dishwasher. Charles came up behind her, wrapped his arms around her waist.

"You can start this project on Monday. Now I have something else for you to think about." Charles took her hand and led her upstairs. He eased her onto the bed and slowly took her clothes off. Charles restrained himself after the shooting; afraid he would hurt Caroline, but not any longer. They made fierce love, which ended the reign of silence between them.

Caroline did go back to work on Monday, but the next several weeks she spent every spare minute on the phone and computer gathering information she would need to make a decision. Caroline had quilted all her life, and opening the shop happened the same way Mickey Rooney and his friends used to 'put on a show'. It just sort of happened. And so the journey began.

Chapter 2

Three years later.

Caroline Clarkson was in the fourteenth day of operation at her new quilt shop, Always in Stitches. The shop opening and the first two weeks went smoothly, to Caroline's delight. This morning she got up after tumbling from one side of her lonesome bed to the other. Charles was in Kansas City on business and wouldn't be back for another four days. She was weary, she was exhilarated, she was anxious and she was eager. She leaned against the railing on the balcony of her bedroom and sipped her morning tea. It was scalding hot.

"Shit," Caroline said when she regained her breath and could speak. And then she smiled. The morning before her was as clear and bright as the tea was hot.

Life was like that. The good and the bad all mixed up together and you hardly knew which you were going to get until it was too late. And it did all turn on a dime.

The phone rang; she hurried to the bedside table and grabbed it. "Good morning," she said in a bright, hopeful voice.

"Mom? Could you stop by the bank and put some money in my account today?" It was Jamie, Caroline's older daughter, now in her fourth year at Bowling Green University. She never managed to get her monthly funds to last as long as the month.

"It's only April 18," Caroline said. "How could you be broke already?"

"I had to have supplies for my art class and then Joellen had a birthday and I had to buy her a gift and we took that trip to Cleveland at the beginning of the month." She let out an exasperated sigh and said, "It goes so fast, Mom. You of all people should understand that."

This was an editorial comment on the fact that Caroline had been broke since she quit her job, her very good job in bank security, to follow her dream of opening a quilt shop. She could no longer be relied upon to fill in either of her daughters' financial blanks like she used to do.

"I don't have the money, Jamie. I've invested it in the Moda dandelion and fig fabric collection. My quilters are going to love it. You'll have to talk to your dad about an advance."

"Should I call him on his cell?" Jamie asked.

"Sorry, honey. He's in Kansas City till Friday. I'll ask him to call you when he gets in."

"Okay," she said with a long sigh. "In the meantime, I get to skip eating." Caroline stifled a sigh of her own. The girl should be majoring in theater . . . or maybe finance . . . instead of education. "Borrow a couple of dollars from Joellen, or eat some of the food you took back with you last weekend; and you know you have a meal ticket at the cafeteria," Caroline said, but Jamie didn't hear. She had broken the connection.

It was financially devastating to open a new business. The money went out so much faster than it came in. The quilt shop was exciting; it was invigorating; it was the answer to Caroline's dreams, but finances were in the toilet. Caroline's advisors told her it could be that way for as long as three years. Maybe she could borrow a few bucks from Joellen, too.

Caroline sighed and went back to sipping her cooled tea on the bedroom deck. A spring storm had blasted through during the night and washed the morning clean. The grass was bright green for the first time since last September. It was the special virgin green that was one of Caroline's favorite colors. The trees were in heavy bloom with wet white and pink blossoms dragging branches toward the ground. The air smelled fresh and clean like dryer sheets engineered by Mother Nature. It was a perfect morning.

Charles' business trip meant Caroline was free to spend twenty-four hours a day at her new quilt shop. The shop had taken every waking moment for the past six months and it didn't look like things were going to change anytime soon.

Months passed, with the display racks stored in Charles' garage. Bolts of fabric lay on the couch for more than a month. Notions were everywhere, boxes cracked open and stacked on the kitchen counter and the dining room table while the shop space was readied for them. Caroline met people at the Small Business Administration, she met people at quilt market in Houston, she met people at quilt guild meetings all over central Ohio and she researched the quilting market till she knew it inside out.

She found what she believed was a near-perfect location, downtown in Buckeye Grove, a small but prospering town just fifteen minutes from Broad and High in Columbus, Ohio. She'd kissed a few frogs before she decided on the restored granary as a likely spot for a quilt shop. And she waited six months longer than she expected to move merchandise into her space and get the shop opened. Schultz, the building owner, ran into a string of remodeling problems that held up the entire project and remained outside of Caroline's control.

She had influence now that the shop was open. At least she

felt like she did. Sales had been brisk, falling under $400 only one of the first fourteen days of operation. That was the minimum required to meet expenses, according to Rumpelstiltskin, which is what Caroline called her small business advisor. She hoped he had the ability to spin straw into gold and in fact was depending on him to help her do that very thing.

She was keeping expenses low by having her family help in the shop. All of them, her sister, her mom, her niece, had been quilters for years and had all agreed to "work for fabric." She also had two paid staff members; Kathy Corbin who was recruited away from another quilt shop in the area who was an expert in the many facets of quilt making and was the backbone of the teaching staff; and Nan, a college student. Caroline was happy to be where she was. It had been a long, hard road. She would not have to worry about bank robbers and shootings any more.

Caroline smiled to herself, walked into the bathroom, turned on the shower, adjusted the water temperature and took a sip of her tea, which had gotten too cold to drink. She dropped her robe to the floor and stepped into the scalding hot water.

"Shit," she said when she could speak. She adjusted the faucets and began to prepare for her day.

⌘

Always in Stitches was the largest tenant in the old granary that was recently restored after dispensing seeds, grain, fence posts and everything else farmers in and around Buckeye Grove had needed for a hundred years. It was closed for fourteen years and the neglect and deterioration that ensued had almost convinced Schultz not to begin the restoration project. But he persevered and now was providing space for Caroline's quilt shop, a yoga studio, an authentic English tearoom, an artist's studio, a small beauty shop and Olyria's new combination manicure studio and palm-reading room. Olyria decided to leave the Buckeye Day Spa and strike out on her own. It was amazing how the building came back to life and how interested the community was in the project. Even the Mayor dropped by the quilt shop the week it opened.

Caroline considered herself lucky to be a part of the project. Going to work was a joy each day. She could hear the phone ringing inside the shop as she struggled with the key. The door handle was loose; she'd asked Schultz to have it fixed, but so far no luck. Her arms were loaded down with her day-timer, her lunch, a quilt she was going to put on display and an extra ironing board she was bringing in for a class that Kathy, her stolen quilting expert, was teaching that afternoon. She dropped the quilt before she managed to jiggle the door enough to get the key to work. By the time she got inside, the phone clicked over to message mode and she could hear Jasmine Carlyle, the owner and proprietor of the tearoom.

"The baker cancelled my scone order again today" Jasmine said. There was a hint of hysteria in her voice. Caroline smiled. Jasmine was a new friend and certainly she had an Attention Deficit Disorder diagnosis in her background. She'd had a tragedy every single day since Caroline opened her shop. The tearoom had been open one more week than the quilt shop and Jasmine was having more problems than Caroline. Both of them were game and the learning curve was steep.

"What good is an English tea shop with no scones?" Jasmine whined over the answering machine.

Caroline emptied her arms onto the end of the service counter and reached for the phone just as she heard Jasmine click off.

"Scones . . .?" Caroline said. "I've got problems of my own."

This morning was the first meeting of the Granary Quilt Guild[1]

1   Quilt Guild - a group of quilters who meet regularly to enjoy the common fellowship surrounding quilting. They work to

Caroline wanted to organize. A lot was riding on this morning's meeting and Caroline was nervous. She set up the ironing board and plugged in the iron that sat on the cutting table. Water dribbled, then hissed out of the iron as it heated up. Caroline bustled about the shop, putting away stray bolts of fabric as she headed to the front door to unlock it and hang out the quilt that symbolized her readiness to do business. It was the flag of the quilt shop. Today she shook out a wedding ring quilt top and pinned it to the wrought iron railing that led up the steps to the front door of the quilt shop.

Cars whizzed by as she worked to get the quilt pinned securely. She didn't want it blowing down if a spring gale went through. She stood, looking across the street to the auto repair and the bowling alley, feeling a bit like the captain of a great sailing vessel and singly responsible for keeping it afloat.

Caroline turned on lights as she went upstairs to the office area to start the coffeepot to provide refreshment for the guild members. Caroline was expecting fourteen women, a core of her quilting friends. This first meeting was by invitation only and Caroline purposefully kept the number small. She hoped it would triple its membership by the end of the shop's first year. It was central to her business goals.

Finally, the shop was organized, the chairs arranged around a table, a box of doughnuts and napkins placed handily for the women to help themselves. Running a quilt shop was like having one big party going on every day. Caroline liked that.

In the hall she could hear the sound of singing. "Oh, what a beautiful morning; Oh, what a beautiful day." It was slightly off key and had to be Goldie, the resident artist. She had a studio in the building and was the most totally upbeat person Caroline ever

improve their quilting skills, to share knowledge and participate in projects of community concern.

met. She liked telling people her legal name was Meg Thomas Jasper Lewis McElroy Jones. She was only forty-eight and had been married four times but was currently single and looking.

"Just call me Goldie," she told folks after she'd gone through the litany that was her name. She poked her head in the quilt shop door, the interior door that connected the quilt shop to the rest of the building. "Good morning," Goldie called out. "You getting an early start this morning?" She wore paint-spattered jeans and a man's shirt.

Caroline smiled. "The first meeting of the guild is this morning," she said. "It means a lot to get this started right. Customer base, you know."

"Thank goodness I don't need a customer base," Goldie said. "I'm just no good at sucking up to other people."

"I don't see it as sucking up," Caroline said. "I'm providing valuable merchandise and a service to some very creative people."

"Yeah, right," Goldie said. "Creative people all have some sort of a screw loose, you know," she laughed. The sound echoed off the ceiling of the quilt shop.

"Maybe so," Caroline said but she smiled again in spite of herself.

"No maybe to it," Goldie said. "It's as sure as a blue moon in October. Come up to the studio. I'll fix you a cup of tea and one of those gooey sweet rolls."

"Can't this morning. I have too much to do before the meeting."

Goldie shrugged. "Life is short." She turned and disappeared down the hall. "I've got a wonderful feeling . . ." hung in the air behind her along with the scent of turpentine.

Nan Roberts came in the back door. She was a tall, thin girl with long black hair that she had swooped into a ponytail that hung from high up on the back of her head. Her arms were loaded with folders and books. She dropped them on the service counter just next to the door. "Whew," she said. "I've got homework. I know the first guild meeting is this morning or I'd have called off."

"I'm grateful you didn't," Caroline said. "Goldie just left and I've got the meeting room set up already. You might catch a minute or two to study while we're meeting."

Nan was twenty years old, a student at Ohio State University, and a fill-in employee for Caroline. She was willing to work for what Caroline could afford to pay.

"My English lit professor is really pouring it on. Stuff not on the course outline." Nan raised her eyebrows. "Rumor has it her boyfriend broke up with her and she's taking it out on her students."

Caroline laughed. "English lit professors have boyfriends these days?" She remembered the day when professors were a hundred years old and didn't like anybody.

"Some of them do," Nan said. She was shuffling through her books and folders and set two off to the side.

"Well, could you hold off on reading till we get the meeting started? I need a dozen fat quarter bundles cut from the new batiks we just got in and I want you to be at full attention in case somebody wants to buy something before we start."

"No problem," Nan said. She carried her other books to the storage room.

⌘

Annie Wilkins was the first to arrive. Annie was fifty-eight-years old and took up quilting after she retired from teaching. Caroline was surprised she'd brought her husband Walter along. Annie and Walter met on a seniors cruise to Holland and surprised everyone by getting married before the ship even returned to the dock. Caroline hadn't met Walter, so Annie introduced them. Annie's arm was twined through Walter's, and her admiration for him shown in her eyes. Walter was handsome, George Hamilton handsome, with a full head of white hair and a tan that wouldn't quit. He was a bit taller than average and trimly built. He was in his mid-sixties, a fact Caroline heard from the scuttlebutt among the women who frequented the shop. She also heard he was a bit of a ladies' man.

Walter bowed from the waist and took Caroline's hand. He kissed the back of it like a full-fledged Frenchman. "Finally, we meet, dear lady," he said. Annie hung onto his arm and smiled. She was trim and attractive herself. They made a very cute couple, Caroline thought. Annie was wearing a coordinated pants suit in shades of pink that highlighted her bottle-red hair.

"Isn't he the gentleman?" she said.

Caroline welcomed them. "Welcome to Always in Stitches, Walter. Are you a quilter?"

Walter chuckled. "No, afraid not. I tagged along with Annie, but my real goal is to meet the yoga master and sign up for some lessons. Yoga is wonderful exercise, you know." He preened before the women and turned just slightly to show off his trim physique. "It allows me to enjoy the apricot scones and jam from the teashop which have become a habit. Yoga helps keep me fit."

"And very relaxing," Annie piped in. "I may take it up myself one of these days. Walter introduced me to yoga and fine Dutch chocolate on the cruise after we met." She smiled at Walter, and Caroline smiled at the two of them. It was never too late for love.

Nan directed other ladies to the classroom area as they arrived.

Jeanine Burke, a retired airline accountant/bean counter, and Samantha Winters, a younger woman who worked as a cosmetologist but not in the granary, entered the shop together and headed for the meeting area. They had Caroline's friend Olyria with them. "Good morning," Jeanine called out. "Look who decided to come along with us?" Caroline was thrilled Olyria was here; it would help fill up the room. It was nice to have friends you could count on.

Olyria smiled, tilted her head to the side and followed Jeanine and Sam through the fabric rounds and displays to the steps leading to the mid-level of the shop where the other ladies were gathering. Walter kissed Annie on the cheek and left the classroom area as the ladies clambered up the stairs. He headed towards the yoga studio. As he passed the newcomers on the stair, he bowed his head slightly in acknowledgment and turned to watch them from behind as they went up the stairs. Olyria stopped on the stair and stared at Walter. Her mouth dropped open and Walter winked boldly at her.

"What are we doing today?" Jeanine asked.

"We have lots of start-up business to take care of this morning. We have to elect officers, establish dues and consider some projects. I thought we'd get started right away on a project to help somebody else," Caroline said. "That is, if everyone agrees. She held up a photo of a log cabin quilt in shades of brown and cream. "Quilts of Valor[2]," she said. "Guilds and individuals contribute quilts for wounded soldiers in military hospitals. I thought it would make a great first project for our guild."

"I love it," Olyria said. "Isn't the log cabin one of the oldest

---

2   Quilts of Valor - an organization that oversees the distribution of quilts to wounded military veterans. The mission of the QOV Foundation is to cover ALL war wounded and injured service members and veterans from the War on Terror whether physical or psychological wounds with Wartime Quilts called Quilts of Valor.

patterns there is?" She ran her fingers through her spiked auburn hair and gave Caroline a tight hug. "This is a wonderful turnout," she whispered in her friend's ear.

"Better save this quilt discussion for the group," Caroline said to Olyria. She offered coffee and doughnuts as more guild members began to arrive.

The women teased Annie good-naturedly about her marriage to Walter. "Your husband sure is handsome," Jeanine said. Annie blushed girlishly. She was happy to be married after a spinster's life and happy to be retired after years of dealing with other people's children. She accepted the teasing with a smile, though marriage hadn't turned out to be the picnic she had expected.

Old friends and fellow quilters Aggie McDaniel, Alice Stone, Georgia Beasley, Linda Hutton, Nina Bradley, Tina DeStocki, Sheryll Douglas and Pat Carter, Caroline's mom and biggest supporter, aside from Charles, came in. They milled around the coffeepot and helped themselves to refreshments before they took seats around the big table in the classroom. Caroline counted thirteen, an unlucky number she thought, as she cleared her throat and began to speak.

"Good morning," she greeted them. "I am so happy to see you all this morning and excited we are forming a new guild. We have lots of business to take care of this morning so I think we should get right to it."

There was a bit of commotion as Michael Lomard came running in late. He and his little dog Stella always ran late. Stella was in the doggy carrier Michael had slung over an ample shoulder. "Sorry," he panted as he pulled out a chair and plopped down in it. "Had a breakfast buffet for two hundred to get going before I could leave this morning." Michael was a tall, solidly built man, a chef who obviously tasted most of what he cooked. He was also a computer nerd, a quilt historian and an e-Bay junkie. Caroline thought he would add a lot to the group. She was glad to see him, and he broke the unlucky thirteen number. Jeanine Burke raised her eyebrows and frowned. Her pet peeve was people who arrived late.

Michael ignored her and pulled Stella out of her carrier. He ruffled her fur and then petted it almost flat again. Stella had a white curly coat that made her look like a snowball. Her hair was tied on top with a pink ribbon festooned in miniature hearts that tinkled with every move she made. Michael nuzzled her head and allowed her to lick his face. Her little black eyes sparkled. "She's been in her carrier for over an hour," Michael said. "She needs to stretch." He situated Stella on his lap and turned his eyes toward Caroline.

"I was afraid you might not make it this morning," Caroline said. She went on from Michael's small disruption. Aggie McDaniel was elected president; Michael became vice president; Jeanine, with her accounting background, agreed to be the group treasurer; and Sheryll Douglas was secretary. After much discussion and begging, Olyria agreed to be program chairman for the first year. It was a good group and Caroline was happy with the results. The officers would make the difference between the guild flying high or struggling along. Aggie led the meeting as the group decided to affiliate with The Quilt Guild of America[3], which had recently moved its national headquarters to Columbus, Ohio. They agreed on annual dues of $13 which was payable at the next regular meeting. When the essential business was complete, Aggie turned control back to Caroline who explained the Quilts of Valor project and then asked the women to choose the fabric for the lap quilt to be assembled and then sent off to a wounded soldier.

---

3   Quilt Guild of America - a fictitious name of a national quilting organization.

The women chatted and roamed through the shop in small groups, as they selected fabric for their quilt. They decided on shades of brown, green and gold as masculine enough for an injured soldier, even if it was a woman. Aggie and Annie began to cut strips for the log cabin quilt.

Caroline took photos of them while they worked and chronicled the amount and type of fabric being removed from the shop's inventory. She felt a warm glow of satisfaction as she watched the members work together and their first project begin to take shape. Quilting was all about community and Caroline felt it strongly this morning. Michael and Stella panned for the camera while Michael fingered fabric, making several selections for his personal stash.

The fabric selection and cutting went well and some of the guild members agreed to take strips home and others agreed to work at putting the blocks together when the time came. They were going to paper piece the blocks in an effort to get them a uniform size, which is sometimes difficult when several people work on a quilt.

"I've never done paper piecing," Annie Wilkins said. She was the newest quilter in the group.

"You're going to love it," Caroline said. "If you can stop in tomorrow, we'll help you get started."

"That is, if you can pull yourself away from Walter," Jeanine said. She laughed and Annie blushed.

"I probably will stop in," Annie said. "I feel like everything goes easier if I have a little bit of instruction before I go too far."

There was a little flurry of purchasing by the women who attended the guild meeting. Caroline hoped it would increase her daily business income. Michael and Stella rushed out as soon as his fabric was rung up but most of the women were still lingering in the shop when Sam Winters said, "I smell smoke." The women remaining sniffed the air.

Caroline said "What?" to Jeanine who was close by.

"Smoke," she said. "Sam smells smoke and so do I."

At that moment, Jasmine came running into the quilt shop yelling, "Fire! Fire! Evacuate the building." Her auburn hair was in a tangle and her eyes were wild with excitement and fear.

Caroline called for Nan and herded women toward the door.

This could be worse than getting shot.

Chapter 3

Caroline stood across the street from the granary taking tight, thin breaths. Her mom and Olyria stood with her. Pat held her daughter's hand in her own damp one. Pat hopped from foot to foot with anxiety. Her curly grey hair bounced along with her.

"Mom, relax," Caroline said. "We're insured and besides we don't know how bad it is."

"I don't see flames," Olyria said. She was frowning as she spoke.

Some of the guild ladies left when the fire emergency occurred and Caroline sent Nan home to study for her English exam. Every emergency vehicle in Buckeye Grove responded to the emergency call and they surrounded the granary. Caroline wondered if the sprinklers engaged, drenching her books and ruining her fabric. Firefighters ran in and out of the building carrying extinguishers while others attached hoses to the hydrants in front of the building.

Caroline's mom was no longer hopping from foot to foot, though she still clung to her hand. Caroline only faintly heard Jasmine when she ran across the street twenty minutes later yelling, "It's okay to go back inside." Her shoulder-length auburn hair was blowing wildly and her eyes had a slightly mad gleam. Jasmine was twenty-eight, with the youthful energy to wring every ounce of emotion out of any situation. On some days Caroline was jealous of the energy, but today was not one of those days.

"Thank you, God," Caroline whispered as she walked through the front door of her shop and looked around. Everything was in place, nothing was destroyed. The sprinklers hadn't gone off? She sunk into a white wicker chair with a quilt draped across it. She collapsed against the back of the chair, realizing she'd dodged a bullet this time. It felt good. Her mother hugged her before she left and Olyria departed to her nail and palm-reading studio, in another part of the building. Caroline thanked the fabric gods for her good fortune and began to straighten and put away the stacks of fabric bolts the guild ladies had left behind.

The shop was empty and the smell of smoke hung in the air. Caroline opened both the front and back doors, hoping a breeze would clear the air. She was sorting an order of quilting magazines when the phone rang.

"Thanks for calling Always in Stitches," she said.

"Who else would I call?" Charles said. He was on his lunch break out in Kansas City.

A bit of warmth twirled through Caroline when she heard his voice. She laughed seductively. "Nobody," she said. She tucked a strand of hair behind her ear.

"How did the meeting go?" he asked.

"There were thirteen women and Michael here," Caroline said.

"A bit better than you were hoping for?"

"Yes, and it went well. Aggie was elected president, which almost assures success. Olyria is going to be program chairman. She'll work hard and do a wonderful job. I'm excited and the women liked the idea of collaborating on a quilt to send to the military hospital. Almost everybody took strips home to make blocks for next time."

"Good," Charles said.

"I asked everybody to bring a friend along next week. Michael is going to bring an egg casserole and some muffins for breakfast."

"Every group should have an executive chef as a member," Charles said. "How long do you think you'll be meeting every week?"

"At least the first two months. Until we get up and running and programs planned for the rest of the year." Caroline laughed, "I consider Michael a stroke of luck on several levels. He has such a sense of color, that outrageous sense of what matters; and of course, the women love him." She paused. "Things went really well till the fire."

"The fire?" Charles said on the other end of the line. "You had a fire?"

"Just a little one," Caroline said. "It started in the tearoom kitchen and nearly scared Jasmine to death. The fire department was here and put it out in five minutes with a fire extinguisher. All the rent-paying tenants are up in arms and have called a meeting for tonight. I think they want to draw and quarter Schultz."

"That poor man. I'd hate to have to deal with all you women about building maintenance."

"We pay our rent. He promised us a reasonable place to do business. You should have seen my customers hightail it out of here when Jasmine ran in this morning yelling 'FIRE'."

"Was there any damage?"

"The wall in Jasmine's kitchen is scorched and her stove will have to be replaced. My shop smells like a cigar store instead of a quilt shop, but I have the doors open and it's starting to dissipate." Caroline stopped talking and sniffed the air. "I think it will be fine by tomorrow."

"I wish I were there to help out."

"I do, too. You know Schultz doesn't relate that well to women. You'd be a big help talking to him about the problems. But there is something else you can do. Jamie called this morning. She's broke again." Caroline sighed. "Could you call her? Maybe talk a bit about budgeting?"

"I'll call. Don't worry, Caroline, we'll get through this. Schultz will get the building into tiptop condition and the money will begin to roll in. You'll see."

"It's going to be a wonderful shop. I just never thought it would take so long to get started, and I never thought we'd owe everybody in the western hemisphere before it was even up and running."

"We both knew retail was like that. Besides, it's your dream. Dreams need to be respected."

"I love you," Caroline said. "You are the absolute best."

"I love you, too. I'll take care of Jamie. You have a good afternoon and I'll call you tonight to find out how the meeting went with Schultz."

"Bye," Caroline said. "Thanks." She wasn't sure he'd heard. Cutting off the conversation was like being cut loose in the universe. Caroline's stomach dropped but she never had to worry about Charles' loyalty. Not one second since they'd met. A good marriage was a gift from God.

⌘

The tenant meeting was being held in Caroline's shop as she had the most room, the most chairs and tables; and she was the most willing. It would take place in the same room the guild members met in earlier that day. Jasmine arrived carrying a sign that said SCHULTZ A FIRE HAZARD. She bounced it over her head moving from Olyria to the yoga master trying to stir up sympathy for her situation. Her hair still stood in a tangle and her eyes glared wildly. Her day had coasted downhill from the missing scone order to the fire.

"I have to shut down at least for two weeks," she said, "while I wait for a new stove."

"Schultz is going to pay for it," the yoga master said. "That seems fair to me." He was a tall man with well-muscled arms and legs. A black moustache and beard made him look older than he really was. His clothes hung loose on his spare frame like he was a window mannequin. He'd stayed mostly to himself since the building opened and Caroline was surprised to see him at the meeting. "My name is David Williams," he said. "Sorry I haven't met all of you before this."

"It's Schultz's fault," Jasmine said. "The wiring was at fault. I could have burnt to a crisp. We all could have lost everything if it had happened when the shops were closed."

David Williams shrugged.

"You have a few mats and rubber blocks," Jasmine said. "Not much at risk in a yoga studio. I have equipment and food supplies and Caroline has bolt after bolt of fabric. Tell him Caroline..." David narrowed his nose and curled his eyebrows across his prominent forehead. His ears were flat to his head but had elfin points on the top. They gave him a rakish look that contrasted sharply with the beard and moustache that covered most of the bottom of his face. Caroline thought it might be hard to take him seriously.

"I have vitamins and dietary supplements. I have inventory and equipment just like everybody else." He started to rise from his chair, but Jasmine pulled Caroline up from her seat and stopped talking in an effort to give her the floor. The yoga master sat back down. He crossed his legs and folded his arms across his chest. He looked for all the world like a pouting child.

"Well, ummm . . ." Caroline began and at that moment Schultz came into the room. Schultz was a tall man with a body padded from too much schnitzel and beer. He was vigorously chewing gum that he said helped calm his craving for cigarettes. He stopped smoking years before but said the craving never ended. Each step was deliberate and he gave the impression that he thought about each one from beginning to end before he took the next one. It gave his gait a jerky cadence.

Jasmine was on him like white on snow, exaggerating the estimate she had received. "Two weeks," she said. "It will be two weeks before I can reopen my tearoom. I had to cancel my scone order. I need a new stove. I had to put a notice in the paper. Thank goodness the reporter who showed up to cover the fire was able to give me the information I needed and the fire fell at a good time for the weekly deadline of the paper. I had groups scheduled in. I had to cancel them, too. I expect a return on my rent. I may never recover from the . . ." She was shooting machine-gun accusations at the blue-eyed building owner.

Schultz waved Jasmine away and took center stage among the shop owners, who were all women except David. Schultz didn't have much patience with women. His aggravation was obvious.

"The wiring has been completely inspected," Schultz told the group. "The Fire Marshall says the rest of it is perfectly safe. The fire in the tearoom kitchen was caused by an old section of wiring that wasn't properly repaired when the building was rewired. I will be holding the electrician responsible financially. None of you has anything to worry about." Schultz pulled a wrinkled handkerchief from his back pocket and swabbed his forehead.

The women's voices erupted in a torrent of chatter. Jasmine was cheerleader for the disgruntled shop owners. "I have light bulbs that need replacing," said Goldie.

"My water is intermittent and the temperature doesn't stay consistent through the length of a shampoo," said the cosmetologist.

David rubbed his beard and shifted on his folding chair. He and Caroline alone were silent.

Schultz shook his head. He needed a haircut, Caroline noticed. Maybe he was having some sleepless nights and scheduling problems, too. His German accent became more pronounced when he was excited, and the screaming women had him excited. "I'm doing my best," he said. He sounded breathless as if he might explode at any moment.

Caroline didn't care to see the generously built, grey-haired old man go through the roof. She walked to the front of the room and stood next to him. The women quieted for her. "We've had a rocky opening," she said. "All of us have, but we're here now, and there are bound to be a few small problems that need to be worked out the first year. We all have to work harder and be patient until the kinks are worked out." She looked at Schultz sympathetically. "Mr. Schultz has sunk a bundle of money into this project."

Schultz nodded; the women grumbled . . . "small problems?" . . . "tell that to my stove" . . . "I need reliable shampoo water."

Caroline couldn't help but think about her loose lock, but she continued speaking on Schultz's behalf. "I say we need to be patient. The building passed the inspection by the city building department. All things are meeting code. The fire today was minor and that particular problem is on the way to being solved. We need to be grateful for that. We'd all be shut down, otherwise."

Schultz nodded.

"We're here. We're open. Jasmine is going to lose a few days' business, but Mr. Schultz has guaranteed she will not bear the financial responsibility."

Jasmine crossed her arms and in the process knocked her sign over. The noise echoed off the high ceiling of the quilting classroom. Caroline spoke again. "I say let's go home and get a good night's sleep. Think about what we need to have done in our shops and give Mr. Schultz a complete list by the end of the week."

"I need my hot water before the end of the week," the cosmetologist said.

Schultz had regained control of himself. "I'll have the hot water tanks adjusted first thing in the morning," he said. "I will get to the rest of it as soon as possible. I promised all of you a reasonable place to do business and you will have it. Think of me as your father, or a doting uncle," he amended. "I want you to succeed. I won't succeed unless you succeed. We're in this together."

Caroline clapped her hands together and the sound echoed off the ceiling just as the fallen sign had a few minutes earlier. Nobody else joined in.

"I'll take care of it." Schultz said. "I'll take care of it all and I'll start first thing in the morning."

He beat a hasty retreat, taking each step individually, and the disgruntled shop owners left soon after. Caroline loaded her arms up with a table runner she hoped to finish at home that evening and a couple of leftover doughnuts from the morning guild meeting. The doughnuts would be supper. She hoped she would be able to stay awake to finish the table runner.

Chapter 4

Caroline swore softly under her breath as she jiggled the key in her lock the next morning. The knob went to the top of her to-do list for Schultz. Finally she got the door opened and dropped the load she carried onto the check-out counter. Half her job seemed to be ferrying things between home and the shop. She needed a carrier on wheels. She made a note in her head to pick one up later in the day. *MAYBE . . . IF SHE HAD TIME.*

Nobody gets extra time. Only twenty-four hours in a day for each of us. Caroline thought of it as the great equalizer. She was feeling less equal than most this morning.

Charles had called last night like he promised. She told him about the meeting with Schultz, de-emphasizing her role in the peacemaking. He was staying an extra day in Kansas City and wouldn't be home till late Saturday. He talked to Jamie, promising her extra money. He even called the bank and made the transfer to her checking account.

A trunk show was coming in and Caroline had to finish the table runner, which she worked on but had not finished last night. She prayed for the strength to get through another busy day.

Jasmine stopped by her house after the meeting with Schultz last night. She cried and yelled and finally the two of them mellowed out over a bottle of wine, crackers and stale doughnuts. Caroline was feeling rocky this morning as a result. She had several years on Jasmine and late nights and poor diet cost her more in terms of recovery time.

Still, she had work to do, and nobody else really cared about her problems, so she hurried around the shop turning on lights, counting change into the cash register, and hanging out the quilt in the warm morning air. It smelled of spring. She felt lucky to be alive. She was ready to work hard all day long to catch up from yesterday.

Nan wasn't coming in this morning. She had her English exam and Caroline hoped she had gotten enough time to study well for it. She hoped Jamie was taking the time to do her studying up in Bowling Green. Jamie was always on her mind since she had gone off to college. Caroline thought it might be worse than having a newborn. At least a newborn couldn't get up and walk herself into trouble or danger. You put a newborn down someplace and that's where they stayed till you moved them.

Caroline was ready to sit down at the sewing machine and work on the table runner when the phone rang. She picked it up and said, "Thanks for calling Always in Stitches. This is Caroline Clarkson. Can I help you?"

There was silence on the other end of the line. "Can I help you?" Caroline said again. She could hear breathing, but nobody spoke. "I don't have time for this," Caroline said. "If there's something I can do for you . . ." Caroline received so many sales calls, so many foreign people calling to sell merchant services, Internet services, mailing services, you name it.

There was an intake of breath and a husky voice on the other end said, "If I had you alone I'd show you how you could help me," and there was more raspy breathing.

Caroline sucked air into her lungs. She held the phone in front of her and looked at it like it might make sense if she could just see through the phone. She couldn't and it didn't. "Kids," she said to herself and clicked the button that disconnected her from the voice out there someplace.

She lay the phone down on the table by the sewing machine and began to sew the binding on the table runner. It was a prototype for the Table-Runner-of-the-Month group Kathy was teaching. This one was all pink, yellow and green with florals and solids. It was very summery and the ladies were going to love it.

The hum of the sewing machine soothed Caroline; it put her into a Zen state. Her toes tingled, peace possessed her soul. Quilting was better than a glass of really good wine.

She was finishing up the binding when Annie and Walter came in. Walter guided Annie by the elbow. He was all decked out in exercise clothes and Annie had her log cabin strips in a plastic bag. The colors showed rich and clean through the plastic.

"Good morning," Caroline said. "You here for your paper piecing lesson?"

"She sure is," Walter said. "I'm having a yoga session and Annie needs to be finished in forty-five minutes, which is how long my practice lasts."

Caroline smiled at Walter and then turned her eyes to Annie. "We'll do our best." Annie smiled back and Caroline thought she pulled her arm a bit to release her elbow from Walter's grip.

Walter smiled at the women and bowed slightly from the waist. He was dapper by any standard and his yoga pants fit tight as his skin. He looked to be in good shape and the hair on his arms was grey, not platinum like the hair on his head. Caroline thought the platinum must be chemically enhanced.

"See you shortly, pet," he said to Annie. She nodded demurely and laid her bag of log cabin strips on the sewing table. Walter left through the door that attached Caroline's shop to the rest of the building. He looked back over his shoulder as he pulled the door closed.

"Walter sure seems to be enjoying yoga," Caroline said.

"He is," Annie said. "He started onboard the cruise ship where we met and has been driving twenty miles north of town until this yoga master opened his practice. He says he feels a special bond with the new master, and it's so much more convenient."

"Hmmm," Caroline said.

"He says there is no better exercise for mind and body than yoga. He's also convinced it helps his golf game. I'm considering taking up the practice, too."

"Do you think you will?" Caroline asked.

"Not right away. I have to learn to do this quilting before I start anything else."

Caroline and Annie lost themselves in making the log cabin squares. Annie sat at the machine, shortened her stitch length and stitched the strips together along the stitching line on the paper pattern. She was an apt pupil and had two perfectly shaped squares done in no time at all. Her shoulders tensed up as she worked and Caroline touched her from behind. "Relax," she said.

Annie jumped like she had been shot. "Oh, sorry," Caroline said. "I didn't mean to startle you."

Annie laughed. "It stresses me, trying to do something new. I'm such a dunce sometimes."

"Honey, you're not a dunce, not at all. Look how perfect your squares are."

Caroline held up the blocks and they were exact twins. "Now you have to pull the paper off the back. Do it one strip at a time and be careful of your stitching."

Annie did as she was told, and the paper came off along the perforations made by the needle. It was like peeling skin off sunburn. "Perfect," Caroline said. "How many squares are you making?"

"Just four," Annie said. "I thought that would be enough for my first time."

"We still have a bit of time before Walter comes back. Want to start another?"

Annie nodded and aligned the center strip with the first side strip. She hunched over the machine and began to sew. As she worked, the starched collar of her blouse pulled away from her neck. Caroline was still standing behind her and saw what looked like a fresh bruise on the side of her neck. "Annie," she said. "What happened to your neck?"

Annie's hand went up and adjusted her collar. "It's nothing," she said. "I fell getting into the shower this morning and hit my neck on the faucet. It looked fine earlier but I guess I'm getting a bruise."

"You sure are," Caroline said.

At that moment Walter pushed through the door. "I'm back," he said. He had a healthy glow about him and was smiling. "It was a great workout. David is a taskmaster as well. Remind me to bring in some of that special dark Dutch chocolate for him next time we come, Annie."

Annie smiled at her husband. "I will," she said and then put her finished squares into the plastic bag along with the half-finished one and the one she hadn't had time to start. She went to Walter's side.

"If you have any problems, come back in," Caroline said. "If I'm not here Kathy is and she can help you probably better than I can." Caroline straightened the sewing table as she spoke.

"I think I've got it," Annie said. "Thanks so much for your help."

Caroline patted Annie's shoulder. Annie winced and pulled away. "Oh, sorry," Caroline said. "Take care of that shoulder."

Walter took Annie's elbow and guided her toward the door. "I will," Annie said.

They were just out the back door when David Williams came in through the connecting door, waving a pamphlet above his head. "Walter forgot his vitamin information."

"They just went out the back," Caroline said. She hurried toward the door, the yoga master leading the way. He came out just in time to see Walter jerk Annie's arm as he pulled her toward the car. She was clutching her plastic bag of quilt squares in her free hand. Walter opened her car door and pushed her into the car.

Caroline saw it, too. She started hurrying toward the car but David caught her by the arm. "Never mind," he said. "I'll give it to him tomorrow."

"He pushed her," Caroline said.

"Family matters," David said, but there was a storm in his eyes when he looked at Caroline.

⌘

Caroline put the finishing touches on the table runner. She was thinking about Walter and Annie when Olyria Brown came through the connecting door.

"I love it," Olyria said as Caroline held up the finished table runner. "Perfect for summer." Olyria was wearing a pink-and-orange flowered turban and a flowing skirt that matched the orange in the turban. Her blouse was white and gathered at the neck.

"You look like a gypsy," Caroline said.

"Do you like it? I'm trying to look more the part for my palm readings." She folded her arms across her chest and leaned back against the cutting table. "I'm doing two palm readings for every manicure these days. Moving into this place has done wonders for my business. Life is all about change."

"It's good to have you close by," Caroline said.

"It will be good if we don't all burn to a crisp in this old building," she said.

"I think we'll be fine," Caroline said. "I did expect to see Schultz first thing this morning. He seemed as upset as anyone at the meeting last night."

Olyria shrugged.

"He has more to lose than any of the rest of us," Caroline said. "Do you have any idea what he's got invested in this building?"

"Not a clue," Olyria said. "And it's not my problem, either."

"We're all lucky to have him spending money so we can all have this charming place to do business. I appreciate his dedication," Caroline said.

"You call it charming, I call it risky," Olyria said. She adjusted her turban and brushed some invisible something off the front of her skirt. "Really," she asked, "do you like the look?"

"I do," Caroline said. "It fits right into the atmosphere of the building. Unique, a bit off the beaten path and yet comfortable to browse around in. It's why I love you, Olyria. You've never been ordinary."

Olyria laughed. "Well, I want to sign up for the mystery night class," she said. "I might want to schedule a mystery night for a guild program."

"That's a great idea," Caroline said. She led Olyria to the check-out desk and clicked up the class schedule on the computer. "We still have four empty spaces. You want to bring a friend along?"

"No," Olyria said, "I'll just meet my friends there or make some new friends." She fingered a green floral fabric on a round table close to the check-out desk. "This has a very nice hand. I may have to have a half yard to add to my stash." She carried the bolt to the cutting table and laid it down.

Caroline measured off the half yard and folded it neatly. "That's all?" she asked and headed back to the check-out.

"I was wondering," Olyria said. "Has Annie been in to work on her quilt blocks?"

"Yes, she and Walter were in earlier this morning."

"Walter was with her?"

"Yes, it seems he's struck up a relationship with the yoga master. He came in for a workout while Annie and I worked on her blocks. Why, does it matter?"

"It doesn't really, but I knew Walter before he and Annie met on that cruise and I just feel like I should say something to Annie about it."

"She doesn't know?"

"Not yet," Olyria said. "Would you want to know if Charles had dated a friend before he met you?"

"You dated Walter? I don't remember that. Surely I would remember someone who looked like Walter. When did you date?"

"Hmm, Walter really was too interested in himself to actually do what I would call dating, but we went out for supper a couple of times. It was about six months after my husband died and I thought I might be ready to step out into the world, but I wasn't yet. I probably never mentioned him to you." Olyria smiled coyly. "Besides, I didn't tell you everything and some things just aren't worth talking about."

"You don't think much of him?" Caroline wanted to share her concerns about Walter and Annie with Olyria but decided against it as the conversation went on.

"He likes the ladies just a little too much to suit me." Olyria fingered her new fabric as Caroline rang it up. "And I kept losing things when we were out together. My grandmother's brooch disappeared and a diamond bracelet my husband gave me right before he died."

"Are you suggesting Walter took them?"

"I couldn't say for sure; but every time we were together, something I valued disappeared." Olyria looked down at her hands. "So . . . would you want to know about Charles?"

"I think I'd let sleeping dogs lie," Caroline said. "Annie is so crazy about him, and they are still sort of honeymooning."

"A year is a long time to honeymoon," Olyria said.

"Still, it seems they don't want to be out of one another's sight."

"Yeah, I thought that, too." Olyria picked up her bag and headed for the door. "I have a palm reading and a manicure this morning so I better get my shop opened up and get ready for business. Ta ta!" she said and saluted with the bag as she left.

Caroline sighed. It was the first moment of peace she'd had since Charles left for Kansas City. She loved her shop, she loved the people who came in, she loved the challenge and the freedom of her own business; but nothing had prepared her for how hard it was going to be or how many hours she'd have to put in to get it to be a paying proposition. She was surprised she could feel so lonely with all the people coming and going. The responsibility lay heavy on her shoulders and she'd be glad to have Charles home on Saturday. She needed a hug.

Caroline worked fast and furiously and when she next checked the wall clock, it was almost noon. Kathy would be coming in soon for her Stack 'n' Whack class. It was for beginning quilters and filled up the first day the shop opened. Buckeye Grove had a lot of people with time on their hands. She thought she'd get a bite to eat, maybe some of the salad fixings she knew were wilting in the classroom refrigerator upstairs. They were left over from the first-week open house.

The afternoon was busy and by the time she left the shop that evening she was exhausted. Budd and Caroline dined on leftovers and then Caroline sewed furiously on her table runner, which she still had not managed to finish for Kathy's class.

The next morning Caroline went through her routine opening the shop. Things were moving along like clockwork when the phone rang.

"Always in Stitches," she said. "May I help you?" On the other end of the line was a softly sobbing girl.

"Mom?" she said. "It's Jamie. I've been mugged. Can you come and get me?"

Chapter 5

Jamie's voice was dry and raspy.

"Jamie, where are you? Are you all right? Did you call the police? Where is Joellen? Were you alone? How many times have I told you not to be alone? Do you need to go to the hospital?"

"Mom, calm down. I am at Wood County Hospital here in Bowling Green, just come and get me. I want to come home."

"Ok, just tell me what happened."

"Well, today is the day I need to be at Belmont for student teaching, but poor ole Louie the Buey was low on gas. Dad said he'd deposited money in my account, so I was at the ATM getting money for gas and out of the blue these guys tackled me from behind. My face is swollen, and they said I'll need some stitches, my back hurts…" Jamie started to sob, "One grabbed the cash and the other grabbed my book bag."

"What was in your book bag?" Caroline asked.

"Oh," Jamie whined, "only about $500 worth of books that I need to study for midterms next week."

"What about your car and house keys?" Caroline asked.

"No, I had my key ring and lanyard wrapped around my wrist. My wallet was in the car. I don't have to worry about their breaking into the apartment or having my driver's license or credit cards."

"Can you call Tommy?" Caroline asked. She wasn't crazy about Jamie's boyfriend, but he was better than nothing at a time like this.

"I called him already. He'll be here as soon as he can get somebody to replace him at work. He's probably on his way right now. "

"I have the same problem here, Jamie. I'll get on the road as soon as I get someone to cover the shop for me."

"Okay, Mom. Just get here as fast as you can." And she broke the connection.

Murphy's Law kicked in and things continued to go sour. She soon had Nan on the phone asking her to come in. Her morning test was over, but she had studying to do for the midterm she had the following day. Nan agreed to come in as long as she could study in the shop.

Caroline had no choice but to agree. She dropped the phone back into its cradle; just then the UPS man came in with a huge Moda order. He was a new guy and he was a hunk. Black hair with Superman-blue highlights. A firm little butt that pulled his brown pants taut as he bent over to deposit the boxes at the check-out counter. Caroline couldn't help but notice. She really couldn't. He looked to be about twenty-five.

"You're new, aren't you?" Caroline said.

"I've been on vacation for two weeks," he said. "I just missed your opening. Joe has been filling in for me." He extended a hand. "I'm Stan Darling, your regular delivery man."

Caroline took his hand and shook it. "Good to meet you Mr. Darling." She said it with a flirty twitter.

"Stan," he said. "Please call me Stan." He smiled as he spoke. His teeth were white as Walter Wilkins's hairy arms and they shone in the shop lights. He extended his signature machine and Caroline signed. "Thanks," he said. "I'll see you tomorrow."

Caroline couldn't even remember what she was working on before Stan Darling came in. He was the cutest thing she'd seen since she met Michael Lomard's little Stella. It didn't matter what she'd been working on because there were a number of unfinished projects scattered about. She started putting fabric away and used her cell phone to call Charles. He answered after two rings; Caroline told him about Jamie's dilemma. He remained maddeningly calm.

"Computer? Money? Books?" he rattled off questions about what was stolen and then proceeded to remind Caroline that he didn't want Jamie to go "so far away" and this probably wouldn't have happened if Jamie had gone to Ohio State. Caroline, not wanting to hear a lecture, cut Charles off mid-sentence to ask his opinion on picking Jamie up.

"Well, do what you want; but it doesn't sound too bad, and we want her to be able to handle her own problems. Do you have someone to cover the shop? What is she going to do when you pick her up? When will she go back?"

"Charles, this is our daughter. She's been attacked. She needs her mother."

"Hmmm, well, yes, you're right. Of course you should go."

Charles also promised to change his flight and come home early instead of a day later. The two exchanged quick good-byes and Caroline hung up. She began checking the newly delivered boxes of merchandise.

The phone rang, startling Caroline. It was Jamie again.

"Mom, who was on the phone?" she asked in an impatient voice.

"I was talking to your father. Call me on my cell phone next time. Did you talk to the police already?"

"No, I just wanted to let you know that Joellen is here with me." Jamie's voice had lost its hysterical tone and she was making more sense.

"Okay, call me when you finish talking to the police." She hung up the phone again.

At that moment Annie and Walter walked through the door. Walter was carrying a small plastic bag of dark chocolate squares.

"Hi," Annie said. "I came for more help with my paper piecing. I hoped we could work on it while Walter has his yoga class."

"Oh, honey. Not today. Jamie just called; she's in the emergency room at school. She was robbed and injured. She needs me to get up there as soon as possible. Nan is on her way in to relieve me. Charles is still in Kansas City and he's trying to change his flight to come home early." Caroline looked at Walter and felt his eyes caressing her in a way that gave her the creeps.

"It's time for my class," he said smoothly. "Wish I could help, of course, but I need to get to my class."

"Yes, go ahead," Annie said. "I'll stay here with Caroline."

Caroline was pacing and checking her watch. She used a pair of scissors to open the UPS boxes and laid two calico bolts on the counter. "I could look after things for a few minutes," Annie said.

Caroline looked around. The shop looked like a quilter had gone on a rampage. Caroline knew she couldn't leave poor Annie in this chaotic mess alone. Annie didn't even know how to run the register.

"Or maybe Olyria or Goldie could come in until Nan arrives," Caroline said. She needed someone to help and she needed them now. She picked up the phone and dialed a number. "Olyria, are you busy?" Caroline frantically asked. "Oh . . . okay . . . thanks." Caroline hung up. "She's in the middle of a French manicure."

Annie nodded. Caroline punched in some more numbers on the phone. "Goldie, this is Caroline, are you busy, I really need some help? Oh great. Could you come over and watch the shop till Nan gets here?" Caroline took a deep breath, then continued; "Jamie just called. She's been mugged at school and needs me."

Caroline hung up the phone. "Yes," she said to Annie and the room. "She'll be right over. She has to finish a background she's blocking in and clean her brushes. Annie, could you stay with her? And don't worry about the mess." Annie nodded again.

"Thanks so much," Caroline said. "I just have to let Budd know so she can spend the night at a friend's house and then I can go."

Just then the back door opened and in walked a group of the Circle Time Quilters[4], some of Caroline's friends from a neighboring town who had a guild that was over thirty years old. They were a great group of girls, hard workers who loved to have fun. They were all master quilters and had been great supporters of the shop. Caroline yelled out a quick hello, and continued opening up the new fabric. She knew the quilters would want to see what had just arrived. Her cell phone rang.

"Mom, have you left to come pick me up yet?" asked the familiar voice of her daughter.

"Ok, Jamie, I'm on my way! I just have to wait for Goldie to get here and I have Nan coming in for the rest of the afternoon."

When she hung up the phone, she glanced at the clock again. Only five minutes had passed since Goldie said she'd be over. Caroline walked toward the group of quilters who had recently won an award at the National Quilters Association show. She apologized for not getting to them sooner.

Caroline cut fabric and rang up sales for the guild girls. Then she

---

4   Circle Time Quilters - fictitious name for a guild in a neighboring city.

began making a list of things for Nan to do during her downtime. Annie stood by, not knowing what she might do to help. Caroline hopped from foot to foot and finally told Annie, "I can't wait another minute. I've got to go." She grabbed her purse, dug out her car keys and hurried out the back door without so much as a glance over her shoulder.

Goldie was there two minutes after Caroline left. Kathy came in right behind her to teach the Stack 'n' Whack class. Annie told them the little bit she knew about Jamie's situation. "Families," Goldie sighed. "Can't live with them, can't live without them. Husbands and children can break your heart."

"I'd agree with that," Kathy said. She was a tall, thin woman with curly brown hair and long slender fingers that Caroline was convinced were artistic. "My eighteen-year-old son and my husband bicker constantly. It makes me absolutely crazy." She shook her head and, after stashing her purse, went upstairs to the classroom.

"Maybe I'm finding that out," Annie said. "I always thought a husband would protect his wife no matter what." She circled the boxes of new fabric and lowered her eyes.

"Some of them do. One of mine was a protector like that. Mr. McElroy..." Goldie's eyes went soft. "He was special but basically they're more alike than different. Be sure to keep them fed and petted and they are pretty tame." Goldie picked up two bolts of fabric from the cutting table and returned it to the shelf.

"That seemed true with Walter, at first . . . but now . . ." Annie hesitated, bit her lip, ". . . but now . . . I don't know, he just seems so angry."

Goldie spoke in soft tones. "Don't ever, ever let it get physical," she said. "Nobody else is going to stand up for you . . . and especially in marriage." Her eyes clouded. "Mr. Lewis would let it get physical. He even broke my arm once. Soon as I healed up I snuck up behind him with a twenty-pound hammer and broke his shoulder. It didn't take him long to get the message and he was meek as a movie star's wife ever after." It was clear Goldie was proud of her ability to look after herself. She gathered up four scattered pattern books and returned them to the bookrack. "It looks like a bomb dropped in here," she said.

Annie didn't respond.

"Does Walter hit you?" Goldie asked, turning to look Annie in the eye.

"He's never hit me. I don't think Walter would do that," she said. "But . . ."

At that moment Nan came through the door. "Hey," she said. "I got here as fast as I could. Where's Caroline?" Her hair was pulled back in a straggly ponytail and she looked tired.

"She left already," Goldie said. "Annie and I were holding down the fort for you. And Kathy came in to teach a class. I bet Caroline forgot she was coming, in all the excitement."

"What happened? Caroline sounded like someone died."

"Jamie was robbed at an ATM," Goldie said. "She was injured and is in the emergency room. She was crying for her mom to come and hold her hand."

Nan shuddered. She pushed fabric out of the way and dropped a pile of books on the cutting counter. "I don't blame her," she said. "Thank goodness, it's slow in here. I'm in the middle of midterms and I have to study."

Goldie left to go back to her studio. Annie decided to down to Walter's yoga class and watch his workout. Nan got busy with her schoolbooks.

⌘

Annie slipped through the yoga studio door as quietly as she could. Walter and four ladies were in Downward-Facing-Dog position. David walked from person to person, adjusting their poses as he went. He glanced at Annie and then went back to the class members as if she were of little or no consequence.

She sat on a bench along the wall, folded her arms across her chest and watched as the practitioners bent themselves into more and more impossible positions. Oriental music played softly in the background and Annie felt herself relax from all the excitement in the quilt shop.

The women were trim and looked experienced in the poses they were taking. Finally, David directed them to totally relax and feel the benefit of their morning's practice. The room was silent except for the exotic music. After several minutes David called them back to movement and the rest of their day. He ducked behind the screen in the corner of the room and left the students alone.

"What are you doing here?" Walter asked when he noticed Annie.

"Caroline had to leave and nobody was able to help with my quilt squares so I came down to watch you."

The ladies rolled up their mats and chatted with one another as they prepared to leave. Walter rolled his mat and watched the ladies. His eyes twinkled with the challenge some men send to some women. "I'm aglow from my workout," he said to nobody in particular. He ran a hand up one of the women's arms as she passed by him. She jerked her arm away and gave Walter a scathing look.

He neither apologized nor withdrew his hand. "David loved the chocolate. He gave me vitamins to sample in exchange," he said to Annie. "They are guaranteed to improve flexibility and energy level. He swore I'd begin to feel like a twenty-year-old."

"How nice," Annie said. "But shouldn't you check with Dr.

Harris before you take more drugs?"

"They're vitamins," Walter said. "Not drugs. Vitamins," he said close to Annie's face. His tone suggested Annie might be dumb as a rock. "Most of David's students take them. He blends them special for us."

"It was just a thought, Walter," she said back. She glanced at the women and stiffened her back. She stuck her hand out to the woman Walter had caressed. "I'm Annie Wilkins, Walter's wife," she said.

"Nice to meet you," the lady said. "I'm Alice Stotts."

Walter scowled and took Annie's arm above the elbow. "It's time for us to go, my dear," he said with the emphasis on my dear. Annie tried pulling her arm away but did not succeed. Walter smiled at Alice Stotts as he pulled Annie closer to him, put his arm around her shoulder.

Annie jerked her arm again and this time she pulled it loose. It was red where Walter's fingers had dug in. His arm was still around her shoulders and he ushered her towards the door. The women stood watching as Walter lead Annie out the door and let it swoosh closed behind them.

Chapter 6

Caroline was deep in thought as she made her way north to Bowling Green. The school always seemed so close – only two hours away; but today the drive was taking an eternity. Her mind was jumping with so many fears and doubts; it was good she was on autopilot. She drove through Findlay and hardly remembered how she got there. Her thoughts were of Jamie. How would this incident affect her spirit? Charles and Caroline raised their girls to be confident, self-assured young women. They had guided them and tried helping them understand the consequences of their decisions but left decisions, in most part, up to them.

Caroline pulled into the emergency room parking lot. She ran to the lobby and asked for Jamie Clarkson.

"You'll have to wait, Ma'am; the police are with her now," said the receptionist.

"You don't understand, she's my daughter, she's been mugged. I need to see her now."

The receptionist looked at the monitor on her desk. "She's in room twenty-five, fifth room down the hall on the right. But I'm telling you there's an officer with her now. You're gonna have to wait."

"Thanks," Caroline whispered. She walked down the sterile

hallway, pushing back thoughts of her last visit to the ER, the day she'd been shot. The antiseptic fragrance heightened her anxiety. Jamie's best friend, Joellen, was standing outside the curtained cubicle. Caroline hugged her tight and allowed herself to be hugged.

"I'm so sorry, Mrs. Clarkson," Joellen said. "She's pretty shaken and they really roughed her up."

The curtain was open slightly; Caroline peered in and gasped when she saw Jamie's bruised and swollen face.

"Mom," Jamie sobbed, "I thought you'd never get here."

The police officer looked up with a tentative smile, "We're finished here for now. If you remember anything else, please give me a call." He handed Jamie a card and told her both the station number and his extension were on it. To Caroline he said, "She can go now."

Jamie slid off the cart, but her legs were wobbly and she began to shake again. Caroline and Joellen put their arms around Jamie's small waist and helped her dress and then hobble to her car. Joellen drove Louie the Buey back to the apartment, and Jamie rode with Caroline.

"I think you should come home," Caroline said.

"I don't know, Mom, that's what I thought at first but I can't just blow off my midterms next week," Jamie took in a deep breath. "But I'm not keen on staying here right now. Can you spend the night and let me think about it?"

Tommy arrived at the apartment at the same time as Joellen, Caroline and Jamie. "I got here as quickly as I could," he said.

Caroline was not fond of Tommy. She didn't understand what Jamie saw in him and feared he didn't have the character she'd hoped for in the men her daughters would marry. Oh, he was handsome, tall, dark-haired, with wide-set blue eyes, and that explained a lot; but character was lacking as far as Caroline could see.

Jamie turned when she heard Tommy; she left Caroline's side and hobbled over to him. "I was so scared," she sobbed as he held her. She buried her face in his chest.

Tommy was uncomfortable with Jamie's crying. He was used to the confident Jamie. Caroline was uncomfortable with the distance he tried to put between himself and her sobbing daughter.

Joellen banged around in the kitchen, making her famous Chinese Chicken Salad for dinner. Nobody was hungry but Tommy. The women pushed the food around their plates and Tommy finished off the bowl. Jamie said the attack had robbed her of her feelings of safety and confidence. The women talked about how to stay safe till Tommy changed the subject.

"Hey, Babe, do you have that research paper I need for my Literature class?" he asked.

"Oh no!" Jamie groaned. "It was in my book bag. I'll have to print out another copy. Do you mind if I do that tomorrow? I made some notes on that copy and it'd take me a little time to recreate the changes."

"Oh, man, I really wanted to get it tonight so I could study it," Tommy said with a pouty frown. Jamie shrugged. "Could you get me a beer when you go to print it out?" he asked.

Caroline held her breath during the exchange; she hated that Jamie seemed to be his willing servant. What had happened to her independent daughter, and was Jamie doing Tommy's schoolwork as well as her own?

Jamie winced as she stood. Joellen glared at Tommy and rushed to help Jamie up.

"I'll be right back," Jamie said. When she returned, she handed Tommy the paper and a beer. Tommy drank the beer while he studied the paper. When he got up to leave, Caroline went into Jamie's room to give them a moment of privacy for saying good-bye. Jamie's eyes were dark rimmed and her shoulders slumped with fatigue. Caroline fumed in the bedroom for forty-five minutes while Tommy said good-night. The boy was as sensitive as a bucket of rocks. It was 10:30 before he left.

Jamie plopped down on her bed after Tommy left. She hadn't decided whether she wanted to stay at school or go home. Everyone was exhausted; and finally, at the end of a very long day, they turned in.

In the morning, they met in the kitchen. It was sparse - - like most college kitchens, - - with an overflowing trashcan and last night's dirty dishes in the sink. Caroline resisted the urge to straighten up.

"Good morning, Mom," Jamie said.

"Good morning, honey, how are you feeling today?"

"I'm sore, and look at all the black-and-blue marks." Jamie turned from side to side to show her mother the marks on her face and arms.

"Have you decided what you want to do – stay or come home?" Caroline asked.

"I'm going to stay here. I have too much invested in this semester to miss the midterms," Jamie said. Caroline smiled and admired her daughter's determination, but she remembered how it felt to have a stranger shoot you in the leg. It created more internal change than external. It had caused her to change her life completely. Only time would tell the effect this would have on Jamie.

"It'll take you a while to heal, both physically and mentally," Caroline said. "At least it did me after I was shot."

"I'll be fine, Mom," Jamie said with a half smile. Her blonde hair was full of morning tangles and the bruises on her face were a jarring purple. Caroline wanted to smooth her hair, kiss the hurt away and command her to get her things together and get in the car. But she was aware that the time for taking that action had passed and instead said, "Well, if that's your decision, I guess I'd better get on the road. I'll have to pick up Budd and get to the shop." Caroline hugged Jamie and gently kissed her bruised check.

Tears trickled down Caroline's cheeks as she pulled out of the parking lot of Jamie's apartment. She was frightened for her daughter and knew she couldn't protect Jamie when she was so far away. Probably couldn't protect her any longer if they lived in the same house. She would return to making daily phone calls like she'd done when Jamie was a freshman. It would make her feel better.

⌘

Charles arrived back in Buckeye Grove early that morning with a heavy heart. His family had needed him and he wasn't there.

"Hello, hello," Charles called as the door slammed behind him. He dropped his suitcase and jacket at the door. His words fell into the silence. He felt the house's emptiness. He went to the kitchen and started a pot of coffee. He'd had one watery cup on the plane before it landed and needed a jolt of caffeine to get him going for what lay ahead.

The coffee perked hopefully and the rich smell of his favorite hazelnut blend filled the room before Caroline came through the back door. It had been a long ride home in the morning traffic. Her eyes were red and she was exhausted. She'd aged in twenty-four hours.

"Oh, Charles, you should see her face," she said as he wrapped his arms around her. Caroline absorbed the warmth of his body and felt the safety of his arms. "She has a big gash over her left eye which required stitches and it's all swollen. She has bruises on her chin and her lip is cut." Caroline looked Charles in the eye. "I can't even think about how scared she is. It'll take a while for all her wounds to heal and we'll have to help her through this."

"I'm sorry if I seemed heartless when you first told me the news," Charles said. "I thought you were bringing her home for TLC."

"So did I," Caroline said. "But she decided she needed to stay at school. She has midterms."

Charles put his finger under Caroline's chin and lifted her head so he could see her big brown eyes. "Remember what they say, 'Whatever doesn't kill you makes you stronger'."

"I'm angry. I'd sure like to kill someone," she said. "How dare some street criminal hurt my daughter? How dare someone take advantage of her like this?"

Charles guided her to the kitchen table and they sat down. He held her hand. "We'll get through this, Caroline. You're strong, the girls are strong. Nobody can beat us when we put our minds to it."

"I know, Hon," Caroline said. "I'm just so angry. I wanted to leave right away, drop everything and go, swoop her up and bring her home. But I couldn't leave. I had to wait to get help at the shop." She swabbed her eyes with a tissue. "I felt so helpless."

"It's okay now. She's fine."

"You're right, but it isn't over yet. I'll just bet it isn't over yet."

"You've had a stressful week. You knew there would be challenges opening your own business."

"Yes, I guess I . . . I just didn't realize how tied down I'd feel . . . how hard it was going to be."

"Do you want to get out from under the shop?" Charles asked.

"No," Caroline said after a minute of thought. "I'm not a quitter.

I've dreamed of this for so long. I know things will get easier once we are truly up and running." Caroline said these words with more conviction than she felt. Could she really have it all? Charles smiled and squeezed her hand.

"Could you pick up Budd? She's at Emma Harrington's house. I've got to get cleaned up and get to the shop." He agreed and Caroline showered and changed, then hurried off to Always in Stitches. Caroline's friend, Janet Moeller was holding down the fort. The shop was quiet all day which was a blessing but also a concern.

⌘

The next morning Caroline struggled again with the lock on the shop door. She grabbed a piece of paper and pinned it to the wall inside the door. She'd start her list of needed repairs right now. As she went through the routine of getting the shop opened and ready for business, the phone rang.

"Good morning, Always in Stitches, what can I do for you today?" Caroline chirped into the phone, half expecting it to be Jamie.

"I have several fantasies of what you can do for me today," the deep voice on the other end said.

"Who is this? Why are you calling me? I don't have time for games."

Caroline could hear the heavy breathing and then the phone went silent. He'd hung up again. She struggled about whether or not to tell Charles. In the end she decided not to say anything, at least not right now. She would solve this herself when she had some free time, if that ever happened.

Stan Darling, the UPS driver, rapped on the front door window. The trunk show had arrived. Caroline spent the rest of the morning unpacking quilts. They were beautiful and hopefully would inspire customers; so would Stan if they could see him. Caroline loved Charles very much but Stan was nice to look at. Caroline thought of how well the shop was going, how she loved being around such beautiful fabric all day; Stan was an added benefit

At about lunchtime the bell on the front door rang as the door opened. Caroline looked up to see Olyria and Jeanine enter the shop. Olyria was wearing a red print skirt and white peasant blouse. Her auburn hair was spiked higher than usual and a black scarf was tied around her waist. She was done up like a Halloween gypsy. But her eyes were puffy and her skin seemed to hang from her high cheekbones.

"Hey, kiddo, how's everything going? How is Jamie doing?" the women said in unison.

Caroline told the story of her drive up to Bowling Green, described what Jamie looked like and the odd evening with Jamie and Tommy.

"You look tired," Caroline said to Olyria. " Is the palm reading getting you down?"

"I'm fine," Olyria replied. "I haven't been sleeping very well. Maybe I need to take some vitamins."

"Annie told me Walter is getting vitamins from the yoga master," Caroline said. "You might check with him?"

"I'll stick with the drug store variety." Olyria said.

Caroline said, "Annie was concerned about Walter taking vitamins without talking to his doctor."

"I don't think they care much about natural remedies," Jeanine said. "But you need to take care of yourself." Jeanine was checking out a round of calico. "Have you seen how dark it is getting outside? Looks like we might be in for some rain."

"Oh, look at these beautiful quilts," Olyria said. "Is this the trunk show you were talking about?" Olyria was happy they didn't ask any more questions about her health. She knew it was more than lack of sleep and that she would have to call the doctor to find out the test results. She didn't want to say anything to her dear friends until she knew for sure.

Olyria picked up one of the quilts Caroline had just put out on display; and when she did, a loud clap of thunder shook the building and rain began to pound on the metal roof of the granary. All three women jumped.

"Speaking of rain . . ." Jeanine said and they all laughed.

"Oh, no . . . . . Olyria, can you grab the wastebaskets, Jeanine please help me move the quilts?" The rain had started to seep down through the ceiling and onto the floor. Fixing the roof would go to the top of the list for Schultz.

They scurried around moving quilts and bolts of fabric before anything could be ruined. When they were all done, they burst out laughing. Olyria and Caroline gave Jeanine a curious smile. Did Jeanine have special powers? More to the point, could she get in touch with Schultz and have him do something about the roof before it ruined a valuable trunk show or something else.

When Olyria and Jeanine left, Caroline called Schultz. There was no answer at his business phone. She left a message and made a mental note to have Charles speak with him. He seemed to be able to get so much further with the man. What is it about those Men-Men; male-chauvinistic types that think women belong in the kitchen. Charles didn't exactly like Schultz either, but he was able to talk to him and get repairs done in a timely manner.

⌘

Sunday morning Caroline woke with a start. Her heart was pounding so hard she heard it echo in her ears. She was dreaming about Jamie. She was walking down a tree-lined street and then in slow motion a young man in a hooded sweatshirt jumped out and pulled her into a dark abyss. Jamie screamed and then was gone.

Caroline fumbled for the phone. She had to hear Jamie's voice.

Just before she hit speed dial, Charles asked, "What's the matter? Do you know it's 3:30 a.m.?"

Caroline clicked off the phone and returned it to the dock. "Oh, Charles, I had such a bad dream."

Charles hugged his wife. "It was a dream, sweetheart, now go back to sleep . . . *please,*" Charles whispered. Charles drifted off but Caroline lay awake staring at the ceiling. She finally fell back to sleep just before the alarm went off.

First thing, she grabbed the phone and hit speed dial. "Hi, honey. Did I wake you?" Caroline said when Jamie answered the phone.

"Not really Mom, I've been up for a while. Every time I close my eyes and try to sleep, I feel like I'm spinning. The muggers are spinning and spinning me around and around, laughing, then they knock me down and grab my book bag." Jamie sounded broken down and worn out.

"Oh, Hon, perhaps you should go see the doctor, find someone who can help you through this," Caroline said.

"I'll be fine, Mom. I've got to run though. I have to get to the library to finish a paper," Jamie said.

"Okay, I'll talk to you later. Let me know if you need anything," Caroline said

"Thanks, Mom. I'll talk to you," Jamie said and she clicked off her phone.

Caroline hoped it was her own paper Jamie had to work on and that this Saturday would be as busy as the last two. She needed something to occupy her mind besides her daughter.

Caroline got her wish. Sales were brisk and the time flew by.

Sunday was Caroline's only day off. Charles was out golfing

and Budd went horseback riding with Emma. Caroline had the house to herself and she sat down at her sewing machine. The hum of the motor and the rhythm of the needle going up and down helped soothe her nerves. She called Jamie two times just to make sure she was OK.

⌘

Caroline slept better Sunday night and woke up late. She rushed around getting Budd off and then going to the shop. She jiggled the key in the lock and wanted to kick the door but thought better of it. Finally the shop door opened and she put her things in the storeroom. Caroline decided this morning she would check the inventory and see what she needed to order.

One customer stopped in and by mid-afternoon Caroline was alone again. The phone startled her.

"Good afternoon, Always in Stitches, how can I help you?" Caroline braced herself, thinking it was her anonymous caller.

"Hey, Mom, are you OK? You sound funny," Jamie asked.

"I'm fine," Caroline said, relieved. "I was just in the middle of something. How are you doing? Are you all right?"

"I haven't slept much; and my stomach is constantly in a knot, so I can't eat. I've been thinking a lot," Jamie said. "Mom, I've made a decision."

"Do you want me to come up and get you? Have you decided to come home for a while?"

"No, Mom, that's not it . . . . . I've decided to move in with Tommy," Jamie said.

Caroline didn't respond.

"Mom? . . . Are you there?"

Caroline's voice was measured. "Jamie, have you thought this through? Are you sure?" Caroline went on. "Things will get better, believe me. I know how I felt after the shooting at the bank."

"I love Tommy; I feel so much safer when I'm with him. I'm not sure how to tell Dad."

"Your father will not be happy with this news; but whatever his reaction is, remember he loves you."

"Could you talk to him and kind of prepare the way for me, Mom?"

Caroline sighed. "I'll talk to him tonight. Are you sure you want to do this?"

"Yes, Mom, I'm sure."

Caroline knew that no amount of pressure would change Jamie's mind and she didn't want to start running her life now. She'd just have to be there to support her if things didn't work out.

Caroline had no more than hung up the phone when it rang again.

"Hey, Caroline, it's Annie. I just called to get an update on Jamie, how's she doing?" Annie asked.

How is Jamie doing Caroline thought to herself? Is she healing emotionally or is she hiding from her fears by moving in with Tommy?

"I just talked to her and she's doing well, Annie; it's so kind of you to ask." Caroline went on to tell the whole story yet again.

"Are you ready for the Guild meeting tomorrow?" Annie asked.

"Oh, yeah, the Guild meets tomorrow. I guess I'll see you then," Caroline said as she hung up the phone. The last several days had seemed to blur from one to another. The one thing Caroline was sure of was whatever tomorrow might bring she would be ready.

Chapter 7

Caroline was optimistic when she opened the shop on Tuesday morning. It was still exciting for her every time she put the key in the shop door and surveyed her fiefdom. There was another Guild meeting today and she hoped the quilts from the trunk show would spark some sales.

"Hey there, how's it going? How's Jamie?" called Amy Nye, Caroline's sister, as she walked in the door. Amy had Caroline's sunny disposition but none of her business sense or practicality. She bragged that she sewed every day and if she didn't, she was sick. Nan was busy with midterms and Amy came in to help while Caroline was tied up with the Guild meeting.

"Jamie's doing fine, I guess." Caroline had no time to tell her sister more as the Guild members started to arrive. Caroline's heart actually started to sing as all the ladies arrived. She was so thrilled to be part of the friendships that were forming. Annie and Walter came in together. Walter's hair was well coifed, and he wore his skintight yoga pants. He smelled of expensive after-shave.

"Top of the morning to all my fair ladies," Walter chimed. He beamed his disconcerting smile, and his eyes spoke volumes, as he looked Sheryll Douglas up and down. Sheryll was a beautiful woman and used to the attention of men but the look made her skin crawl. She was shocked Walter would be so blatant in front of Annie. Sheryll gave him a half smile and went upstairs for the meeting.

Walter kissed Annie and headed downstairs for his session with the yoga master. Annie watched him leave. Was he flirting right in front of her? The look he gave Sheryll seemed an awful lot like lust. No, he wouldn't do that, he was just being charming, she told herself.

Michael Lomand, with Stella under his arm, came in late again. Aggie had already called the meeting to order and Jeanine had collected dues as part of her treasurer's duties. There were only four new members, Wilma Good, Patsy Cline, Mary Clark and Charlene Powers. Several of the women had questions about how much the guild would be allowed to grow. "I like a group that stays small," Wilma said.

"We're planning to go no larger than thirty or forty," Caroline said.

Patsy Cline and Mary Clark nodded. "I prefer a smaller group, too," Aggie said.

Charlene pursed her lips. "I actually like bigger groups," she said. "It gives so many more opportunities for alliances."

"We may decide to start another guild if this one fills up," Caroline said. "We're trying to meet the needs of all our quilting friends."

Michael arranged his muffins and egg casserole on the refreshment table and took a seat. He pulled two log cabin blocks out of his jacket pocket and patted Stella while the meeting continued. Jeanine gave him a disgruntled look as she collected his dues. The ladies took a break to help themselves to muffins and eggs. Michael watched with the pleasure of someone who loved food, just because it was there.

Olyria made a program report; she seemed rather stoic today, as if something was on her mind. She suggested a mystery night quilt session for the guild ladies later in the summer and asked who might be interested in having Shirley Stutz[5] come in and speak to the group about free-motion quilting. Shirley was an award-winning quilt maker and teacher from southeast Ohio. She had several program topics the group could pick from but Olyria thought a number of the members were ready for some free-motion tips. She knew she would inspire the guild with her enthusiasm and innovation and had heard through the grapevine that Shirley was sure to make everyone laugh with her funny stories. "Maybe she would autograph her *Easy and Elegant Lone Star Quilt* book for us," Jeanine said.

When Olyria was finished, Aggie turned the meeting over to Caroline, who was leading the Quilts of Valor project. Caroline's face beamed when she saw the number of blocks the group had completed.

"We're making great progress. We should try to have all the blocks made by the next meeting." Caroline said. "Once the blocks are done, we'll need a volunteer to assemble the quilt top."

Jeanine piped up and said, "I'll put all the blocks together."

"That would be great," Caroline replied. "I thought we could take some time this session to have a general discussion on how each of us got involved with quilting and what type of quilting you prefer – patchwork, paper piecing, appliqué, crazy quilting."

The dialogue that ensued lifted Caroline's heart even higher. This is why she wanted to open a quilt shop. This is what made all the struggles of opening the shop worthwhile. She was watching new friendships being forged. She believed friendships were the

---

5   Shirley Stutz - a quilter who became a leader in teaching and display. She uses humor as a teaching aid.

core of the quilting experience. Quilting brought women together the same way sports brought men together. It had been that way forever. She was happy to be part of it.

The women chatted and ate Michael's muffins, basking in the warmth of one another. Michael put Stella down to sniff up crumbs on the floor and began to clear the refreshment table. While Michael worked at gathering up the food, Olyria took the floor again.

"I've got something I'd like to share; it's something very personal." Olyria's voice cracked. She was dressed conservatively today; her hair was smoothed into a do that hugged her head. Caroline missed the gypsy outfit. "I have a tumor, it's cancerous . . . it's in my breast. I'll have a lumpectomy first and then immediately begin radiation therapy within the next week or two." Tears welled in Olyria's eyes and one slid down her cheek. She took a deep breath, lifted her head and firmly said, "I just wanted you to know so you would understand if I go bald."

The members of the guild clamored, "Is there anything we can do to help?" "You'll be in our prayers." "Everything will be okay."

Olyria cleared her throat. "I'm going to be fine. We've caught this early and there is every reason to be hopeful."

"We're all here for you. Let us know if you need anything." Jeanine said.

"I know you're going to be okay; you're a strong woman. Give the doctors a run for their money," Michael said.

Caroline gave Olyria a hug and as everyone got up to leave Caroline said, "Be sure to check out the trunk show that just arrived yesterday. Oh, and next time why don't we bring our favorite quilt book and share why we like it. See you again next week."

Michael reached down to put Stella in her carrier. He looked right and left, then fell to his knees on the floor, looking under the table. "She's gone. Help, help, has anyone seen Stella! She's gone!"

A search ensued. "Here Stella, Stella," echoed through the store. "We'll find her Michael, don't worry, we'll find her."

"Stella, Stella, come here girl." Michael was down on his hands and knees peering under display shelves. The quilt shop had fallen into chaos over Michael's puffy little dog. His tone was getting frantic when several minutes later, the quilt shop's connecting door opened from the hallway and David Williams walked in. "Does this little fur ball belong to anyone up here?" he asked. "I saw her wander over from the tearoom into my studio. I'm in the middle of my yoga session and she's very distracting."

"Oh, thank you, thank you so much," Michael sighed. Jeanine helped pull him to his feet, and he made a lunge for Stella" He looked into her eyes and held her nose-to-nose. Scone crumbs hanging on the fur around her mouth. "Bad doggie, no treats for you today. You scared me half to death." Then he smoothed Stella's fur, gave her a hug and tucked her into the big patch pocket of his coat instead of her carrier.

As things calmed down, Annie went over to Olyria and gave her a hug. "If there's anything I can do for you, please let me know," she said. "I guess now wouldn't be a good time to ask you to help me with my paper piecing?"

"That would be just what I need right now to keep my mind occupied. I don't have another palm-reading appointment until 2:00 so I have some time on my hands." Annie looked at Olyria, studying to see if she was serious.

"It's a little palm-reader joke," Olyria said. "Time on my hands. Get it?"

"I get it," Annie said. "Very funny." The women settled down at a sewing machine and got to work.

As they worked, Olyria studied Annie and noticed some bruises on her arm but didn't ask her outright about them. "How are things going on the home front?" Olyria asked.

Annie kept her eyes down; she didn't want her friend to read what had to be written all over her face. "Fine . . . well, okay, I guess."

"You don't sound too convincing."

"I guess the newness has just worn off."

"Annie, how much do you really know about Walter?" Olyria asked quietly.

"Not much. Not as much as I should have before . . ." Annie's voice trailed off.

"It might be worth your while to try to learn more about the man you're married to."

"I've tried," Annie said. "But he doesn't like talking about himself. All he's ever told me is that he's Dutch. It just seems easier to let the past stay past. I don't really know what else to do." Annie didn't like confrontation, and Walter's reactions were so unpredictable. If Walter didn't want to talk, she wasn't going to push it.

"I've known women who accidentally happened upon things in their husband's sock drawer. You know, strictly by accident."

"I couldn't go through Walter's drawers," Annie said. Her eyes were wide and her mouth hung open.

"Of course, you could. Women do it all the time. It's almost a normal part of marriage."

Annie squared her shoulders. "I would never do that to my husband."

Olyria stopped; she wanted to say more, but she didn't want to cause her friend any pain. Olyria struggled with keeping the secret that she had dated Walter before Annie and he met. "You may change your mind; and if you do, don't think you're spying on Walter, you're just looking out after yourself."

"You might be right, Olyria, but there are some things in my past I'd rather nobody knew. I have the right to keep those things to myself. I believe Walter has the same right." Annie looked down at the floor. It was hard to tell if she was embarrassed or just uncertain. "Thanks for the help. I'm lucky to have such good friends." She put an arm around Olyria's shoulder and hugged her.

A few minutes later Walter hurried into the shop. His eye was bloody and swollen. His platinum hair was tousled and damp.

"What happened?" Annie cried.

"That maniac, Carl Stotts, took a punch at me. Seems his wife told him I was taking liberties, which is ridiculous. You met the woman last week. I'd never take liberties with a married woman."

Annie held her tongue. She didn't want to agitate an already bad situation. "You need to see a doctor," she said.

"I don't need a doctor. I need to get home and clean up this eye. Then I've got a 2:00 tee time."

Annie quickly gathered her things.

"Don't forget what we talked about. I'll talk to you soon." Olyria could see the concern on Annie's face.

⌘

Annie hated the idea that she might need to pilfer through Walter's things, but Olyria was right. She knew almost nothing about Walter . . . really. His getting punched today was a complete surprise to Annie. She paced about their house, walking from room to room, pondering what she should do. Walter had washed his own eye and gone golfing as if getting punched in the eye by an irate husband was a normal event. Annie was thinking this would be a perfect time to begin a search. It's not right, she thought. But what do I know about him. He likes yoga, he likes to play golf, and he likes to go to the gym. Walter enjoys the finer things in life. What she didn't want to acknowledge was he seemed to like the ladies, and he was beginning to show a nasty streak a mile wide.

Annie took a deep breath and went upstairs. She stood holding her stomach, looking at Walter's bureau. Her hand slowly pulled the top drawer open. She lifted the clothes and was relieved; that was all she found in the drawer. She opened the second drawer and, again, only clothes. This is crazy she thought to herself. She opened the bottom drawer and again carefully lifted the clothes and ran her hand over the bottom of the drawer. She felt something firm, not clothes. She gently pulled the item from the drawer. It was an old leather zippered pouch about the size of a book. Well worn.

Annie set it on the dresser and carefully unzipped it. She found a photo of a very young Walter with two little boys and a woman. There was a school picture of a boy who appeared to be about ten years old; the name of the grade school was printed on the bottom with the year 1984. There was also a life insurance policy with a woman's name as beneficiary. The name was Claudia Wilkins. Annie couldn't tell if the policy was still in force but the face value was $10,000, a nice tidy sum. Walter's birth certificate was stuck behind the life insurance policy and indicated Walter was five years older than he had told Annie. His original social security card was tucked between the documents along with his college grade sheets. What Annie found most interesting was a divorce decree with a second woman's name on it. Josephine Wilkins. Could these be Walter's sisters? And if so, what happened to them? Walter told her he was an only child, an orphan with no family. More likely they were wives, but he also told her he had never been married - -

and what about the two little boys? It was clear that Walter had not been honest with her. But then she had secrets of her own.

Annie made some notes; the name of the school, the beneficiary name, the information from the divorce decree and slipped the notes into her purse. She made it a point to return everything to the pouch in the same order she'd removed it so Walter wouldn't know she'd been going through his things. She was startled when she heard the garage door go up. Walter was home. She hurriedly zipped the case closed and returned it to the bottom of the drawer. As she looked over her shoulder to see if Walter was coming the school picture of the young boy fluttered to the floor and slipped just under the bureau. Annie didn't notice.

She stepped into the master bath, flushed the toilet for diversion and walked out of the bathroom as Walter came in. She quickly glanced around the room to make sure everything looked normal. "How was your golf game?" she asked as he kissed her cheek.

"I did okay; it was a little too windy, so we played only nine," Walter said.

"How's your eye," she asked, turning her head to get a better angle on the injury.

"My eye is fine." He turned his back and pulled his golf shirt over his head.

"I'll let you change and meet you downstairs," Annie said. She couldn't wait to get out of the bedroom. She was nervous, afraid that her guilt would give her away.

Walter changed his clothes; and as he did, he saw something peeking out from under the bureau. He picked it up and knew immediately that Annie had searched his drawers. He returned the picture to the zippered pouch. Everything else seemed to be there in its place. He would have to watch Annie, try to figure out what she was up to. His life was very comfortable here. Annie was a good provider. He wasn't going to let anything interfere with his gravy train.

"What's for dinner?" Walter asked, his voice controlled, as he walked into the kitchen.

"I was going to make a salad and spaghetti, I have to get it started."

"What . . . it's almost six o'clock and you haven't even started dinner?" Walter's blue eyes turned a dark grey-blue as his temper rose. He grabbed Annie's arm, an arm that was already sore. "What have you been doing all afternoon? You knew I would be home by six."

"I . . . I . . . was reading a new quilt magazine I bought this afternoon and lost track of time. I'm sorry. It won't take me long." Annie said as she backed away from Walter and grabbed the pasta pot, filling it with water.

Walter spun her around, his fingers digging into her shoulders. "Why can't you have dinner ready on time? You have nothing else to do but run this house."

"Walter, please, you're hurting me. Why don't you go into the living room and read the paper? I'll call you as soon as it's ready. It won't take long, I promise."

Walter released his grip, but his eyes were still dark and the afternoon's injury made them more sinister. He stormed out to the living room. Annie heard the TV blaring as she stood clutching the sink, trembling.

Conversation at the dinner table was nonexistent. Annie was learning how to maneuver through Walter's moods. He was such a puzzle.

They sat quietly that evening, watching TV. Annie could not stop thinking about Walter's other life. There had been other women, yet Walter had never mentioned any other relationship. In fact, he said he had come close to getting married but never made the leap. Now it appeared he'd been married and had children, two boys. What happened to them? How could he walk away? The thought of having a child, two children, and not being part of their lives pained Annie deep in her heart.

Chapter 8

It was Wednesday. Annie Wilkins rolled over in the king-sized bed she shared with Walter, who was still snoring softly. He had been gentle with her last night and loving in spite of his aggravation and the argument about supper. Walter definitely had at least two sides. The sweet, considerate Walter she had fallen in love with and the angry Walter she was just getting to know. She felt guilty for going through Walter's things the day before and hoped he never found out what she'd done. But she wanted to know which Walter was real.

Still she was curious about what she'd found and meant to investigate when she got the chance. She sighed and rolled to the edge of the bed, sat up and went to the bathroom to start her day.

She was being hounded by second thoughts. It might have been crazy to marry Walter so quickly after she met him, but she wasn't getting any younger and he seemed to be so much what she wanted in a man. A good companion, good looking, distinguished, clean. He had seemed the answer to her prayers at the time. Annie smiled to herself as she stepped into the shower, lathered herself up and let the water glide over her. It was a sensuous experience, an erotic experience. She had been taking showers all her life and hadn't realized how wonderful they could be. Since Walter came along, everything seemed sensuous. Annie thought it was unseemly for a woman her age . . . but there it was. She was in the middle of an erotic awakening that had been going on for over a year now. The pinches, the bruises and the rough treatment might just be part of it.

Annie toweled herself off and fluffed her hair. She loved it that Walter paid attention to everything about her, including the shade of her hair dye. It bothered her that he paid the same kind of attention to other women. Perhaps she was just a jealous, possessive woman.

Annie slid her tall, slim body into casual clothes for the day. A pair of soft denim pants and a pink oxford-cloth, man-tailored shirt with the sleeves rolled up to the elbow. It felt good to be a woman, good to be dressing for someone besides students. She'd done her penance for past sins. She'd paid the world back for her mistakes. Now it was her turn to shine.

Still she was confused about the hurting, about the way Walter sometimes shut her out of his life and about the things she had found yesterday in his leather pouch. She had the barest experience with the way things were supposed to be between a man and a woman. Maybe this was normal. Goldie seemed to think there was little out of the ordinary about the relationship, and she should know with all those husbands in her past. She'd have to ask Olyria for her opinion when she got the chance. She was going to the quilt shop this morning when Walter went for his yoga session. It was beginning to feel like a second home.

She woke Walter with a kiss. "Wake up, sweetheart," she said. "You'll be late for yoga. I'll get breakfast started while you dress."

"Nothing for me," Walter said. "The practice goes better on an empty stomach." His voice was gruff and the fragrance of last night's sex tinged the air when he tossed the covers back and climbed out of bed.

It was hard to get her mind around the positive and the negative of Walter. She studied him as he padded toward the bathroom.

He stopped and looked back at her, over his shoulder. "Maybe you should take a picture," he said. "It would last a whole lot longer." There was no softness there, no hint of affection.

Annie averted her eyes and hurried out of the room.

⌘

Across town at Always in Stitches, Caroline was packing up the trunk show. It hardly seemed worth the effort to pack and unpack when it had to go back inside of a week. She'd have to remember that the next time she agreed to take one on, to ask for a month at least. She was hurrying to get it ready for Stan Darling, the hunk of a UPS guy. He'd be in before eleven. Olyria had come in early. She was checking out the florals, looking for something snappy to make some new turbans. Her surgery would be in just one week, and radiation therapy was shortly after that. From what she'd been told, she might lose her hair, she might not. If she did, she'd be leaving hair on the pillow and everywhere else before the second week. By the third week she'd probably be bald as Yul Brynner, and who needed that.

The phone rang and Caroline picked it up. "Always in Stitches," she said. "How may I help you?"

"Good morning, gentle lady. Are you having a good day today?" The voice was oily, like you'd imagine the voice of a guy with a handle bar moustache and bad intentions.

"You need to stop calling," she said into the phone. "This is a place of business and I don't have time for this foolishness." She dropped the quilt she was folding into the packing box and held the phone with both hands.

"Nothing foolish about it, gentle lady," the man said. "I have visions of you. Visions I'd like to share with you when the time is right. When I am ready."

There was a sinister tone in the man's voice. Not the tone of a casual crank. "Who is this?" Caroline asked. Her knuckles were white on the phone and she was angry.

"You'll find out, when I am ready."

She held the phone away from her ear and looked at it like that might help her figure out who was on the other end. Then she clicked the off button and threw it to the floor.

"Are you all right?" Olyria asked. She was standing next to Caroline, holding a bolt of fabric with a purple-and-blue hydrangea pattern.

"This man . . ." she said. "He keeps calling, and he's getting more and more threatening with every call."

"Maybe you should call the police," Olyria said. "Make a report."

"Maybe I should," Caroline said.

Olyria bent over and picked up the phone. "It would save wear and tear on the equipment."

Caroline laughed and that broke the tension. Her shoulders relaxed and she examined the phone for damage. She clicked it on and held it to her ear. "Seems okay," she said and put it back into its base. "But you're right. Maybe I should call the police."

"Any idea who it might be? Olyria asked.

"I've been thinking about it," Caroline said. "The only person I can think of is somebody who was involved in the bank robbery and shooting before I left the bank."

"I thought the guy was in jail."

"Yes, the actual shooter is in jail and will be there a good long while, but they never caught the driver of the car. It could be him."

"Do you think he'd risk it after all this time?" Olyria asked. "Seems foolish."

"Nobody ever said bank robbers were smart," Caroline said.

Olyria laughed and Caroline went back to folding quilts and putting them into the packing box. "What do you think of this for a turban?" Olyria asked. She held the hydrangea fabric up, turned it for Caroline to see.

"It would be great," Caroline said. "And perfect for use as a palm reader when your hair grows back."

Caroline finished packing up the quilts. She dragged the box to the side of the check-out counter as Annie and Walter walked in. Walter watched her struggle with the box but made no attempt to help. "Good morning, ladies," Walter said. He bent over, lifted Caroline's hand and kissed it with a flourish. He was his personable, public self. Olyria clasped her hands behind her back and edged away from him. He nodded in her direction.

"Your eye looks terrible," Caroline said. "Are you going to report it to the police?"

"My eye is fine," Walter said. "I have no intention of bringing the police into the matter. A man has to keep an eye on his wife, and that was what Mr. Stotts was doing." He turned to look at Annie. "Right, my dear?" Then he left for his yoga practice.

Annie flushed and changed the subject, "I must be the slowest quilting student of all time. I need more help." She looked at Olyria.

"I have a palm reading in a half hour. It would have to be after that."

"I can help you, Annie," Caroline said. She put a long piece of tape across the trunk show box. I'll be finished here in just a few minutes."

"Oh, good," Annie said. "I am so happy for the help. I want to get my blocks finished so they'll be ready next week for Jeanine to assemble."

"You'll get them finished," Olyria said. "I thought we made good progress last week." Caroline measured off a yard of the hydrangeas for Olyria who paid her money but stayed around to chat until time for her palm-reading appointment.

Caroline was busy with a new customer who had come into the shop. Olyria said, "Let me help you get started with your block, Annie."

"Okay," Annie said, and she settled at a machine while Olyria instructed her over her shoulder.

"Did you think about what I said yesterday?"

"I feel terrible, but I did look through Walter's drawers yesterday afternoon."

"And . . .?"

"I found several things in an old leather pouch and I don't have to tell you they give me more questions, rather than fewer." Annie's stitches began to wander off the paper line she was supposed to be following.

"Whoa," Olyria said. "Stop. You're going to have to take that out. It will buckle on the front side."

"I told you I was hopeless," Annie said. She found a seam ripper and began to remove the mistaken stitches.

"What did you find?" Olyria asked. "If I'm not being too personal."

"There were some photographs, one of Walter, a woman and two little boys. They look a whole lot like a happy little family. And there was a school picture of a little boy about ten. It had the name of the school on it."

"Did Walter tell you he'd been married before?" Olyria asked.

"No, he told me he almost got married once but didn't." Annie looked up from her ripping and into Olyria's eyes. "I think he may have lied to me."

Olyria smiled. "It wouldn't be the first time a man lied to his wife."

"The worst thing is, I can't even ask Walter about it because then he'll know I've been going through his things."

"For sure, you can't ask," Olyria said. "But we could find out about the child by calling the school. That would be a start."

Olyria took the log cabin strips from Annie. She moistened her finger with her tongue and lifted the stray threads from the fabric. She handed them back to Annie, who turned back to the sewing machine and began re-stitching.

"I have to concentrate," Annie said.

"I know," Olyria said. "And I have to get to my palm-reading session." She looked around the shop. Caroline was still busy with the walk-in customer. "Caroline will be with you shortly." She lowered her voice to a whisper. "I can help you investigate," she said. "I am going to have extra time while I recuperate from my surgery. I can make some calls and maybe find out something for you."

Annie stopped sewing. "Would you?"

"I would," Olyria said. She patted Annie on the shoulder and left the quilt shop through the connecting doors, closing them carefully behind her.

Caroline measured fabric and rang up a big sale for the customer she was helping. Annie finished her log cabin squares on her own. It felt good to have them done. She thought she might make a log cabin quilt for herself, now that she knew how to do it.

Caroline walked her new customer to the door and asked her to come back soon. Then she came to where Annie was packing her squares into their plastic bag.

"May I see?" she asked.

Annie handed her the squares. "I think they came out right," she said.

"They look wonderful, Annie," Caroline said. "You've done a wonderful job on your very first squares."

"Do you think I'm ready to make my own quilt?" Annie asked.

"Whenever you feel ready. A quilt is a commitment," Caroline said. "A promise to the future that you will do the work you need to do and stick with it to the end. I think quilting is a powerful metaphor for life."

Annie was silent.

"Maybe I take it all too seriously," Caroline said. "But that's how I see it."

"I just never thought of it that way," Annie said. "I thought it was just some stitching and ripping."

"It might start out that way but it becomes so much more. It's really all about process, just like raising a family or being a wife." Caroline sighed. "Whether you like it or not, whether things are going the way you hoped, you just have to keep on going till you finish the quilt."

"I think you've changed topics on me," Annie said. Annie had made the decision to marry Walter in haste and now she would have to work through the good and the bad and make it work.

Caroline sighed again. "It's Jamie and I'm so concerned about her. She's decided to move in with her boyfriend, who I see as little more than a freeloader. She asked me to break the news to her dad. I'd rather have a deep cleaning on my teeth."

"Will Charles be angry?"

"Charles will yell and probably curse but most of all he'll be scared. Scared to death Jamie will get hurt. Scared to death Jamie will get into trouble he can't get her out of. Scared to death he will lose control."

"Men are a puzzle, aren't they?" Annie said.

Caroline handed Annie's quilt squares back to her and frowned. "Charles gets confused when it comes to emotions. Scared often comes out looking like anger."

Annie tucked the finished squares into their plastic bag and put them in her tote bag. Annie couldn't imagine Walter being scared of anything, but she had seen his angry side. "I wonder what is taking Walter so long," Annie said. "He's having an extra long session today."

"Maybe you should go drag him away."

"I'd never do that," Annie said. "He'd be furious with me if I tried telling him what to do."

"Hmmmm," Caroline said. "Maybe the honeymoon is over." She smiled to soften the words.

Chapter 9

Caroline closed the front door of the shop and locked it after the last customer left. It had been another brisk day of sales with hardly a minute to think. She gathered up two bolts of fabric that were leaning against the cutting table and returned them to the shelves. The shop was really coming together; sample tops and some quilted samples hung on the walls and from the ceiling beams. Caroline had added light fixtures in corners and alcoves to warm up and highlight display areas, and Charles had finally found the time to move in old furniture from their garage to add a touch of charm to the atmosphere. She was very happy with the progress.

Her mind drifted to Jamie and her living situation. Caroline knew Jamie didn't fully realize the gravity of her decision to move in with Tommy. Jamie had told her on Monday. It was now Wednesday and she still hadn't told Charles. She dreaded the conversation and had been putting it off until the right time. She knew it couldn't wait much longer.

Monday night Charles worked late. He was cranky when he got home and Caroline was chicken to bring up the subject. Tuesday, like always, the shop was open until 8:00. By the time Caroline closed the shop, stopped at the grocery to buy some bread and milk, it was late and she just collapsed into a chair when she got home.

No matter how she felt tonight, she would have to break the news about Jamie and Tommy to Charles. He had a right to know even if it did make him angry. Caroline grabbed her purse and headed for the back door of the shop. She paced back and forth before she worked up the courage to head for home, rehearsing in her mind what she would say to Charles. "Hi, Hon, how was your day? Oh, by the way, guess what's new, you have three guesses and the first three don't count," she whispered to herself testing the words. No, no, no. Charles would never see the humor in the situation. If she was honest, Caroline couldn't see any humor either. If there was any touch of humor, it was black.

She pulled into the driveway, turned the car off, grabbed the wheel tightly, drew in a breath, held it for a slow five count and then let it out slowly. She had nothing else to do but get out of the car and enter the house.

"Hello, Hello," Caroline called as she walked through the back door.

"Hi, Mom," Budd called from the living room.

"How you doing? Is all your homework done? Did you eat dinner?" Caroline said.

"Yeah, Mom, we had sub sandwiches and I had only a couple of chapters to read for my history class," Budd said.

"Where's your Dad?" Caroline asked.

"He's in the den practicing his presentation for tomorrow."

"Oh, right, the big meeting is tomorrow," Caroline said. Charles was the General Manager of the Electronic Motor Division for Bartan Engineering. He started there as an Electrical Engineer after he graduated from college and worked his way up through the ranks. Caroline hesitated just outside the door to the den. Maybe she should wait just one more day?

No, Charles always said family came first. He was going to hit the roof as it was; if she waited any longer, he would go right through the stratosphere.

"Hey, there, how's my favorite electrical engineer?" Caroline asked as she stepped into the den.

Charles looked up and smiled, "How's my favorite business mogul?" He reached out for Caroline's arm and pulled her into his lap.

Charles ran his hand up and down Caroline's outer thigh. Caroline sighed and closed her eyes as she inhaled his cologne. It was a woodsy scent with a hint of spice. Charles and Caroline had had so little time the last three weeks that she didn't want to break the mood but knew there was no getting around it. She would have to tell him tonight.

Charles nuzzled Caroline's neck and asked, "I've hardly seen you since Monday morning. How is everything going at the shop?"

"Business has been brisk; Rumpelstiltskin will be very happy," Caroline said. She curled into the warmth of Charles' embrace. Avoidance was very tempting.

Then Charles asked, "Have you talked to Jamie lately?"

"I talked to her on Monday," Caroline said, trying to beef up her courage.

"How is she doing?"

Caroline took a deep breath, swallowed hard, and then decided to dive into the abyss. "The swelling on her face has gone down and she's not so black and blue." Caroline hesitated, let the information sink in. "She sounded scared, she said she's not sleeping and has pretty much lost her appetite."

"Well, maybe she should have come home for a while," Charles said.

"I told her that. She said she's been thinking a lot."

"So . . . she's coming home?" Charles said.

"Well, no . . . . . she's decided to move in with Tommy," Caroline held her breath for the rant that she knew was coming.

"What?" Charles barked. Caroline nearly fell to the floor as Charles jumped up. "What is she thinking? Did the muggers knock a screw loose?" Charles' eyes were popped wide with the white showing almost blue, and his fists were clenched tightly by his side.

"Charles, she says she loves Tommy. I'm not happy about this either, but she is an adult."

"What does she know about love? She hasn't known him that long. . . . There's something about that boy that bothers me . . . he manipulates her . . . and he's a Browns' fan for God's sake." Charles barked.

"Honey, do you think you don't like him because he's dating your older daughter?" Caroline asked. Charles paced back and forth; he kicked the couch and knocked one of Caroline's half-done quilting projects to the floor.

"No," Charles said firmly, "that's not it. I don't think he treats Jamie with respect." Charles paced some more, kicked the couch another whack and Caroline cowered out of the way. "Well, she'll have to get a job because I'm not paying for her to live in sin."

Caroline shook her head. He was worse than she had expected. "Charles, I think her strength, her independence have been shaken to the core by the mugging. She feels as if she doesn't have any control in her life, as if she's not safe." Caroline's tone of voice was pleading Jamie's case. "After I was shot I had to stay off my feet, I was home with my family around me. The first time I went out by myself I had a lump in my stomach the size of Gibraltar. Jamie wasn't injured to the point she had to stay off her feet, thank God, but that means she had to face the world by herself immediately."

Caroline was pacing now, matching Charles stride for stride. "She's got to be scared. She probably looks over her shoulder no matter where she goes. I'm not happy with Tommy, either; but if he makes her feel safer, if he gives her the courage to go on, I can deal with her move."

"To say I'm unhappy is definitely an understatement. I'm livid. We didn't raise her so she could pull something like this." Charles was shaking. His jaw was clenched and his eyes had gone even wider.

"Why didn't you tell me earlier?" Charles said. His voice was controlled and deep . . . angry. "I had a right to know."

"Well, Monday you worked late and Tuesday night I didn't get home until late." Caroline paused, "I was afraid you'd react like this and I guess there was never going to be a good time . . . . ."

"Don't you realize my family is the most important thing in my life?" He kicked the couch again. "I'm not here just to pay the bills."

Caroline stopped breathing; that remark cut straight through her. She hadn't seen Charles this upset since she was shot. She briefly thought she should tell Charles about the strange phone calls she had been getting but dismissed the thought. Now *definitely* was not the time to bring up another touchy subject to Charles.

"I realize that and I *am* trying to contribute to the finances . . . I think I'm going to go and make myself some toast." She kicked the couch herself for good measure as she left the room. It was childish, it was silly, but it made her feel better.

The rest of the night Caroline and Charles avoided each other. Budd kept to herself. She knew something was wrong and didn't want to get caught in the crossfire.

⌘

The next day Caroline had Nan open the shop. She hadn't slept well after her conversation with Charles. He had left that morning without waking her. A sure sign he was still angry.

Nan was helping Aggie McDaniel just as the UPS man walked in.

The minute Nan laid eyes on him, her world went into slow motion. She stood in the aisle with her mouth open, holding a bolt of fabric. Stan Darling was wheeling two boxes to the back of the store and Nan was blocking his way.

"Hello," he said.

"Hello," Nan whispered. She realized her mouth was a gaping hole in her face, big enough to catch frogs. "Excuse me," she said as she stepped to her right.

Just then Stan stepped to his left. "Oh, excuse me," Stan chuckled as he stepped to his right.

"Are you new?" Nan asked.

"No, this is my normal route; I was on vacation for two weeks. I'm Stan Darling," he said and he held out his hand.

"Stan . . . I'm . . ." for a minute she forgot her own name.

Aggie cleared her throat and said, "I'm Aggie McDaniel and this is Nan Roberts." She smiled as she watched the two of them. She fluffed her hair and met Stan's eyes.

Nan was drinking in Stan's black hair, his expressive brown eyes and watching his tight butt as he walked back to the check-out counter and unloaded the boxes. Inventory deliveries had just gotten a whole lot more interesting.

As Stan walked past her again, he smiled and extended the electronic signature card for Nan to sign.

"Huh?" Nan said.

"Could you sign?" Stan said.

"Oh, yeah, sure." He handed her the stylus and it was all she could do not to kiss his hand.

"Nice to meet you," he said as he retrieved the stylus and headed toward the door.

"Nice to meet you, too," Nan called as he left.

"Whoa, that is one good-looking delivery man," Aggie said.

"Oh, my god, oh my god. He's an Adonis but . . . but . . . I think I'm in love . . . but good looking? Really, I hadn't noticed," Nan said.

Nan turned towards Aggie and they both started to laugh. Just then Will Douglas, a guild member's husband, came in the front door with one of his friends. Both of them wore badges. At the same moment, Caroline came in the back.

"Hey there, ladies," Will said with a big smile, "What's so funny?"

"Inside joke, Will, you would've had to have been here," Nan replied.

"Hey, Will," Caroline said. "Did Sheryll forget something at the guild meeting?"

"Nah," he said. "And just in case anybody cares, we're on our lunch break." Will stepped to the side and introduced his friend "This is my partner, JT Hooks,"

"Nice to meet you JT," they all said in unison. JT was a good-looking man with dark brown hair, graying at the temples. His green eyes sparkled as he smiled and nodded. He looked to be in his late fifties or early sixties. And he couldn't hold a candle to Stan Darling.

"We were at lunch and JT okayed making a stop to buy a gift card for Sheryll. Our anniversary is coming up next week, thirty-three years," Will said proudly.

"Fabric is better than candy to a quilter," Aggie said.

"Is that why they call them fat quarters?" Will said and they all laughed again.

"Hey, Caroline, I also wanted see where you've decided to put my remains when I am gone. Sheryll said she'd ask for a spot for my urn. I'd like to see my final resting place." Caroline had a puzzled look on her face.

"You mean she didn't tell you," Will said. "I figure she spends so much time here she can visit me here rather than go all the way out to Kingwood Cemetery."

"You choose the spot, Will, I'd be glad to have the company," Caroline said with a laugh. "Here, let me get that gift card for you." They headed for the cash register and JT trailed along behind.

"I saw the sign for a yoga studio here in the building," JT said. "I've been thinking about taking up yoga."

Will jabbed JT in the ribs, "Yeah," he said, "all you need is a tutu."

Caroline rang up the gift card and handed it over to Will. "You don't wear a tutu for yoga. I'm surprised at your macho attitude, Will."

Will grinned. He had a very nice smile. She wondered how he dealt with his dangerous profession and figured the smile he was showing the world might be part of it. "I'm just teasing JT," he said. "He knows that."

JT nodded. "But tutu or not, I hear it's very good exercise and relaxing to the spirit."

"Spirit, smirit," Will said. "I think you just want to find out how to tie lawbreakers into knots. Besides, we detectives have no spirit."

Caroline had to laugh at that. "I know the yoga master a little," she said. "I could call him and see if he'd drop over. You could ask him what you want to know."

JT shuffled his feet and looked down at them to see what they were doing. "Hate to be a bother," he said.

"If it's a bother, he'll let us know," Caroline said. She closed the cash drawer and picked up the phone. She pecked in a number from a list posted on the wall. Her eyes met JT's. "Busy. Let's just walk over to the studio. I don't think he has a class this time of day."

JT shrugged. "Sure, okay," he said.

"I'll be right back," Caroline said to Nan and Aggie. They were still conferring over fabric in the front part of the store. "One of our guild lady's husbands is a yoga student. He seems to really like it."

The door was open as if the yoga master was expecting people. He was bent over the sound system twirling dials while he spoke into the phone. A soft Mideastern tune was coming into the room. Incense filled the air. The lights were low and one corner of the room was shielded with oriental screens. Caroline strained to see a sink and counter top with a basket of fruit. There were bottles of vitamins and some other containers on the counter.

"Nice music," Caroline said.

The yoga master turned, surprised that he wasn't alone. He looked curiously to the detectives. "Yes, it is," he said. "Can I help you with something?"

Caroline introduced JT and Will. "JT is interested in the practice of yoga."

"One moment, please," he said. He spoke softly into the phone and then hung it up.

The yoga master nodded to JT; he stroked his heavy, dark beard. "Yoga is a salve to the soul." The teacher bowed from the waist, held the bend for a second and then returned to standing. "My name is David Williams. I am a certified yoga master and I do have a few spots available for new students."

"I don't want to be the only man in the session," JT said.

"I have men in many of my sessions. One is starting in just a few minutes." The yoga master looked around the studio. "Have you ever done yoga?" he asked.

"No, but I hear it is very relaxing," JT said.

"It relaxes the mind and body at the same time it builds muscle and strength. Here's a schedule of my beginners' classes. You're welcome to join whichever time fits your needs."

"Thanks for the information." A pair of women walked into the studio. They had blue mats rolled up under their arms. One of them was Alice Stotts.

"Morning, David," Alice said. The yoga master bowed and the ladies began to arrange their mats on the floor.

"I won't keep you any longer, but I'll probably see you soon." JT folded the yoga schedule and tucked it into his pocket. He turned to leave, with Caroline and Will close on his heels. As they were going up the stairs they ran into Walter Wilkins. The stairwell was filled with the aroma of his after-shave.

"Hey, Walter," Caroline said. "You going to yoga?"

"Why yes, it really makes me feel wonderful. David is the best teacher I've had. " Walter said.

"Maybe you could tell JT about it," Caroline said.

JT looked at Walter's shiner and wondered how a calm, relaxed person acquired such a beauty.

"Be glad to," Walter said. Two more women walked by on their way to class. Walter pulled himself taller and turned his platinum pate from side to side just enough to show he was preening. "But right now I've gotta run, I don't want to be late. Could you give him my number? It's in your file, I presume, what with Annie's quilting mania."

"Sure," Caroline said. She gave Walter an ugly look, but he didn't see it because he had turned and hurried down the steps after the other two yoga class members.

"I don't think you're cute enough for yoga," Will said to JT.

Caroline laughed and led the men back to the quilt shop.

After Will and JT left, the shop was very quiet. Business was slower than Caroline had hoped for. She thought about Charles' comment about paying the bills. Then she closed her eyes and took a deep breath.

"Are you okay?" Nan asked.

"I'm just tired. I see we got our shipment of books and RJR fabric," Caroline said. She started unpacking the boxes.

"Oh, yeah, the shipment came this morning," Nan said.

"So?" Caroline said.

"So what?" Nan asked.

"So, what did you think of the delivery man?" Caroline asked.

"You mean . . . what's his name, Stan . . . Stan Darling?" Nan chuckled.

"That's the one."

"I think I may need to be here for all deliveries in the future, but for now, I've got to run. Are you going to be okay? You seem sorta down."

"I'll be fine. See you tomorrow and thanks for coming in early this morning." Caroline left the unpacking to wrap Nan in a hug.

"Any time," Nan said. Then she grabbed her purse and headed out the door.

Chapter 10

The shop was extremely quiet the rest of the afternoon. Caroline wanted to sit down and sew, but she finished unpacking the UPS shipment. She replayed the fight with Charles last night over and over in her mind. She'd never seen him so upset. Caroline delayed going home, afraid of a repeat of the night before. Having a root canal would be better. When there was absolutely nothing else to be done, Caroline sighed, locked the shop up for the night, grabbed her purse and headed for the back door. She was almost out the door when the phone rang. She went back in, locked the door behind her and answered the phone.

"Hi, Mom, I'm glad I caught you," Jamie said. "Did you talk to Dad?"

Caroline closed her eyes and sighed, "Yes, we talked last night."

"How did he take it, Mom?"

"He's really upset, honey. How are you feeling?" Caroline asked.

"I'm . . . I'm doing OK, Mom, but it's hard to go out. I keep thinking it's going to happen again," Jamie replied. "I went to see Joellen today. She said it is too late to get another roommate, and they can't make the rent without my share. She's been such a good friend. I can't leave them hanging. Then Tommy said he wants me to contribute to room and board. He said the other guys are upset because I'm using the water and other utilities. Mom, I feel obligated to both of them, I . . . I know I shouldn't ask but I need $300."

"Oh, Hon, your Dad is so upset. I can't ask him for more money now. "

"Mom, I'm desperate. I've been looking for a part-time job but that will take a few weeks before I get paid, and they need the money now. What can I do?" Jamie asked.

"I don't know how, but I'll find the money for you somewhere." Caroline said.

"Thanks Mom, I really appreciate it. I've got to run. I'll talk to you soon. You're the greatest," Jamie said as she clicked off the phone.

Caroline put her elbows on the counter and her head in her hands, then groaned. Where would she get the money? Perhaps Rumpelstiltskin could spin her some gold. Charles would really be upset if she gave Jamie money, but she couldn't turn her back on her daughter when she was in need. Caroline thought for a few minutes and then realized there was no way around it. She would have to dip into the secret funds she had, the funds she had put aside to buy Charles an anniversary gift. She would stop by the bank tomorrow morning before the shop opened and transfer the funds. She prayed Charles wouldn't find out.

⌘

"Hello, hello," Caroline called in a downtrodden voice as she entered the house.

"Hi, Mom," Budd called from the living room. "How was your day?"

Caroline plopped down in a chair in the living room. "Long;

I'm really tired. Is your Dad home yet?"

"No, he called a little while ago and said he'd be late. He said he'd grab a sandwich at the office so I guess it's just you and me tonight," Budd said.

"Let's do something easy. Do you want pizza or should we go for sub sandwiches?" Caroline asked. A part of her was relieved that Charles would be late.

"I vote for pizza," Budd replied.

"Pizza it is," Caroline said as she picked up the phone to call Emelio's, their favorite pizza/bar. Longtime family friends owned the bar; and the pizza wasn't cheap, but it was very good.

"Mom, are you and Dad okay? Your voices were muffled last night, but it sounded as though you were both really upset," Budd said sheepishly.

"We're going to be fine; we just have a few things to work out," Caroline said. "Is your homework done, young lady?"

"Yup, finished it as soon as I got home."

They watched the news while they waited for the pizza. After they ate, Caroline read a quilt magazine while Budd watched TV. It was 8:30 when Caroline heard Charles come in the back door.

"Hi, Dad," Budd called.

"Hi, Budd, what ya up . . . " Charles' voice trailed off as he entered the room and saw Caroline, "to?"

"Not much," Budd looked from her Dad to her Mom. "I . . . I think I'm going to go and read over my notes from English again." She left.

"How was your day?" Caroline asked in an even tone.

"Fine," Charles said a little more sharply than he wanted.

"How did the meeting go?"

"We made progress but still have a lot more work to do. I've got a couple of reports to read over before tomorrow. Don't wait up for me." Then he turned and went into the den, which doubled as his office.

Caroline nodded; and after Charles left she closed her eyes, holding back tears. She picked up her quilt magazine again and tried to get her mind on something that would soothe her.

⌘

Caroline got up early the next day and went to the bank. She took a deep breath as she transferred the money to Jamie's account. She knew she was doing the right thing and Charles would eventually realize it also.

Caroline got into her car and dialed Jamie's cell phone. "Hi, Jamie, it's Mom. Just wanted to let you know I made the transfer this morning. Talk to you later." Caroline hated to just leave a message but it was important this time. She wanted to make sure Jamie knew the money was there as soon as possible because once Caroline got to the shop she wouldn't have time to call.

Caroline jiggled the key in the lock, jiggled the handle and pushed on the door. When it finally opened she almost fell. She would have to get Shultz to fix the lock TODAY. He had started working on her list, and the building scuttlebutt had it that the water was hot for shampoos these days. Life was smoothing out for the building tenants, but for some reason he hadn't gotten to the damned door.

Caroline turned the lights on, put her things in the storeroom and unlocked the rest of the doors. Every morning when she opened the shop it felt like her little island of tranquility, but today she was anything but tranquil.

"A penny for your thoughts," Olyria said as she touched Caroline's shoulder.

"Huh?" Caroline shrieked. She was not aware anyone had entered the shop.

"I'm sorry, Caroline, I didn't mean to scare you. I thought you heard me come in. You looked like you were in another world."

"Is there one close that I can escape to?" Caroline laughed.

"Don't we all wish," Olyria said. "I just wanted to pick out my fabrics for the table-runner-of-the-month class."

"Oh right . . . that class is this afternoon," Caroline said.

The bell on the door jingled and Caroline and Olyria turned to see Annie Wilkins come in. "Hey there, ladies, what's up?" Annie said.

"I came in early to forage for fabrics for this afternoon's class," Olyria said.

"Me, too," Annie said.

Caroline helped them select their fabrics. The two ladies were as different as night and day. Annie chose a burgundy, blue and gold and Olyria chose an orange, rust and green. It would be interesting to see the finished projects.

"Annie, looks like we have a little time before the class. Do you want to grab a bite to eat? Since the tea shop is still closed, we could go down to Traugott Bakery?" Olyria asked.

"Sure, Walter is golfing again today," Annie said. "Do you want us to bring anything back for you, Caroline?"

"No, thanks, I've brought leftover pizza," Caroline answered.

Olyria and Annie left the quilt shop and walked the block to Traugott. The air was crisp but the sun was warm. They were lucky to get a table outside and were seated right away.

"How are you doing, Olyria?" Annie asked as she laid her napkin on her lap.

A young woman came to take their orders. They both ordered the Reuben sandwich with German potato salad. It was the best Reuben within thirty miles.

"Fine, I guess," Olyria said once the waitress left. "My

lumpectomy is scheduled for next Wednesday. I'm anxious to get this behind me . . . I'm more worried about my Mom, though. She'll be beside herself during the surgery. I'm trying to talk her into staying home," Olyria said.

Olyria felt very alone in her situation. Her late husband, Kyle, was killed in a car accident three years ago. Her twenty-three-year-old son, Holt, was getting his master's at Stanford and couldn't come home. Her father was dead. The only family she had left was her mother, Edwina, who lived with her. She was a very spry seventy-two but lately she had been showing signs of dependency. Her dilemma came through in her tone of voice.

"Do you want some moral support for Wednesday? I could take you to the hospital. Maybe if your Mom knew someone would be with you she'd be willing to stay home," Annie asked. She was genuinely concerned.

"That would be wonderful, but I hate to ask you to do that for me," Olyria said.

"I'd like to," Annie replied.

Olyria took Annie's hands and squeezed them, turned them over and started to study her palms. "You have strong hands," Oyria said as she studied them, then looked up, puzzled.

"What is it Olyria?" Annie asked.

The waitress brought their sandwiches. She looked at their clasped hands and gave them both an odd smile. Both Annie and Olyria laughed. The waitress set their sandwiches on the table. "Anything else I can get you ladies," she asked with the emphasis on ladies.

"We're fine for now, thank you," Annie said and pulled her hand away from Olyria.

Annie took a bite of her sandwich, then asked, "Olyria, you have me curious now. What did you see in my hands?"

"Let me take another look," Olyria said.

Annie held her palm out and Olyria studied it again.

"Well . . . .you have a long Mercury finger, which is your pinky finger, and that shows your good communication skills and your teaching abilities." Olyria hesitated a little because she saw some potentially dark signs in her friend's hand. "Your Heart Line has breaks in it . . . . . which could mean a sudden and dramatic ending to a special relationship."

Annie was quiet. That wasn't what she expected or wanted to hear.

"There's more," Olyria said. "Your Marriage Line curves downward, and it actually passes through the Heart Line which may be another sign of a dramatic ending to your marriage." Olyria took another bite of her sandwich, chewed, and swallowed, giving the issue a minute to rest. "Is Walter feeling OK? This could mean a sudden change of direction of a partner's destiny . . . a divorce. Even death."

"Why . . . I think Walter is fine. He has been doing a lot of yoga and has indicated he is tired, but he is taking vitamins so I am sure he will be fine," Annie said in a soft voice. She looked as though she was going to vomit.

"Palmistry isn't an exact science," Olyria said. "I wouldn't worry too much about this, but there is a definite trend; and what's more curious, Annie, is that your Children Lines, see this faint line under your pinky finger? See how they are straight?" Olyria pointed to the lines on Annie's palm.

"Yes," said Annie as she studied her hand.

"Well, that line tells me that you have a son. Isn't that strange?" Olyria said.

Annie pulled her hand away abruptly and looked at her palm. "Well, how could that be? Why it must mean something else."

Annie nervously rubbed her palm.

Olyria saw how uncomfortable her friend was. "Perhaps I am getting it confused with your stress lines or your worry lines. They're in the same area."

"Well, yes, that must be it. You have worried about your mother and lately I've been really worried about my dad. He has the start of Alzheimer's and I don't know how much longer my Mom will be able to take care of him," Annie said in a quiet voice.

Olyria smiled and patted her friend's hand. "That must be what I am seeing." Olyria couldn't tell Annie of the cross on the "B" section of her Heart Line because that means emotional trauma. She didn't want to upset her friend any more than she already had. "Perhaps I should read Walter's palm," Olyria commented to change the subject.

"Oh, Walter would never agree to that," Annie said. "He's too macho."

"You're probably right," Olyria said.

"Not to change the subject," Annie said, although that is exactly what she wanted to do. "Do you want me to take you to the hospital for the lumpectomy? Think about it and let me know."

"Are you sure you would want to spend that much time at the hospital?" Olyria asked.

"Sure, I'll help you any way I can. It can be a payback for the sleuthing you said you'd help me with."

"Okay. It's a deal and will give me something interesting to do while I recuperate. Maybe we can get together over the weekend to map out a strategy for the investigation," Olyria said. She glanced at her watch and realized the class would start in a half hour. "We better hurry so we can get to class."

Annie ate only a small portion of her sandwich. The facts that Olyria revealed from reading her palm were unsettling and she had lost her appetite. Olyria didn't eat much more than Annie. They hurried to the table-runner class.

The shop phone rang as the two women came through the quiet shop door.

"Oh, no," Caroline said but she went toward the phone and hesitated only briefly before she picked it up. "Crank calls," she mouthed to Annie; then she clicked it on.

Annie nodded. She and Olyria watched for a minute before going upstairs for their class

"Oh, no," Caroline said again. "I'm so sorry, Michael. Is there somebody there with you?" . . . . . "Please stop crying." . . . . . "What did the vet say?" . . . "Yes". . . . . "Yes," . . . . . "A memorial service?" . . . . . "The guild ladies all loved her." . . . . . "I guess we could do it here." . . . . . "Yes, okay, on Tuesday?" . . . . . "Refreshments would be nice."

Annie stopped on the stairs up to the classroom and watched Caroline with all her attention.

"Please stop crying, Michael" . . . . . "The twenty-third Psalm?" . . . . . "Do you think that's appropriate?" . . . . . "I guess, it couldn't hurt. Okay, Michael, I'll see you on Tuesday. In the meantime, if I can do anything don't hesitate to call."

Caroline ran a hand through her hair. She gently put the phone back in its cradle and spoke to Annie. "Stella died in her sleep. She was only five. The vet said she was poisoned or maybe she bled to death. They can't tell for sure, yet. Michael is bereft. Said she was never out of his sight except for the few minutes she was lost here this week. Schultz is going to have to do a search and be sure there is no poison anywhere in the building." Caroline paused, took a deep breath. "Michael wants me to read the twenty-third Psalm at her memorial service, which he wants to have at next week's guild meeting."

Annie walked to Caroline and put her arms around her. She gave her a hug. "It will be all right," she said.

"The twenty-third Psalm . . . for a dog," she said.

Caroline, in her spare moment, said a little prayer for Michael. She didn't know what he would do without that dog. And she didn't even want to think about what Schultz would have to say when he found out Michael was filing a lawsuit against him. Then she went up to start the table-runner class.

After the class Annie said her good-byes and hurried out the door. "See ya next week," she called over her shoulder to Olyria.

Caroline's heart was uplifted by the flurry of sales that took place after the class. She so wanted the shop to be a success to help take the financial burden off Charles. There had been a steady stream of customers all afternoon. Just before closing the business slowed down and the shop was quiet. The shrill ring of the phone broke the silence.

"Good afternoon, Always in Stitches, may I help you?" Caroline said with a cheery smile.

"You help me every time you answer the phone, my fair lady," a deep, breathy voice said. "Soon you will do more than answer the phone."

"Who is this? Why are you calling me?" Caroline said.

"You have caught my eye and are taking over my heart," the gruff voice said.

"I'm going to call the police if you don't stop," Caroline shrieked.

"I wouldn't do that if I were you. Your daughter . . . what's her name . . . it's an unusual name . . . oh yeah, Budd. She reminds me of you. Perhaps I could get to know her better."

Caroline slammed the phone down. Her adrenaline was pumping. She raced to the front door and then the back door and locked up the shop. Threatening her was one thing but to think of Budd . . . she shook her head as if to shake that thought right out of her head. There was no getting around it; she would have to do something and do it soon. She looked at the clock; she wanted to make a note of the date and time of the call.

⌘

Walter got home about 3:30 and had been pacing the floor looking at his watch every fifteen minutes since he arrived. What was Annie doing with all of her time? Walter had to be careful. He would have to keep his eye on her. Walter knew when he had a good thing, and he didn't want to rock the boat. He knew Annie was an only child and stood to inherit a lot of money. Walter had his eye on the successful horse-breeding farm Annie's parents, John and Eleanor James, owned in McConnelsburg, Maryland. Annie's father was showing signs of Alzheimer's and who knew how long her mother would live; but he was going to be around when that ship came in.

"Walter, I'm home," Annie called as she came in through the garage.

Walter entered the kitchen. "You're a little late, aren't you?" he barked.

"I left right after the class. Have you been home long?" Annie asked. She immediately went to the sink to wash her hands so she could start dinner and put some distance between herself and Walter.

"I've been home for over an hour. What are you making for dinner?" he said.

"I thought I'd make one of your favorites . . . Liver and onions," Annie said. "Why don't you relax in the den and I'll have dinner ready in a little while." She could see him relax just a little.

"Make it quick. I'm hungry," Walter said as he left the kitchen.

Annie stood at the sink and took in a deep breath. Annie realized she had dodged Walter's fury. Tears came to her eyes as she made dinner, not from the onions she was slicing but from thoughts of her conversation with Olyria. Could Olyria be right? Annie shuddered at the thought of what might lie ahead.

"I had lunch with Olyria today," Annie said as they sat down to dinner. "She's going to have surgery next week. I told her I'd take her to the hospital."

"Isn't there anyone else who can take her?" Walter asked curtly.

"No . . . there really isn't," Annie replied.

"You're spending a lot of time with her," Walter said.

Annie's heart constricted, she didn't want to stir Walter up but had to stand by her friend at her time of need. "Olyria's a good friend . . . she needs me now," Annie said.

"I guess," Walter said rather flippantly.

They finished their dinner in silence and spent the rest of the evening each in their own chair, watching TV. Each lost in their own thoughts.

Chapter 11

Dinner at Caroline's house was not going any better. "I've been getting some prank calls at the shop," Caroline said. After the words left her mouth she braced for Charles' reaction.

"What do you mean 'prank phone calls'?" Charles' face was red and he was standing beside the table with his napkin clutched in his fist.

"Calm down," Caroline said. "You're scaring Budd."

"Budd needs to be scared if some scum bag is calling. I won't have it, I tell you. I just won't have it."

Budd's face was white; she was trying to hold back the tears that threatened.

"Look at her," Caroline said. "You're the one who is scaring her. You're the one who is scaring me. The phone caller isn't half as bad as you are."

The color drained out of Charles' face. He threw his napkin on the table and sank into his chair at the head of the table. His shoulders were shaking and Caroline hurried to stand behind him. She rested a hand on his shoulder.

"Budd, go to your room," Caroline said.

"I was supposed to go to . . ."

"Not tonight," Caroline said. "Whoever it is, call and tell them you can't make it."

"Mom, it's Friday night."

"I don't care. Go to your room."

Budd nodded and left the table.

"I don't understand what's happening here," Charles said. "My family is in jeopardy and nobody tells me. Nobody asks my advice. First it was Jamie and now it's you and Budd. It's like I'm the invisible man." Charles was in pain and Caroline was shaken seeing him this way. The phone calls were bad, and she'd had to tell him; but his reaction was more frightening than the calls.

"Charles," Caroline said, "we're all fine. Tommy is looking after Jamie and nobody has raised a hand to Budd or to me."

"Tommy is a goofball. He couldn't look after his own ass and I may not be much better." He wiped a hand across his forehead. It came away damp and he wiped the hand on his napkin. "This has to stop, Caroline. I won't have any of my girls in jeopardy. The quilt shop was supposed to keep you safe. Remember? It was to get you out of harm's way where strangers came in and tried to shoot you down." Charles' eyes were bulging and his complexion was back to red. "Remember?" he said again.

"Oh, Charles. None of this has anything to do with the bank. The bank was years ago." She patted his shoulder, tried to soothe him. "I've almost forgotten about the bank."

"I haven't forgotten. I'll never forget what it felt like to get the call you had been shot; and now the girls have been dragged into it." A lump formed in Charles' throat. How could he forget that frightening day? It was seared in his memory. He couldn't prevent Caroline from being shot, but he would now prevent some lunatic from hurting the ones he loved. He didn't know how but he would not let them get hurt. He banged his fist on the table.

The dishes shook and Caroline jumped.

"Charles, you're really scaring me."

Charles sighed. His shoulders slumped. "I don't mean to scare you. It's the last thing I want to do, but this has to stop."

"You're right," Caroline said. "It's Friday. Nothing big is going on at the shop this weekend. Let's take Budd and drive up to Bowling Green. We'll check up on Jamie, see her new digs with Tommy and just relax for a day. We can even spend the night in one of those Holiday Inn Expresses and the girls can go swimming. Remember how they loved to do that when the weather was bad outside? Do you remember, Charles?"

"I remember," Charles said. He stood, put his arms around Caroline and hugged her to himself. "Jamie was twelve, Budd was seven, and it was a different world."

"Oh, Charles," Caroline said. "It was a different world." Caroline looked into his eyes, begging him to help her turn back time while the juices on the roast turned white and congealed, while the potatoes turned grey-brown and, the peas collapsed and puckered in their bowl. Finally, they went upstairs together.

⌘

Budd didn't want to go to Bowling Green, Jamie didn't want them to come; but on Saturday morning, Caroline made arrangements for her sister, Amy, to take care of the shop; then Charles and Caroline tossed bags in the trunk of the car, called for reservations for four at the Holiday Inn Express and began their journey back toward a simpler time in their lives.

Caroline sang, 'She'll be coming round the mountain', just like she'd done when the girls were small, from the front seat, while Budd sulked in the back seat. Charles sat in stony silence behind the wheel. Caroline reached across the console and took his hand. He suffered a small smile onto his face and in that smile Caroline saw the future. Just the two of them with no girls left to drain off the stress that developed between them. The girls would be off with their Tommy's or Jim's or Ralph's, having discussions of their own. There'd be nobody for either of them to turn to but each other.

They checked into the motel and Caroline called the number Jamie had given her for Tommy's apartment phone. It rang twenty times before the electronic operator came on the line to tell her nobody was answering and for a fee they could call back later. Deregulation had absolutely ruined the phone system in this country. The anonymous voice was still speaking when finally someone answered, sleepily. "Hullo."

"Is Jamie home."

"Hold on, I'll check," the slurry voice said.

Caroline smiled and did eyebrow tricks for Charles while she waited. Budd had slumped into a chair by the gold-and-orange drapes on the sliding door that opened onto a small balcony overlooking the pool and the open play area in the middle of the motel.

The sound of children's laughter broke through the soundproofing.

"Hullo," Jamie finally said.

"We're here."

Silence on the other end.

"At the Holiday Inn Express."

"Mom, I told you I had to study today."

"You still have to eat. Come and have breakfast with us. Your Dad needs to see you."

"Is he still mad?" Jamie asked.

"Maybe a little, but seeing you will fix things, I think. Can you come have breakfast?"

Caroline could hear Tommy in the background. He was growling like a tiger. Oh, god, she thought. Oh, god. They're in bed together – alone. Oh, god.

"Let me check," Jamie said. Then she giggled.

Caroline could hear Tommy's angry voice, but not what it said. She could hear Jamie trying to console, but not the words.

"We can come for breakfast, Mom," Jamie said, "but that's all the time we have this weekend. Tommy has to go to work at two and I really do have to study for midterms.

"Jamie, I didn't actually think about Tommy coming with you. I'm not sure your Dad is ready to see him."

"*Mommmmmm?*" Jamie said. It was the whine she'd developed at about the age of six to express displeasure.

"This isn't easy for your father and me," Caroline said.

"I'm the one who got mugged, Mom, I'm the one who can't sleep at night. Forgive me if I lack the proper sympathy for you and Dad."

Caroline's voice took on a sharp edge. "Just hop into old Louey the Buey and come have breakfast, Jamie. Tommy can come if you can't put him off, but he does so at his own risk."

So the arrangements were made and an hour later Charles, Caroline and Budd were seated together in the restaurant of the Holiday Inn Express in Bowling Green, Ohio, waiting for Jamie. In just a couple of minutes Jamie walked up to the table, no Tommy. Charles stood and hugged her tightly. This was the first he'd seen her since she was mugged. With his hands on her shoulders he held her at arms length and looked at her. His right hand touched her forehead. He pulled her to him and hugged her again and shuddered.

As Charles released her Jamie looked at her watch and said, "I'm sorry but I don't have a lot of time today. I wish I did but I have a big project due on Monday."

They sat down and Charles clenched his jaw. "Are you all right? I've been so worried about you."

"I'm fine, Dad," Jamie said; her voice clipped.

Charles hesitated; there was so much to say but this wasn't the time or place. "It's good to see you."

The waitress came and took their orders. They sat at the table, each miserable in his own way.

⌘

Back in Buckeye Grove, Olyria and Annie were having brunch, too. Annie had the notes she had made on Walter's hidden possessions. "I don't really believe it's right for a wife to spy on a husband, like this," Annie said. As a schoolteacher, Annie always tried to instill honesty and integrity into her students. Something about rummaging through her husband's things didn't square with her values.

"It isn't right for a husband to hide things from his wife, either," Olyria said. She was dressed in a red-and-black gypsy outfit with her hair spiked. Obviously she was feeling better. Annie nodded and laid the paper with her notes on the table.

Olyria picked it up and looked it over. "The divorce information is a matter of public record. We can get copies of everything for a fee from the Bureau of Vital Statistics. The divorce took place in Indiana. I'll look into that right away," she said. "When we get the names we can check marriage records and birth records."

Annie nodded. "The school picture should be fairly easy to trace, too," Olyria said. "Directory information about students is public record. I never heard of Economy Elementary School and, thank goodness, the photo has the year. I can check the Indiana and Ohio State Departments of Education. If there's nothing there,

I can move on to a larger geographic area."

"I wish I could see the photos," Olyria said.

"There is no way I can get them out of the house," Annie said. "I'd be terrified that Walter would find them missing." It was hard enough going through Walter's things. She knew both sides of Walter and she couldn't risk it.

"Yeah, I know," Olyria said. "Maybe you could make copies and we could work from those."

"I'd still have to take them out of the house and get them returned without Walter finding out."

"Does your computer have a scanner?" Olyria asked. "You could scan them in and make copies that way."

"We don't have a computer. Walter says they're the devil's tool and he won't have one in the house."

"The devil's tool?" Olyria laughed. "He is old-fashioned, isn't he?"

"Only about some things," Annie said. "And that's part of what is so confusing about him. In many ways he's the nicest husband a woman could want and in others . . . well, let's just say . . . I never expected marriage to be like it's turned out, confusing. That's the only reason I've agreed to look into this stuff. I don't think Walter has been completely honest with me."

It was all Olyria could do to keep from making a smart remark but she didn't want to hurt Annie. Instead she reached over and patted her hand. The women had their assignments and Annie was planning to do her computer work at the library with the help of the experienced researchers there. It would speed up their search into Walter's past.

⌘

Jamie and Charles had words at breakfast about Tommy and

what he meant to Jamie's future. Jamie believed it was everything, Charles thought it was nothing. The meal ended when Jamie stomped off. The family checked out of the hotel and headed south in silence. Only Budd could find anything good in the situation. When she got home she'd be able pick up her weekend plans that were so abruptly interrupted.

Charles buried himself in work all day Sunday and Caroline worked on another table runner sample and scanned quilting magazines for projects for her newly formed guild. Both were happy when Monday morning arrived and they had something scheduled.

Caroline arrived at Always in Stitches early. She put her key in the lock and it opened without a bit of trouble. Schultz had finally fixed it. She dropped the load she was carrying on the counter and went through the shop turning on lights, straightening shelves and trying to maintain a feeling of control in her life. She unlocked the front door and secured a tumbling-block baby quilt to the railing. It flapped and sparkled in the early morning breeze. She stood on the steps and sighed. A deep feeling of satisfaction came with the sigh. She owned this feeling and hoped it would last out the day. She looked across the street and could see the Schneider Funeral Home. There was a parking lot full of cars, and police motorcycles were positioned to lead a procession to the graveyard. She turned and glanced up the street and could see Schultz stepping out of his wife's German Deli, planting his feet solidly on the ground with each step, the way he did. Things could always be worse.

A soft breeze stirred the baby quilt as she was turning to go back in the shop. She stopped when Nan called out, "Caroline, Hi!" Nan skipped up the sidewalk, full of youthful exuberance and entered the shop through the front door with her boss.

"I didn't know you were scheduled this morning," Caroline

said.

"Oh, I'm not," Nan said. "I just dropped in. Thought maybe the UPS guy would be here."

Caroline laughed. It was a great healthy guffaw. "You are really smitten with him."

"Well, yes," Nan said. "He's better looking than Brad Pitt and he frequents Buckeye Grove. What more could a girl want?"

"I can't imagine." Caroline sorted the pile of books and magazines she had brought in with her this morning. "Look at this," she said. "Do you think it would be a good guild project?" Caroline showed her a quilted apron with a pocket across the front.

"It might," Nan said.

"Why don't you choose some fabric and make up a sample? It would help me decide."

"Sure," Nan said. "I'd be glad to. I'll try to get it finished by the end of the week. School is slow right now with midterms over." She pulled a couple bolts of fabric and cut some off. She tucked it all into her bag. "Do you think he's married?"

"Do I think who is married?" Caroline asked.

Nan put a hand on her hip and crooked her elbow, "The UPS guy," she said. "Mr Darling . . . Stan." the names rolled off her tongue like honey, sweet and slow.

Caroline laughed again. "I have no idea," she said.

"Are you expecting him this morning?"

"Not really," Caroline said. "Fabric shipments usually come in on Tuesday and notions and stuff come in on Thursday. Trunk shows and special orders are less predictable but if you want to stalk the UPS guy, the best days to do it are Tuesday and Thursday."

"Good information to have. Good information to have," Nan said. She wiggled her eyebrows like Groucho Marx used to do.

Maybe the generation gap wasn't as vast as Caroline was thinking these days. She decided to talk to Nan about the weird phone calls.

"Have you had any funny phone calls here in the shop?"

"Funny how?" Nan asked.

"You know like threatening or sexual or somehow off?"

Nan looked at the ceiling, thinking. "Not really," she said. "I've had a lot of hang-ups lately. You know, when you hurry to answer the phone, say hello and there's nobody there. It's really aggravating when we're busy. Why?"

"I've had a few," Caroline said. "I'm thinking of involving the police. The last one was Friday and the man – it's always a man with a raspy, deep, scary voice - -mentioned Budd. I'd even say he threatened her."

"Did you talk to Budd about it? Maybe it's some weirdo who is interested in her or some crazy from school."

"We didn't really talk about it . . . . . but the man's voice sounds much older than Budd. I thought he was using Budd to threaten me."

"Hmmmm," Nan said. "I think I'd talk to the police. At least make a record with them. That sort of thing can become important to verify just in case something happens down the line."

"You think it could be serious then?"

"The world is weird sometimes. People are weird sometimes. I'm not a baby but look what happened to Jamie when she just went to the ATM."

"Maybe I'll talk to Will Douglas about this," Caroline said.

"I would," Nan said.

The bell on the shop door rang as a group of quilters came in and began asking questions, so the conversation with Nan was over. Caroline pushed her troubled thoughts to the back of her mind, smiled and helped her customers; some of them hadn't been in the shop before. Nan pitched in and helped the ladies. It was obvious she was stalling hoping to see Stan. She finally gave up and left.

Tomorrow was another day.

Chapter 12

The he best and worst day of the week was the day the guild met. Caroline could depend on a good day of sales and the time flew by. Today was no exception. She had been going full bore since before she walked into the shop.

Nan stopped in and dropped off the apron she had stitched up the evening before. It could be a good project for the guild women. Nan hung around longer than she needed to, hoping for a Stan sighting, but he didn't materialize.

Michael came in early with his significant other, Adrian Smith, who also happened to be the County Coroner. Adrian had obliged his lover by doing an autopsy and toxicology screens worthy of a first-degree murder case on poor little Stella. Adrian was a trim, good-looking fellow and he wore a red bowler hat and black spats. Though Stella was definitely Michael's dog, Adrian also felt the loss.

"Caroline, meet Adrian," Michael said. He was rolling a serving cart into the shop from the back parking area. It was loaded with smoked salmon croquettes, cucumber-and-cream-cheese sandwiches in a bone shape, sauerkraut balls and chicken livers in bacon. "I've made all of Stella's favorites," he said as he rolled by. "Adrian is going to help me up the steps with this cart and we'll be right back."

Nan stood with her mouth hanging open, watching the guy in spats lift the front edge of the cart while Michael got the back. They had no trouble getting up to the level of the guild meeting. And in no time they were back at the counter. "I want Adrian to see the scene of the crime," he said. "Is the building owner here?"

"I don't think so," Caroline said. "He usually doesn't come in till about noon and then he's pretty hit-and-miss. Why do you need to see Schultz?"

"Adrian has some questions. Murder is his business, you know." Michael looked at Adrian with undisguised affection. "Adrian, this is Caroline Clarkson."

Adrian removed his hat. He held out a hand and Caroline connected with it so they could shake. "Nice to meet you, Mrs. Clarkson."

"Please, call me Caroline." Adrian nodded and Caroline went to Michael and hugged him. "I'm so sorry about Stella," she said.

"Thank you. I know she'd want me to go on and I will, but I feel as though I owe her a proper send-off; and it only makes sense we should do it at the guild meeting since this is absolutely the place she got into whatever poisoned her."

"Do you know yet what it was?" Caroline asked. She looked at the coroner as she spoke.

"Not yet," Adrian said. "We're running a complete battery of tests to try to discover what it was." He shook his head. "My office doesn't usually work on animals. We usually send them out to the vet clinic at OSU, but for Michael . . ." He let his voice drift off. "It could take a week or more."

Nan was standing by, shifting from foot to foot.

"Oh, this is Nan Roberts. She's one of my employees."

"Hey," Nan said and stuck out a hand to the coroner. "Any

friend of Michael's."

"I couldn't get a preacher to come in and read the scripture, so I'm going to do it myself," Michael said.

"I didn't know you were so religious," Caroline said.

"Well, I'm not really. But death, you know. It's so final and this is the time to take a shot. Just in case." Tears formed in the corners of Michael's eyes and Adrian patted him on the shoulder.

"Stella is fine," he said to Michael. "And feeling no more pain. She's eating chicken livers with God."

"Watch out for the lightning," Caroline said. Both men shrugged.

Just then Aggie McDaniel and Jeanine came in the back door and saved everybody from further conversation about how Stella might be spending her post-life time.

"Hey, ladies," Caroline said. Michael and Adrian went off in search of Schultz. Aggie and Jeanine waved hello and went up to the classroom to set up for the meeting.

"I've got to run to an English Lit class," Nan said as she headed out, having given up on Stan making a delivery.

Other guild members began to arrive. Caroline rang up a few sales; and when Kathy arrived, Caroline went up to join the guild meeting. Aggie had just called it to order. Michael and Adrian were back and dragged out chairs to sit at the end of the table.

Jeanine gave Michael a disapproving look for being late, even after arriving early.

The previous week, the women had agreed to bring names of favorite quilting fiction books and there was a lively discussion about authors Earlene Fowler, Jennifer Chivarini and Emilie Richards. Each had a group of devotees and the discussion was spirited.

The main topic for the guild was assembling the quilt for the

Quilts of Valor project. There were twelve blocks to be joined before the quilting could begin.

"I'm very proud of my squares," Annie said. "Olyria and Caroline helped but I finally got them put together. They are nearly exact in size because of the paper piecing." She held them up for everyone to see.

"Very nice," the ladies murmured and "My first squares weren't nearly as well done." Annie glowed in the praise from her fellow guild members. Jeanine agreed to take all the blocks for the week and assemble them into a lap-quilt top that could then be quilted and bound.

"I love to bind," said Wilma, a recent member of the guild. "I'll sign on right now to do that part when the time comes."

"I'll make a note of that," Olyria said. "But first Jeanine has to put the squares together and it has to be quilted. Any one volunteering to do the quilting." No hands went up and Olyria said, "Well, think about it. We'll need someone to volunteer by the time Jeanine gets the quilt put together. Could be next week?" It was a question and Jeanine shrugged in response.

"It could take me two weeks," she said.

Olyria suggested some future projects for the group: a mystery night, a first quilt show and tell, an ugly fabric swap; and then Caroline shared the apron Nan had made.

"I love the apron," Michael said. "I could make one of these for each of my cooks as a Christmas gift. I think we should make this our next project."

"Do you want to work on them at a meeting or do you want to do them at home?" Olyria asked.

The women and Michael agreed the meeting time was really too valuable to spend on sewing and if Caroline would bring the patterns, they could choose fabric and begin working on the apron project after the next guild meeting.

Jeanine reported they already had $290 in the treasury and would have to decide how they wanted to use the money before too long.

Aggie closed the meeting and then gave the floor to Caroline as she had been asked.

"We've had a very sad situation develop," Caroline said. "Michael's sweet little Stella has died and Michael asked if we could have a Memorial for her after the meeting today. I told him I thought that would be fine and hope you all agree."

There was a low mumble of sadness and condolences to Michael. Those women who were close enough reached over and touched Michael's shoulder or his arm. "We're so sorry," several of the ladies said.

"Thank you, ladies," Michael said. "It makes this easier to have you share my sorrow. Stella was a wonderful dog, as you all know, and wouldn't have hurt a flea, even if it bit her first. Though Stella never had a flea in her life." Michael took a deep breath before going on.

"This is my friend Adrian. He's involved in forensic medicine, and he did an autopsy on Stella for me." Michael laid a hand on Adrian's shoulder. "He believes, and I do, too, that Stella was poisoned when she escaped from her carrier those few minutes last week at the guild meeting." The women looked from Michael to one another, with surprise in their eyes.

"Don't worry ladies," Adrian said. "I'm sure there's no threat to the rest of us. By that, I mean the poison isn't airborne. I think Stella accidentally got into something not meant for her. Perhaps rat poison or something like that."

Michael spoke up. "Nothing against Caroline or Always in Stitches, of course, but I think the building owner has a responsibility here. If there are rat poisons, or any sort of poisons on the premises he should have warned customers of the possibility of damage from that poison."

"But the main thing I want to accomplish today is the Memorial to Stella. I have an inspirational reading I want to share and I've prepared some of Stella's favorite treats that I'd like to share with you all. If you will indulge me . . ."

Caroline looked around the table and though there were some blank looks on faces, no one seemed disagreeable to giving Michael a few minutes to remember his dear pet.

Michael opened a Bible he took out of his shoulder bag and flipped through the pages. He began to read, "The Lord is my shepherd, I shall not want . . ." The ladies sat in respectful silence till he reached the end of the passage and then chairs scraped and scratched against the floor as the women crowded around Michael to hug him and offer tissue so he could dry his eyes. Adrian stood to the side and Caroline did, too, as the sympathy and the snacks were passed.

"The salmon croquettes are fabulous," Annie said to Michael. "The best I ever ate. Would you be willing to give me some tips so I could make them for Walter?"

"Well, I don't usually share recipes, but if you promise not to let the secret out I guess I could do that," Michael said.

Olyria praised the liver-and-bacon rollups and Michael thanked them all. "Stella would have liked sharing these with you," he said.

Caroline was just about to wrap things up when Schultz came striding up the stairs. "I heard someone up here was looking for me," he said.

Michael didn't even try to contain himself. "Murderer."

Schultz looked puzzled, "What are you talking about?"

Tears filled Michael's eyes. Sobs wracked his throat. He couldn't speak coherently.

"Michael's dog has died," Caroline said. "The coroner," she indicated Adrian with a tilt of her head "believes she was poisoned. She got loose here in the building last week and Michael says that is the only time she could have gotten into some sort of poisonous substance."

"I have no poison in the building," Schultz said.

"No rat poison? No insecticide for spiders. Nothing to kill off bats?" Adrian said. "I'm presuming whatever the dog got into was accidental, not something that was done with malice toward the dog."

"I didn't even know we had animals in the building, ever," Schultz said.

Michael had pulled himself together. "If Stella got into it, so might a small child and then you'd have a problem on your hands. Think of that."

Schultz put his hands on his hips. "You're crazy," he said. He surveyed the room. "All of you. There is no poison in the building."

"Are you sure?" Caroline said. "Could one of the tenants have put something out without your knowledge?"

Schultz relaxed a bit. He ran a hand through his grey hair front to back. "I doubt it. Nobody wants to do anything for themselves. They expect me to take responsibility for every little thing around here."

"Will you check?" Caroline asked. "Could you do that for Michael? Just check to see if anybody has ant traps or rat poison or anything like that that Stella could have gotten into."

"I could do that," Schultz said.

"You'd better," Michael said. "And be warned that you'll be

hearing from my lawyer about Stella. I know we have a wrongful death suit in this situation. I just know we do." Adrian took Michael's arm and pulled him away from Schultz.

"For a dog?" Schultz said.

"Stella was no ordinary dog," Michael said.

All the women nodded, then gathered around Michael and Adrian and what was left of the refreshments as Caroline escorted Schultz down the stairs and out of her shop. She thought this would be a good time to set up a meeting to discuss all of the unfinished projects and things that needed to be corrected in the quilt shop.

⌘

Annie dropped Olyria and her mother, who could not be talked into staying home, in front of the hospital on Wednesday morning, then searched for a parking spot. It was storming out and Annie had damp spots on her blouse that had turned cold when she entered the prematurely air-conditioned hospital lobby. It was only May and someone must be testing the thing for hot summer days.

Annie stopped by the cafeteria for a cup of coffee and then hurried to the second floor in search of Olyria. By the time she found Olyria she was already in the pre-op cubicle.

"They already gave her a shot of something to sedate her," Olyria's mom said. She smiled at Annie, and Edwina seemed as reasonable as anybody. Maybe Olyria was imagining her neediness.

Nurses were in and out, checking Olyria; and the anesthesiologist came in and introduced himself all around. Olyria answered all his questions without confusion.

"It'll be about twenty more minutes," the nurse said. She had popped her head between the curtains that surrounded the bay Olyria was in.

"If you don't mind, I'd like to start over to the waiting room,"

Edwina said. "I'm getting a little tired of sitting on this straight-backed chair."

"Sure, Mom," Olyria said. Her mother stood, bent over and kissed Olyria on the cheek. "I know you'll be fine," Edwina said. "And I'll see you when it's over."

"See you then," Olyria said, with a giggle. She grabbed hold of Annie's hand as Edwina left the cubicle. "You'll stay with me, won't you?" She giggled again. Clearly the sedative was taking effect.

"As long as they'll let me," Annie said.

"We have so much in common." Olyria said.

"You're right, we do. Quilting and friends and our ages."

"And don't forget Walter," Olyria giggled again.

"Walter?" Annie said confused. "You mean spying on him together?"

"Spying?" Olyria put a hand over her mouth. "Like James Bond? I don't think so. I meant both of us dated him." Olyria giggled again. She put her hand over her mouth and whispered, "Except you married him and I didn't."

"You dated Walter?" Annie cried. "*You* dated Walter."

"Shhh! Somebody might hear."

At that moment the nurse came in. "Time to go," she said and with a burly orderly's help wheeled Olyria out of the room toward her cancer surgery.

⌘

It was a slow day at Always in Stitches. Caroline was grateful. She was coming to appreciate slow days as an opportunity to catch up on all the housekeeping things that had to be done, even though the low sales totals were hard to take.

It was still early when the phone rang. Caroline picked it up and Jamie was on the other end. "I got a job, Mom, at the Electric

Quilt Company[6] here in Bowling Green. This could solve all my financial problems."

Caroline cleared her throat. She hadn't heard from Jamie since the blowup between her and her father in the Holiday Inn Express dining room. "That would be a start," she said.

"Come on, Mom. Be happy for me. I'm doing my best."

Caroline sighed. "I know you are, but you should call your dad. Mend fences with him before they get too high to get over."

"He needs to understand Tommy and I love one another. We mean to be married one of these days and it just would be better if he had some respect . . ."

"Jamie . . . Jamie . . . we don't need to have this same discussion again. I'm very happy you got a job and the Electric Quilt should be a great place for you to work. You have the background for it."

"Thanks. That's what the owner said, too. She even said she'd heard of your shop. Can you imagine? You've only been open a couple of months and already other shops around the state have heard of you."

"It's a small world, Jamie. And we quilters keep an eye on one another. Knowing what the competition is up to, you know."

"I'm excited," Jamie said. "Dad will see I'm serious about Tommy and my life and he'll have to stop thinking of me as a kid."

---

6   The Electric Quilt Company - the leading quilt design software maker in the world, with wholesale customers and distributors in the U.S., Canada, Great Britain, Japan, Australia, New Zealand and South Africa. In the 13 years the company had been in business, it has produced 29 software editions and published 12 books. Located in Bowling Green, Ohio, it is the brainchild of Penny Morris and Dean Neumann.

"Just think about calling him, Jamie, and making up. Your dad loves you more than anything. He's really hurt by the problems between the two of you."

"Yeah, I will. I just wanted to let you know about my job. I have to go now. I start work on Friday and that's just two days away. I have to get everything else organized so I'll have time to go to work. Tommy has a paper due Friday and I promised to help him with it and there a lot to do around here. I'll talk to you later, Mom. I love you."

Jamie hung up and Caroline felt exhausted by the conversation. Youth is so suited to the young, Caroline thought. Nobody else has the energy, and besides, we know too much by the time we begin to send children out into the world.

The phone rang again, almost immediately. Caroline thought it must be Jamie calling back with some forgotten detail. She picked up the phone, "Did you forget something, Honey," she said.

A moment of silence followed. Then the familiar raspy-voiced man said. "I haven't forgotten a thing and I must say, that's more like it, my dear."

Caroline sucked in air. "What do you want?" she yelled into the phone. "Leave me alone. I'm going to call the police."

"That would be a mistake," the man said. His voice took on a hard edge. "A big mistake for you and for that little Rose Budd of yours."

Caroline slammed the phone down and panted to get her breath going again. She felt like she might lose her breakfast, but finally she got control back and went to her data base and looked up Sheryll Douglas's number. Caroline didn't want to call Will at the police station as it might upset whoever was calling her. She dialed and when Sheryll answered she said, "It's Caroline Clarkson, Sheryll. Could you ask Will to give me a call? I need some advice."

"Of course, I will," Sheryll said. "Are you okay? You sound sort of breathless."

"I'm okay for now, but I think I may need some help. I think Will could tell me what I need to do."

"Soon as he gets home, I'll have him call," Sheryll said.

Caroline hung up the phone and got furiously busy clearing counters, putting away fabric bolts and rearranging the pattern books.

Chapter 13

Annie sat in the hospital family waiting room with Edwina, waiting for someone from the hospital staff to give them an update on Olyria. Annie's mind replayed Olyria's remarks over and over in her head and they still didn't make any sense. Olyria dated Walter? How could that be? Annie convinced herself that it was the medication talking, that Olyria was confused. What if it was true? Why hadn't Olyria mentioned this earlier? Did she think Annie would be jealous? Is that why she encouraged Annie to spy on him?

"It's taking a long time," Edwina whispered, breaking Annie's train of thought.

"I'm sorry, Edwina, what did you say?"

"I thought they would be through by now."

"Oh, I'm sure it won't be much longer, Edwina; it's been almost three-and-a-half hours so someone will come out soon."

Edwina turned to Annie and squeezed her hand. "Thank you for being with me, dear. I don't think I could've . . ."

Just then Olyria's doctor came out, "The surgery went very well. We removed the tumor and three lymph nodes for testing. She's being moved into recovery now but it will be a couple more hours before she can go home. I'll give her a prescription for some medication to ease the pain." He hesitated a little to let this sink in and then smiled and added, "Olyria is in good health; hopefully, her recovery will be quick. I'll see her in ten to fourteen days and by then I'll have the results of the test."

"Thank you, Doctor; when can we see her?" Edwina asked.

"The nurse will let you know."

Finally the nurse came out and said they could see Olyria, one at a time. Edwina went first. She didn't stay long as Olyria was sleeping. Annie went back a little later thoughts of Walter and Olyria swirling in her mind.

"Hey, kiddo, how are you feeling," Annie whispered close to Olyria's ear.

Olyria reached up to grasp Annie's hand. "Like a Mack truck just hit me," she said with a weak smile.

"You'll be home soon and on the road to recovery." Olyria smiled and drifted back to sleep. Annie gazed down at her friend, contemplating their earlier conversation.

It was still daylight when Annie dropped Olyria and Edwina off at Olyria's house. It had been a long day and Annie thought about how good it would feel to sit with her feet up. Annie helped Edwina prepare the ice pack to put over Olyria's incision. She made sure Edwina and Olyria had something to eat and then said good-night.

It was almost 7:00 p.m. when Annie got home. Walter met her at the door and was clearly upset. "Where have you been?" Walter paced in the kitchen, running his fingers through his hair.

"At the hospital with Olyria and her mother. I explained the other night." Annie pleaded with her eyes. "I couldn't turn my back on her."

"So you turn your back on me instead?" Walter said. He banged a fist on the kitchen counter. "I haven't had my supper yet."

Annie's first thought was 'well, too bad' but she held her tongue and bustled about the kitchen throwing together a chicken sandwich and some potato salad for her pouting husband.

They spent the rest of the evening in cold, stony silence.

⌘

It was Jamie's first day at Electric Quilt. Her schedule was afternoons on Monday, Tuesday, Thursday and Friday then all day on Wednesday. When Jamie got home she was exhilarated and exhausted. Tommy was agitated.

"I don't like the idea of your working. I needed your help on a paper today and you weren't here," Tommy barked.

"I'm sorry. You know I have to work. My parents can't afford the additional cost of my living here."

"Oh, yes, . . . your parents. Evidently they couldn't afford to pay for one more breakfast on Saturday either, so you had to go without me." Tommy's voice was sharp. "You sure didn't stand up for me."

"I didn't have a choice, Tommy. My dad's still upset about the mugging. He just wants to keep me safe. And, yes, he's upset with my decision to move in with you. It will take him some time to get used to it." Jamie went to the fridge to get some iced tea for herself. "He'll come around, I'm sure of that. We just have to give him time."

"He'll never accept me. I know he doesn't like me. I can see it in his eyes every time he talks to me." Tommy's voice was getting harsher now, his jaw rigid.

"Tommy, please. I'm sorry, just give him some time." Jamie said. They stood glaring at one another.

Jamie gave in first. "You said you needed my help today. What did you need?"

"Help with my Modern Physics project. Don't worry, I went to the library and Roberta was more than willing to help me."

Jamie was taking a sip of tea just then and it caught in her throat. The idea of Roberta, a beautiful brunette who worked at the library and at one point had dated Tommy, going out of her way to help Tommy was the last thing she wanted to hear. Jamie went over to Tommy, put her arms around his neck and said, "I'm sorry I wasn't here to help you. Please let me make it up to you."

Tommy's facial features eased as Jamie kissed him. "Well, now that you're here, there is something you can do for me," Tommy said as he led Jamie to the bedroom. Jamie was exhausted from work, had a ton of homework to do, but did not want to lose Tommy, especially to Roberta, so she went along.

⌘

Will Douglas called Caroline Wednesday night. Caroline carried the phone into the bedroom in order to speak freely to Will and to avoid upsetting Budd. "Will, I don't know if I'm doing the right thing, but I'm at my wits' end," Caroline said quickly and drew in a breath.

"What are you talking about?" Will asked.

"I've been getting phone calls from some weird man. I have no clue who he is but, he keeps insinuating things he wants me to do for him," Caroline said. "He even knows Budd's name and I can't bear the thought of her getting hurt."

"And you don't have any idea who it might be?"

"No. The voice seems somewhat familiar but I can't place it."

"Does he call at the shop and at home?"

"I get the calls only at the shop."

"Well, then getting an answering machine isn't an option. I'll stop by and make out a report and I'd suggest you call the phone company. They should be able to set up a Trap on the phone for a couple of weeks." Caroline was confused. "The Trap is different from a tap. The Trap allows the phone company to determine the telephone number from which the harassing calls originate. A tap would require a court order. They'll ask you to keep a log with the time and date of the harassing phone calls and that should help us figure out who it is." Will's words were giving Caroline some comfort. "Is there anyone who might be upset with you?" Will asked.

"Not that I know of. Do you think this could be related to the robbery at the bank? Perhaps the accomplice that wasn't caught?" Caroline said.

"Anything's a possibility, but that seems like a reach since it was so long ago. Talk to the phone company and we'll take it from there."

"Thanks, Will. I feel better, but the caller told me not to go to the police. If you come by he'll know I disobeyed."

"Don't worry Caroline, in most cases it's just kids. They get their thrill and don't go any further."

"Thanks Will, I'll talk to you soon."

Charles came in the bedroom and saw Caroline sitting on the bed still holding the handset. "Is everything all right?" he asked.

"That was Will Douglas. I talked to him about the phone calls. He suggested I call the phone company."

"I'll take care of that for you tomorrow. I can't just sit here while my girls are being threatened." Charles sat down next to Caroline. By the set of his jaw, Caroline could see the stress in Charles' face.

"I know you would do anything you could to protect us." Tears filled Caroline's eyes.

Charles pulled Caroline to him; he put his arm around her and lifted her chin so he could look her in the eyes. "I'd walk to the ends of the earth for you. You must know that. Soon Budd will be away at school. I can't imagine what I would do if anything terrible happened to you or the girls."

"I know, Charles, I know," Caroline said as Charles kissed her. Charles made love to her; she absorbed his warmth and strength and he absorbed hers. This was something they both needed. It had been too long. Afterward Caroline nestled next to Charles.

"You're right, Charles, it won't be long before we're alone. Budd will be off to college and it'll be just you and me." Caroline said. "It's scary on the one hand and exciting on the other. It's been so long since we've been alone." Charles squeezed his wife tight.

"Shhhh, don't worry about that tonight. We'll manage somehow." He kissed her good-night and they fell into gentle slumber.

⌘

When Caroline woke up Thursday morning, everything seemed brighter. She was preparing breakfast when Budd walked into the kitchen.

"Hey, Mom," Budd murmured.

"Good morning, honey. Did you sleep well?"

"Yeah," Budd said with a yawn. "I'd like to talk to you. I've been thinking about getting a job this summer as a camp counselor. I could use the money I earn toward my college education. I know things are hard with the shop just getting started, and I'd like to help."

Caroline wrapped her arms around Budd and held her close. She was grateful for Budd's willingness to help and at the same time was sad that Budd would even have to think about such things. "Oh honey, your Dad and I will manage your tuition. If you want to work for some extra money, that's up to you."

"I'll see about the job today. I think it would be fun," Budd said.

"That's fine with me. Your Dad's already gone to work, so let's eat before breakfast gets cold. I've got to hurry to open the shop."

⌘

The shop had been open only twenty minutes when Michael came in. He was clearly still agitated about losing Stella. "Caroline, have you seen Schultz?" he asked. "I want to know what he's done about the poison."

"I think he's around this morning. You might check his office in the back."

Michael stormed through the granary, hunting Schultz down. He finally found him in his closet-sized office. Schultz's more-than-ample form was shoehorned into a chair behind a metal desk. His hair was disheveled and his eyes looked crusty. He was showing every day of his age. "What have you found out about the poison?" Michael said. "I'm not giving up on this until I know what happened to Stella."

"Yah, yah, yah, I know you're upset. I've checked the facility and there is no poison in the building," Schultz said, his words clipped.

"Is that all you're doing? Something happened to Stella and it happened here. She was never out of my sight except Tuesday at the Guild meeting and she wasn't gone long. Something in this building caused her death and you better find it." Michael's face was red and his eyes were wide, glaring at Schultz.

"Okay, okay, I'll talk to the tenants. It's not doing any good to get so excited. She was just a dog, not a child," Schultz said. He shook his head.

"Just a dog . . . .you have no idea how much I loved her. She was my companion. She gave me great comfort and because of you she is dead. I'll show you how much she meant to me. Just you wait." Michael was visibly shaking now. He stormed off.

⌘

Nan came into the shop shortly after Michael left to find Schultz. "Good morning. Hope I'm not too late," Nan said.

"Late?" Caroline asked. "You're not scheduled to come in until 11:00?"

"Oh, I know, I'm early for work, but I hope I didn't miss the UPS deliveries," Nan said with her eyebrows raised.

"You mean you hope you didn't miss seeing Stan?" Caroline chuckled.

"Well . . . yeah. Has he been in yet?"

"No, but he should be soon."

Michael came back through the door. Caroline had never seen him so upset. It was obvious he'd found Schultz. "Well, I talked to him and he just doesn't get it. He will soon . . . I've got to run but I'm not letting this drop." Michael left in a flurry, just the way he had arrived.

⌘

Schultz hurried into Always in Stitches on Michael's heels. "That man is crazy," he said to Caroline. "You'd think a person had died, instead of a dog. He swears he will show me how much the dog meant to him." Schultz shook his head. "I just don't get it, but I'm going to call a tenants' meeting to get to the bottom of this."

"We can do it here," Caroline said. "So long as I don't have a class going on."

"How about two o'clock this afternoon?"

Caroline consulted her class schedule. "That would be fine."

"I'll notify all the tenants. Nothing but problems around here. My wife is even having trouble at the deli because of this place."

"What sort of problems?" Caroline asked.

"That old yoga guy, the one married to the lady who quilts, he has been stopping in and harassing the girls who wait tables. My wife asked me to talk to him, and he couldn't care less what I had to say. I may have to take more action."

"That has to be Walter. He considers himself quite a ladies man."

"Snow-white hair?"

"That's him. Annie is sweet as sugar and he's a bit hard to take."

"He better watch himself or I'll give him something that's hard to take." Schultz made a fist and plodded off in his strange, determined gait.

Nan was busy cutting fat quarters and Caroline helped two groups of customers who breezed in and out over the next hour. Nan came to attention each time the bell on the door jingled. Finally, it was Stan Darling. She smiled and tried to look busy with her fat quarters. She did her best not to stare. Stan wheeled the boxes to the back counter where Nan was standing.

"Good morning," he said. His brown eyes were gleaming.

"Were you talking to me?" Nan said, immediately feeling like a fool, as there was no one else around.

"I sure am," he said as he unloaded the boxes. Nan couldn't take her eyes off his strong arms. Stan smiled. "I was wondering if you'd like to go for coffee or to have a drink tonight?" he asked.

"That would be nice."

"I could meet you here at 6:00 if that's okay?"

"That'd be fine." Nan allowed her fingers to touch Stan's as she signed the electronic signature pad and handed it back.

Stan walked out of the shop.

"See you later," Nan whispered.

It was a little before 2:00 when people began arriving for Schultz's meeting. Jasmine came in first. "Hi, Caroline, how's everything going with you?"

"Pretty good, and with you?"

"I'm still not back to normal. They're just finishing up the wiring now and I should be able to get my stove hooked up tomorrow. I hope to be up and running again by Monday."

The back door to the shop opened and in stepped Goldie. "Hey, how are you two gals?" she said in her ever-cheery voice.

"I can't wait to get my hands on Schultz. It's taken them far too long to get things done," Jasmine said.

"I'm fine, too," Caroline said with a chuckle.

"I hope this doesn't take long," David Williams said as he entered. "I've got another session this afternoon."

Schultz was the next to arrive, and he led everyone up to the meeting area. "Are they going to be done with the wiring today?" Jasmine asked him.

"The electrician said they should finish up today," Schultz said.

"Well, I expect to have my rent reduced for the amount of time that I've been shut down. It'll take me some time to build my clientele back up." Jasmine said curtly.

Caroline had purchased scones from Jasmine while she'd been closed down, in an effort to support her, and they were darned good -- especially with her homemade jam. She knew Walter had sweet-talked her into some apricot scones and jam too. It wouldn't be long before Jasmine was at full speed.

"Yes, yes, don't worry. I'll take care of it. I told you before, I'd take care of everything. Haven't I fixed the problem with the hot water? And I added more lights for you, Goldie. Caroline, I fixed your lock," Schultz said. His voice showed his irritation. "But I have something else I want to talk to you about." He took in a deep breath and then went on. "It seems that a dog got loose in the building last week and ended up dead."

David sat straight up in his chair. His moustache wilted as he listened to Schultz. Everyone else listened quietly.

"Is anyone using poison without telling me? Maybe for rats or insects?" Schultz asked.

"Rats, I can't have rats if I'm serving food. Do you know what that would do to my business if people thought there were rats here?" Jasmine's voice rose and her cheeks took on a pink glow.

"I just asked if anyone had problems, I didn't say there is a problem." Schultz's brows furrowed; his voice was gruff.

"Why do you say the dog was poisoned?" David asked. He rubbed his beard and waited for an answer.

"Because they actually did an autopsy on the dog. Can you believe it? On a dog! Supposedly this is the only place the dog was out of the owner's sight," Schultz said.

"Was it rat poison?" Jasmine asked.

Schultz looked to Caroline for an answer. "The results aren't complete yet," she said. "I don't think they know what kind of poison yet."

David nodded and leaned forward, putting his elbows on his knees. He crossed his arms and rested his head in his hands. It wasn't exactly a yoga pose, but it required some advanced flexibility. His eyes closed in a meditative mood.

"If anyone has a problem with any kind of pest, I want to know about it. I'll get a professional company in to exterminate. I don't want poison used in this building without my knowledge." Schultz pounded on the cutting table to emphasize his point.

A busload of quilters entered Always in Stitches and Caroline said, "Could we break this up? I don't want these women to hear us up here talking about rats, poison and dead dogs." She had a pleading look in her eyes and Schultz took pity. The meeting broke up and Caroline hurried down to the sales floor to help Nan.

Chapter 14

Nan was primping in front of a small compact mirror. She spit on her fingers and twisted a curl at her ear. "You look great," Caroline said.

"Do you think so?" Nan turned her head from side to side, straining to get a total effect in the tiny mirror.

"Stan already knows what you look like," Pat Carter said. She was helping in the shop during the evening hours while Caroline taught a one-session tote-bag class. The women had begun to arrive. Goldie was taking the class and considering the tote an art project. "He's going to love you, Nan," Goldie said. "Stop worrying. Worrying will give you wrinkles."

Pat laughed. "Don't listen to her. Time gives you wrinkles."

"Don't even think about wrinkles," Caroline said. "You're twenty years old, for heaven's sake."

The women were circled around Nan when Stan came in the back door. He was wearing a pair of khakis and a blue-and-white striped golf shirt. His forehead shone like a mirror and the women could smell his after-shave, which was minty and fresh.

"You ready?" he said to Nan. She smiled and reached out to take the arm he offered. They left the shop through the back door. Nan threw a glance over her shoulder. She made a hubba-hubba sign with her eyebrows and the women laughed when the door slammed shut behind them.

"Oh, to be twenty again." Pat said.

"I wouldn't want it for anything. My life has been too much fun to wish it away." Goldie said. She was fingering a turquoise-and-brown print on the brights round just next to the check-out counter. "You can only go forward. There is no going back."

"We have to get started," Caroline said. "This tote is going to take the entire class time and we're already late getting started. "We'll find all about Stan tomorrow when Nan comes in to work."

Six women followed Caroline upstairs to the classroom.

⌘

Caroline was exhausted when she got home. Charles had made lasagna for supper, the take-it-out-of-the-box and stick-it-in-the oven kind, and he heated some up for Caroline while she sat at the kitchen table and drank a glass of Chianti. It was good to have made up with Charles. He was a fine man and she loved him.

"You want garlic bread?"

Caroline shook her head. "No, thanks. I'm not even sure I can stay awake long enough to eat this."

"No wonder you're tired. You were at the shop from open to close today."

"I have to do that some days, Charles. We both knew it when we started." Caroline yawned, sipped her wine, rubbed her forehead and then dug into the lasagna. "Mmm, good," she said, smiling at Charles.

Budd entered the kitchen. "Hey, mom. Long day?"

Caroline nodded.

"I got the job."

"What job?" Charles said.

"The camp counselor job. Mom and I talked about it this

morning." Budd looked at her mother. Caroline looked up from her plate of lasagna and nodded.

"That was fast," she said after she swallowed.

"Mr. Collins interviewed me today at school. He's the camp director and I had him for geometry last year. You remember, Mom?"

Caroline nodded again.

"It wasn't like starting out flatfooted. He already knows me and all we had to talk about was my kid skills."

"Kid skills?" Charles asked.

"I'll be working with nine-to-twelve-year-olds and he has to be sure I won't eat them or something." Caroline laughed. "I could be a kid-hater," Budd said. "Mr. Collins said his first responsibility is to the children; and now that I'm a counselor, that's my first responsibility, too."

"Where's this camp?" Charles asked.

"Twenty miles north of Columbus. It's a sleepover camp with two five-week sessions, so I'll be home a few days in the middle."

"Oh, honey, I didn't know you'd be gone all summer. I didn't even know the camp was an overnight," Caroline said.

"I thought I mentioned that," Budd said. "I'll have to have a permission slip signed by you or dad and then it'll be official."

Charles scowled and poured himself a glass of the Chianti. "I wish somebody would include me in what's going on around here."

Budd shrugged. "I'm including you. I let you know I got the job." Budd kissed her mother on the forehead and patted Charles on the shoulder before she left the room.

Caroline wiped her mouth, took a large glug of Chianti. "She's going to be all the way gone soon, just like Jamie."

"It's gone so fast, Caroline. I can't keep myself from thinking about when the girls were little and thought I had all the answers."

"I know, honey." Caroline covered Charles' hand with both of hers. "It will be just the two of us before we know it."

"That's how we started out, just the two of us. It's only right that's how we should end up, but I'm not really ready for it yet. "

Charles carried Caroline's plate to the sink, rinsed it and put it in the dishwasher. He took Caroline's hand and together, they went upstairs to bed.

⌘

Friday Caroline had to go to Always in Stitches early again. It would be two more days before she had a day off. At least the lock was working and the door opened right up without jiggling or cursing of any kind. She was still in the process of turning on lights and unfurling quilts when Nan came in.

"How was it?"

"It was wonderful," Nan said. Caroline could see she still had stars in her eyes for Stan. "He's very smart. We went to Plank's for a soda and a sandwich. He got Final Jeopardy right and I didn't have a clue."

"What was the question?"

"Heck if I know," Nan said. "It was about geography. I don't do geography."

Caroline laughed. "Me neither," she said. "So . . . we know he's good looking and smart. Anything else?"

"He has a three-year-old son."

"Whoa," Caroline said. "What about a wife?"

"He and the little boy's mother were never married. It was an accident that he says shouldn't have happened, but now he's really happy about it. He pays child support and sees the little boy whenever he can. His name is Jack."

"Jack Darling? Cute! Reminds me of the song, *You Call Everybody Darling*."

Nan had a blank look on her face.

"It's an oldie," Caroline said.

"Must be a *real* oldie," Nan said. "I had a good time, and he seems like a really nice guy."

Annie walked in at just that moment. Walter was with her and had hold of her elbow. It always seemed to Caroline that Walter was driving Annie, like a car.

"Hi, you guys," Caroline said. "You have yoga again today?"

Walter bowed slightly. "Yes," he said. "It's doing wonders for my golf game. Improved flexibility and I'm beginning to see a change in my strength level. The vitamins are also working wonders. I think your friend, JT, will find it very beneficial."

"I'll be certain to tell him what you've said," Caroline said. Walter left the quilt shop and Annie filled Caroline in on Olyria's surgery and recovery. "Walter and I are going to see her after Walter's yoga."

"Walter's going with you?" Caroline asked.

"I think he's a little jealous of the time I've been spending with Olyria," Annie said. "Men can be such a puzzle."

This brought the conversation back to Stan and Nan's date. Nan told Annie about the romance and Annie asked, "So . . . are you going out again?"

"On Sunday afternoon. Stan has Jack for the day and we're going to the zoo."

"You're meeting his son already?" Caroline asked.

"Yeah," Nan said. "It's how things are these days. Lots of people have children and no husband or wife. The children don't know a world that's different."

"I think that's a problem," Annie said. "Children prosper in a family setting. In the old days children without two parents were put up for adoption and it was the best thing for them." Annie could almost always pick out the kids in her class that were being raised by a single parent.

Caroline and Nan were both taken aback by the intensity of Annie's statement. "Well, sure," Nan said. "That works, too, if you don't want to raise the child."

"Raising the child is hardly the issue," Annie said. "Some women think it's the best thing for the child." Annie's face got red and she was clearly agitated.

"We don't have to decide this. Jack's mother already did that," Caroline said. She changed the subject to the table runner Annie was working on for her class, and Nan went off to the cutting table to cut some skinny bolts into fat quarters. There was a fat quarter sale coming up.

⌘

Walter and David Williams had finished their yoga practice, which included an extended sun salutation. It went way beyond warming Walter up. They finished with several difficult triangle poses and two inverted poses. The calm in the yoga studio and the oriental music all contributed to the success of the practice.

"Your balance will come," David said. Walter had just toppled out of a headstand.

Walter nodded and took a deep breath. He was frustrated when he couldn't hold his pose as long as David.

"Go into child's pose to rest and cool down," David said.

Walter took the position and practiced his breathing while the yoga master came out of his inverted lotus and went into child's pose, too. The morning exercise was nearly over.

When it ended, David turned off the music and raised the lights in the room.

"How are the vitamins working for you?" he asked Walter.

"I shot a seventy-four yesterday. That's my best this year. I think the exercise and the relaxation techniques are helping."

"Yoga is about life, not just golf, you know," David said.

"Golf is what I'm interested in right now, though I am enjoying a new level of calm in my life."

"That's a good thing," David said. "We have nothing to be if not ourselves. Yoga is all about equilibrium and bringing balance to your life. It is about connection with others and getting to the root of problems."

"I have no problems," Walter said.

David lowered his eyes. "We all have problems with ourselves and others. It is the nature of things. Family, friends, illness, all are problems for the perfectly balanced system."

Walter didn't always understand what the yoga master meant and this was one of those times.

"Enlightenment will come," David said often.

"Will we practice tomorrow?" Walter asked.

David consulted his schedule. "I have special hours on Saturday and won't be free till ten if you want another private session." He handed Walter a vial of tablets as he spoke. "Glad the vitamins are making a difference. Most of my clients believe they are a benefit."

Walter nodded and felt the tension begin to return to his shoulders and back as he left the studio, walked toward the quilt shop. He met Schultz on the stairs. Schultz snarled at him. "You've been making trouble for my wife, bothering her help. I want it stopped immediately."

"Bothering them? A smile bothers them?"

"You know what I mean, the way you look at them. You think

you're the answer to every woman's prayer. You'd better think again."

Walter grumbled and continued up the stairs. If there were problems in his life they were caused by people like Schultz. The calm he had gained in yoga now eluded him.

⌘

Olyria's front door was unlocked. Annie cracked it open and called out, "Olyria, it's Annie and Walter." There was no answer and Annie stepped inside the house. "She said she'd have her mom unlock the door before she left for bridge and I should just come on in," she said to Walter.

Walter didn't speak, but he was close behind Annie as she edged into the entry hall. "Olyria," she called again.

"Annie?"

"Yes."

"Come on back." Olyria was propped up in bed reading the morning newspaper. It had been only two days since the lumpectomy and Olyria was still tired. "I wasn't sure that was you. Well! Walter! I wasn't expecting you this morning."

Walter bowed slightly and Olyria indicated a chair with her hand. Walter took the chair and Annie scurried around straightening the spread on the bed and offering to fluff Olyria's pillows.

"Relax, honey," Olyria said.

Annie giggled and asked, "Is there anything I can do for you?"

"I hoped you might run over to the drugstore and get a refill on my pain meds. I've been taking more of them than I expected to and the prescription was only for ten pills. I take them about every six hours and I have only one left."

"Is it very painful?" Annie asked.

"Like a poke in the eye," Olyria said. She laughed, and then winced. "They whacked part of my boob off and stole a lymph node or two. Of course it hurts."

Annie glanced at Walter to see how he was taking Olyria's attitude. He seemed unaffected. Maybe he would run out and get her prescription. She hadn't talked to Olyria about her dating comments before her surgery and didn't feel really comfortable about leaving the two of them alone. "Walter would you mind getting the refill?"

"I'm pretty worn out from my yoga practice," he said.

"Oh," Annie said, "of course," her voice flat.

"I've always wanted to read Walter's palm. Maybe he'd let me do that while you run to the drugstore," Olyria said.

"I don't think so," Walter said.

"What can it hurt?" Olyria said pressing him when Annie didn't.

"Why not?" Annie added her voice to Olyria's.

"All right," Walter said, "but I don't believe in this stuff." His lack of eagerness put Annie at ease about leaving. Olyria was just talking crazy at the hospital, she thought. "Olyria will do a wonderful job and I'll be gone only a few minutes," she said.

"Pull your chair up close to the bed," Olyria said. Walter took a deep breath and leaned away from her.

"She read my palm the other day," Annie said. "It was fun."

"Come on," Olyria said. "You've nothing to be afraid of."

"I'm not afraid," Walter said. His teeth were clenched and his lips hardly moved.

He pulled his chair closer to the bed and stuck his hand toward Olyria. She took his hand and turned it in hers till the palm was up. Olyria glanced toward Annie, "The prescription bottle is on the counter in the kitchen," she said. Annie nodded and beat feet out of the room. Walter and Olyria sat side by side with their heads together, leaning over Walter's palm. The sight did not fill Annie with confidence but she continued on her way, fast as she could.

Annie wanted to know what Olyria would see in Walter's hand but knew Walter wouldn't allow Olyria to do it in front of her. Annie was barely out of the door when Walter moved in on Olyria. "What do you think you're doing?" he said. "Do you want Annie to get suspicious, or are you trying to make her jealous?"

"Walter, you're married now and I wouldn't do anything to hurt Annie. She means too much to me. You don't have to worry that I have designs on you. I'm just interested in reading your palm." She looked at Walter from under her blinking lashes. "I just want to read your palm," she repeated. "I'm learning new techniques and need the practice."

Olyria turned his hand from side to side. "You have very strong hands," she said. Walter leaned back into his chair and let Olyria have her way with his hands. Walter's fingers were short and thick. Olyria knew this was a sign of someone who is impatient and rash but she said, "I see a spirit of peace." Walter's hands had a well-developed Mount of Jupiter, which is the area under the index finger. This told her he was using his ambition and ego to his own best interests and that he had an authoritarian nature. In fact, Walter's Mount was over-developed, which confirmed what Olyria knew about him. He was selfish, arrogant and a bully.

Olyria noticed short branches that curved down from the Heart Line, which could possibly mean short-term relationships. She told Walter his love line was deep and multifaceted, which meant he had a real way with the ladies. Walter accepted all she said because he believed it was true.

Annie was back, clutching a paper prescription bag in her hand, before fifteen minutes had passed. "I'm back," she called before she went into the bedroom. Olyria dropped Walter's hand and he allowed it to rest on the bed where it fell. "How'd the palm reading go?" Annie asked. She was more than curious but knew Olyria couldn't say much in front of Walter.

"About as I expected," Olyria said. And at the moment she spoke, Walter clutched his stomach and fell sideways off the chair.

"Walter! Walter!" Annie cried. She looked at Olyria with her eyes showing white. "What did you do to him?" she yelled.

Chapter 15

Annie rushed to Walter and fell to her knees. "Walter, Walter, are you okay?" she sobbed while she stroked his forehead. His cheeks were slightly flushed, which was a good sign. "Walter, please open your eyes, talk to me."

Olyria scrambled out of bed and put her robe on. She was weak. She was tired. She was scared.

"Walter, oh, Walter," Annie cried. He finally opened his eyes. "Are you okay?"

Walter looked up at Annie through blurry eyes. "What . . . what's the matter," he asked as he swatted her hand away. "What are you doing?"

"Oh, Walter, when I came in you stood up and then just fell over," Annie said. "Olyria call an ambulance . . . hurry . . . please." Olyria grabbed the phone.

"No, no, no, I don't need an ambulance," Walter said. He started to sit up but felt a little dizzy and leaned against the chair.

"Please, Walter, you need to see a doctor," Annie said.

"I'm fine . . . just tired from my yoga workout. Don't make a big fuss over this," Walter said. He sat on the floor next to Olyria's bed for a minute, holding his foggy head in his hands.

"Walter, please listen to reason. Let me take you to the

Emergency Room and have someone check you."

"I'm not going to any Emergency Room. Stop fussing over me." He started to stand and then sat down in the chair behind him. He scowled at Annie as she tried to help him. He hated her fussing so much in front of Olyria. He wasn't an invalid.

"Promise me you will at least see a doctor next week," Annie said firmly.

"All right, all right, but for now let's just go home," Walter replied.

When Annie looked up at Olyria, her face was tight with tension. "Olyria, I was going to prepare you something to eat before we left but I need to get Walter home. Let me get him situated so he can rest and then I'll drop something off for your lunch. I need a couple of things from the grocery store, so I can swing by later after things calm down."

"Oh, don't worry about me, you have enough on your hands," Olyria said.

"That's all right, it will take only a minute or two to drop something off. You need to eat so you can get your strength back."

Annie and Walter left. Clearly shaken, Annie almost missed the turn for their street. Once in the house she watched Walter walk to the den and plop down in his chair. He immediately put his head back and closed his eyes.

"Is there anything I can get you, Walter, before I run to the store?" Annie asked.

"Maybe a glass of cranberry juice and just a little peace and quiet." And with that, Walter drifted off to sleep.

Annie sat across from him and watched his rhythmic breathing. His color was good. Perhaps he was just tired, but she'd keep an eye on him for the next couple of days. She got his glass of cranberry juice and set it on the table next to his chair. He could sleep while she ran her errand.

Annie grabbed a cart and raced through the grocery aisles like an Indy car driver. She found her few items and a container of chicken from the deli and headed back to Olyria's.

"Oh, Annie, this is so sweet of you," Olyria said.

"I brought you broasted chicken from the Deli," Annie said as she carried it into the kitchen. "It's supposed to be quite good."

"Is Walter okay?"

"He's sleeping, so I can't stay long. I just want to apologize for accusing you of doing something to him. I know you would never hurt him."

"Annie . . . if Walter is sick and he has family, don't you think they should know?"

"I think he does have family. It looks like he has been married twice. He has two sons from his first marriage. At least that's what I believe. I was able to get some sketchy information about possible relatives and cities where he might have lived," Annie said. Annie simmered inside with the thought that Walter had kept so many secrets from her.

Olyria's eyebrows rose, making her blue eyes even bigger.

"I think he may have lived in Ashtabula, Ohio, which is where the insurance policy was purchased and New Castle, Indiana, where his divorce took place and where the young boy's school picture came from. I have such mixed feelings sneaking around and researching my own husband," Annie said.

"If something is wrong with Walter, he might need them now. You never know."

"You're probably right. But I've got to run for now and check up on Walter." She gave Olyria a hug and quickly left for home.

When Annie got home she dropped the bag of groceries on the counter and went into the den. Walter was sleeping, but his glass of cranberry juice was half gone. His color was much better but still Annie worried. She feared his heart caused the fainting spell. She decided to make Aglio-Olio, sautéed garlic and olive oil over pasta, as she knew garlic was supposed to help prevent hardening of the arteries; and for tonight it would be quick and easy.

Walter woke to the pungent aroma of garlic cooking. He loved garlic. He headed for the kitchen.

Annie turned as he walked into the kitchen. "You're awake! How are you feeling?"

"I'm fine, that nap is just what I needed. How long before we eat?"

"Less than five minutes. Why don't you pick out a wine for dinner? I'll be serving it up in just a minute."

Annie served up dinner while Walter poured a full-bodied zinfandel. Walter ate his pasta heartily, but he picked at his salad. After dinner they retired to the den to watch TV.

"Seems my glass is empty and the bottle as well. Want some more wine, Annie?" Walter asked.

"No, I'm fine, Walter, and you should probably go easy on the wine."

"Don't be silly," Walter said as he popped the cork from another bottle. He poured himself another glass, and then another, and another. He finished the second bottle all by himself and fell asleep in his chair. Drunk!

Annie sat in her chair, studying Walter. Bruises had formed on his arm from the fall. She would have to watch him more closely over the next couple of days.

⌘

Friday afternoons were usually busy at Always In Stitches, and today was no exception. Several of the new guild members came in to browse through the rounds of fabric.

"Hello, my dear friend," Michael said to Caroline as he came through the door.

"Michael, it's good to see you smiling," Caroline said.

"It's a half-hearted smile – smile on the outside," he made a plastic looking smile. "Sad on the inside."

"Things will get better, Michael, you . . ." Michael cut Caroline off before she could finish.

"Things are already getting better, Caroline. I've talked to a lawyer about what happened with Stella and he thinks I have a case. He's looking into it and should be drawing up papers soon."

"You're serious about filing a lawsuit?" Caroline asked.

"You bet your sweet bippy I am. I'll show Schultz that Stella wasn't just a dog," Michael said. "But for now I want to pick out some fabric to make a remembrance quilt for Stella."

As Caroline was helping Michael pick out fabric, the phone rang. Nan answered and then brought the handset to Caroline. With her hand over the mouthpiece she whispered, "It's Jamie."

Caroline excused herself from Michael and let Nan step in and help him. "Thanks, Nan."

"Hi, Hon, what's up?" Caroline asked. There was no response, just a whimper. Caroline walked to the back of the shop so she would have more privacy.

"Jamie, talk to me. Has Tommy done something?" Caroline asked, sensing Jamie was upset and trying to get the conversation started.

"No, Mom, Tommy didn't do anything . . . well, yeah, he did. Well, I mean we did . . . oh, Mom, I think . . . . ."

"What Jamie, what is going on?

"Mom, I don't know how to say this . . . but I think I'm pregnant," Jamie said in a weak voice. "I'm past due . . . I bought a pregnancy test this morning but I'm afraid to use it." Jamie had always valued her mom's input and this was a time she really needed it. Since the mugging, Jamie's own confidence had been shaken.

"*What????*" Caroline yelled. Everyone in the shop turned to look at her. Caroline turned and went into the storage room that doubled as an office, for more privacy. She took in a deep breath and closed her eyes to think. "How could this happen? When did you find out? Doesn't Tommy use protection?"

"Mom slow down. I'm a little late and I'm always very tired and I'm not even sure yet. I just don't know what to do if it turns out I am pregnant. I've got one year to go before I graduate. If I'm pregnant, that would throw a monkey wrench in everything."

"How does Tommy feel about this? Have you talked about what you will do?"

Jamie started to cry. "Oh, Mom, . . . I don't know what I'm going to do. I haven't said anything to Tommy yet. I want him to marry me because he loves me and not because he feels trapped."

"Tommy has the right to know. It's his child, too." Caroline was sure Jamie's inability to cope came from the attack at the ATM. The loss of control she felt was a result. Caroline remembered the feeling and was happy to be through with it.

"Everything is all messed up. Tommy is going to graduate this month. He has a couple of good job prospects lined up. He'll resent the baby. He'll resent me," Jamie sobbed.

"A baby is a major life change but, Hon, if Tommy loves you he'll love the baby," Caroline said. "We can't always control the curves life throws us. You need to tell Tommy when you're sure."

"I know, Mom, and I will; but will you tell Dad? I just can't. If I thought Dad was upset about me moving in with Tommy, I'm afraid of what he will do when he hears I think I'm pregnant."

"Maybe you're just tired because you're working now. You've

taken on a lot these last few weeks." Caroline tried to sooth Jamie's nerves. Caroline took several deep breaths to soothe her own nerves.

"What are you going to tell Dad?" Jamie asked.

"Well . . . for now, let's just wait and see what happens. We don't need to start down that road yet." Caroline cringed at the thought of telling Charles of yet another life-changing event. His response to Jamie moving in with Tommy had put the family on edge for several days. This could cause him to burst a gasket. Caroline didn't know what she would do if anything happened to Charles. No, she wasn't going to go down that road unless she needed to.

"I've got to run Mom, I'm on my break and I have to get back to work," Jamie said. "Thanks for listening. I just needed to tell someone. I'll talk to you soon."

Caroline sat in the office trying to compose her thoughts, a baby, no not just a baby, but a grandchild, Jamie's plans for the future, no insurance. Oh, when were they ever going to get ahead financially? But then again, a grandchild.

Nan stuck her head in the office "Excuse me, Caroline, Michael's gone and I need a bolt of fabric that was put back for one of the block-of-the-month kits. Are you okay?"

Caroline managed a smile and said, "I'm fine, just some family issues." Nan and Caroline left the storage room; and before Nan could ask any more questions, the bell on the shop door rang. Jasmine wandered in. She had a plate of scones and a pot of tea with three fancy porcelain teacups on a tray. She put the tray on the counter by the door. Nan took her tea and a scone to the worktable where she was sewing on the table runner Kathy needed for her class.

"My new stove was delivered," Jasmine said to Caroline.

"Finally, I know you have been waiting."

"It took so long because of all the inspections that had to be done. I hope to reopen by the first of the week. Schultz has been hard at work on this for me." Jasmine sipped her tea. "I have to give the old guy credit, but on the other hand he has insurance for just such an occurrence."

Caroline's mouth was full of scone. She couldn't remember the last time she had tasted something. Her mind was filled with thoughts of Jamie. She nodded at Jasmine and wolfed more of the scone.

"How's it going for you?" Jasmine asked.

Caroline brought Jasmine up to speed, omitting the latest development with Jamie, and they finished their snack. Caroline didn't want to share the possibility of Jamie being pregnant with anyone. If she wasn't going to share it with Charles, she wasn't going to share it with anyone.

Chapter 16

The next morning Annie was having a bowl of cereal with strawberries for breakfast. Walter was just having juice to keep his stomach empty for yoga practice. "Do you think you should go to yoga today?" Annie asked him.

"I scheduled a session and I mean to keep it." He scanned the morning paper while he sipped his cranberry juice.

"I'm worried after the spell you took yesterday."

"I didn't take a spell, I was groggy and fell over. It was nothing." He folded the paper in half to read something.

Annie slurped milk into her mouth from the almost-empty bowl. "Do you have to make that racket," Walter said. His temper was short and the day had just begun.

"Sorry, dear." Annie wiped her chin with a napkin and put her dishes in the sink. "I'm going to the library to do a bit of research on their computer this morning."

Walter laid the paper on the table and stared at her. "What are you researching?"

"Quilt patterns," Annie said without a moment's hesitation. She surprised herself with what a good liar she was becoming. "I'm looking for an Ohio Star pattern. It's the pattern I've decided to use for my first quilt." She smiled in what she hoped was an honest way.

Walter shook his head. "This quilting is becoming an obsession with you. Don't they have pattern books at the quilt shop?"

"They do, but I want to paper piece and need something I can duplicate. I thought something off the World Wide Web would work well."

"Fine. I'm going to the golf course after my yoga practice and I'll be tied up there till probably two or later."

"Okay dear," Annie said. She bent and kissed Walter on the forehead. "Please don't wear yourself out."

Walter left the house and Annie put the breakfast dishes in the dishwasher before heading for the library to snoop into her husband's background.

⌘

Caroline was in the tea shop. "These scones are the best yet," she told Jasmine. Jasmine shrugged. "It doesn't matter how good they are if there's nobody here to eat them."

"It's early." Only one other table was occupied.

"I put a big sign out in front so people would know we've reopened. I'd hoped we'd have a lot of people eager to get back in here."

"You were barely open when you had to shut down," Caroline said.

"I know. I hold Schultz responsible for that. It's hard enough to get a new business up and running without having to close down three weeks out of the first six for repairs and refurbishing."

"It could have been a lot worse," Caroline said.

Four ladies walked in and Jasmine had to greet them and seat them, so Caroline had a chance to slip away. She could sure sympathize with Jasmine but she had problems of her own. She was in the back hall when she passed Walter Wilkins. He was just standing on the steps that went down to the yoga studio. He had a glazed look in his eyes, but his hair was neatly coiffed and his yoga pants were snug.

"Walter," she called. "Annie didn't come in with you this morning?"

He startled at the sound of her voice. "No, she had to go to the library to look for a quilt pattern on line . . . or something." He was clearly befuddled and confused. His fingers were white on the railing going down the stairs.

"Are you okay?" Caroline asked.

"I'm fine. Why does everybody keep asking me if I'm okay?"

"I don't know about everybody, Walter, but you seem confused . . . or something."

"I'm not confused. I'm on my way to . . . yoga."

"Right." Caroline stood and watched him as he stepped carefully down the steps while maintaining his white-knuckled grip on the rail.

Caroline's mother had opened the shop and was already hard at work cutting fat quarters. The sale was only a week away and Caroline didn't know how many fat quarters they might sell at a dollar apiece. She'd had everyone cutting furiously for the past week.

"Thanks for coming in today," Caroline said to her mother.

Pat Carter shrugged. "Happy to help out. I notice Schultz finally got the lock fixed."

"Isn't that a treat?" Caroline said. "How's dad?"

"He's working on the bathroom today. We're putting down new tile."

"It really never ends, does it, mom?"

"Nope, it really doesn't. There's always something to fix, or some problem to solve or some work or other to be finished up."

"I'm tired," Caroline said. "I wonder every day if I will get through the day and if we'll ever have any money again. Budd got a job for the summer and Jamie . . ." Caroline hesitated. She couldn't tell even her mother about Jamie's latest dilemma. She'd have to keep that completely to herself.

"What about Jamie?" Pat asked.

"Oh nothing, really. Just growing pains, I guess."

She was saved by JT and Will Douglas coming in the back door. "Hey, you guys need another gift certificate?"

"Not this time," JT said. "I have an appointment for yoga this morning and we're early. Will decided to come along and watch. He said he had some information for you."

Caroline looked at Will. "Yeah," he said. "I got some information for you about that phone problem you were having."

"Oh, good." She pulled Will by the sleeve outside her mother's hearing. "I don't really want my mom to hear this," she said.

"You haven't told other people in the shop?" Will asked.

"I just asked Nan if she'd had any strange calls. I didn't want to upset anyone."

"Has anyone else received calls?"

"I don't think so," Caroline said. "They surely would have said something."

Will raise his eyebrows. "Like you did?"

"I guess you have a point. You think I should see if anyone else has had the same sort of calls?"

"Makes sense to me," Will said, and JT nodded.

"Mom?" Caroline called. "Have you had any funny phone calls here in the shop?"

"Well, yes," Pat said. "Last week there were three calls in one afternoon when the line was just open and nobody spoke. I thought it was strange. Is something wrong?"

Pat left the cutting table and walked over to where Caroline and the two detectives were standing. "A police matter?"

"I don't know, Mom, but I've had several calls of a threatening or harassing nature and I've asked Will's advice on how to handle it."

Pat nodded, "Kids, I'll bet."

"Probably," Caroline said.

Pat went back to cutting fat quarters and Caroline showed Will the call log she'd been keeping. "The phone company told Charles it could take as much as two weeks for them to set up the trap."

"That's what I understand," Will said. "But if they catch this guy, it will be worth the investment of time and energy. Has he said any more about Budd?"

"No, but it scares me that he knows her name and that she's connected to me. I wonder what sort of a thrill he can get out or making me uncomfortable." Caroline picked up a bolt of fabric and moved it off the counter.

"Who knows what motivates some people," Will said.

"Mostly a sense of not being in control," JT piped in. "Not having enough money, not being the biggest kid on the block any more, not having people do what you want them to."

"Hmmmmm," Caroline said. "I thought criminals were people with anger problems or drug addicts who needed a fix."

"It usually goes deeper than that," Will said. "Not that we ever really get to the bottom of it. People usually become criminals when they are children and things go against them more often than they should or they fail to learn to cope in a socially acceptable way."

"You've been reading again?" JT asked his partner.

Will laughed and Caroline had to laugh, too, at the good-natured banter between the two.

"I don't really care what causes the problem," Caroline said. "I just want it to stop."

Will grinned. He was a very nice man and Caroline was glad to have the connection his quilting wife gave her. "That's how most people feel," he said.

"We'd better get going," JT said. He looked at his watch. "Just a couple of minutes till my yoga practice starts."

"Are you thinking of doing it, too, Will?" Caroline asked.

"When pigs fly," Will said. He laughed and the two burly guys left to go down to the yoga studio.

JT and Will went out the back door and headed toward the stairs. They hesitated when they heard harsh male voices in a heated discussion. When they turned to go down the stairs, they saw Walter Wilkins being pushed against the wall by a man with a red face. The two men were oblivious of everyone else.

"Stay away from her," the red-faced man shouted.

"You don't know what you are talking about," Walter replied.

"I know you are making her uncomfortable with the way you look at her and I want it stopped. NOW!" The red-faced man pushed Walter again.

JT stepped in, showed his badge. "What's going on here?"

"I had a delivery for David and a message for Walter," the man said. Some of the wind had gone out of his sails.

"I suggest you both tone everything down, boys, or we'll have to take you in and sort this out." Will said.

"No need for that. I'm just leaving," Walter said as he pushed past his verbal sparring opponent.

⌘

Annie stopped by Olyria's after her trip to the library. Edwina was home and insisted on fixing the women a soft drink and snacks while they visited. Olyria was dressed and sitting on the sun porch.

There was a soft breeze blowing and it carried the scent of new-mown grass from somewhere in the neighborhood. Olyria wore a multi-colored caftan in an African print. Annie complimented her, asked how she was feeling and then jumped right into a report of her morning's work.

"I used the people finder," Annie said. Tears filled her eyes. Walter was married to Barbara Stillman in 1968 and they had two sons. One in 1973 which would make the boy about thirty-three now. The younger boy was born in 1977. He died in 1979." She wiped her eyes. "Imagine the pain of losing a child. That could hurt a person so they might never recover."

"It is a terrible thing," Olyria said. "Everybody has pain, but it's no excuse to hurt other people."

"I know, I know," Annie's face was still contorted by Walter's imagined grief.

"Did he and Barbara get a divorce then?"

"I didn't find any record of that, but I did find that Barbara Wilkins died in 1981. She was only thirty-eight years old. I found the obituary in the Ashtabula paper, but no mention of Walter or a son as survivors. Just her parents and one brother."

"Walter's had such a sad life."

"Any clue about the other boy or the second wife?"

"I didn't find anything. It's like the earth closed in over all of them after the wife died. I didn't find anything about Walter, either, from that day forward. No mention of a second marriage or any other children."

"Not even you?" Olyria asked.

"Me!"

"Yes, is your marriage listed?"

"No, but I'm sure it occurred. I was there."

"Who performed the ceremony?" Olyria asked.

"The Captain of the ship, who was an old school friend of Walter's. Walter had been on several of his cruises."

"Have you seen him since?"

"Well, no, but . . ."

"I think you should check with the Bureau of Vital Statistics and see if you and Walter are really married," Olyria said.

"Of course, we're really married. How could we not be?" Annie's hand went to her mouth as if it might stop the thoughts that were going through her head as well as the words that were coming out of her mouth. "Really, Olyria, we're married."

"You have the marriage certificate?"

"Of course I do, it's in a folder in Walter's file cabinet." Tears were springing up in her eyes again. Her hands were balled into fists and she did her best to control herself when Edwina came in with drinks and cucumber sandwiches for the two women. Edwina served and the women made polite conversation.

"Great sandwiches, Mom," Olyria said.

"Yes, they're very good," Annie said. She bit off a tiny corner. The thought that she and Walter might not be legally married turned her mouth dry and she took a sip of iced tea to wash the bit of bread down.

"I could use some more sugar, Mom," Olyria said.

Edwina smiled and went toward the kitchen to get sugar for the tea.

"Just check it out," she said to Annie. "Maybe the license didn't get properly filed. That happens sometimes." Edwina returned with the sugar before Annie could say anything else. Annie played with the sandwich while the other two women talked, and as soon as possible she excused herself and headed back to the library to find out if she was married.

⌘

On Sunday, Nan and Stan took Stan's son, Jack, to the zoo. Jack was full of energy. He and Nan hit if off from the start. He was blond, wearing bib overalls and a plaid shirt. Stan already had him seat-belted into the back seat of his Jeep when they picked up Nan.

"My daddy says you're his friend," Jack said.

Nan smiled. "He's right," she climbed into the back seat with the little boy. Jack's eyes got bigger when Nan pulled the belt across her lap and snapped it into place. Stan grinned over his shoulder at her, started the car and headed for the north end of town. It was a twenty-mile drive, and by the time they arrived at the zoo Jack and Nan were solid friends.

"You're good with him," Stan said as he helped both of them out of the Jeep's back seat. It was a perfect day for the zoo, with a clear blue sky and a few puffy white clouds. A breeze ruffled the boy's hair, causing it to change from gold to white in the sunshine.

The fertile fragrance of large animals hung in the air and reminded Nan of her grandfather's farm back when she was a little girl. She took Jack's hand and they walked until he wore out, then Stan carried the boy and Nan held Stan's hand. It was a good day for all of them.

⌘

Annie didn't find her marriage recorded on the Bureau of Vital Statistics web site. At home she went through Walter's file cabinet and couldn't find the wedding certificate that should have been there. She had searched everywhere by the time he came home from the golf course. She stared daggers at him and counted the minutes till Monday when she could visit the Bureau of Vital Statistics and check this out in person.

Walter drank two bottles of wine with supper again and fell into a restless sleep in front of the television before eight o'clock.

⌘

Caroline avoided Charles because she didn't want to risk letting her fears about Jamie's possible pregnancy slip out. She looked through a baby-quilt book and dreamed of the grandchild she might have. A baby was never really bad news but it sure would complicate everybody's life. Caroline put the quilt book down and soothed herself by sewing. Her thoughts drifted while she worked on a pillow top. She got the entire thing, including the machine quilting, finished before Budd got home from her friend Emma's house. She'd have plenty of time to make a quilt for the baby, if there was one. The thought comforted her.

⌘

Monday was clear and cool. Charles kissed Caroline good-bye in a better mood than he'd been in since Jamie was attacked. Caroline hoped he was beginning to feel a bit more in control of the family again. She'd continue to shield him from Jamie's possible pregnancy as long as possible although it wouldn't be easy as she was bursting to tell someone.

Caroline lingered over a second, and then a third, cup of coffee. It felt luxurious.

Budd came downstairs ready for school and asked Caroline to sign her job application. Caroline hesitated only a moment, sighed and then scrawled her name across the paper.

Letting go wasn't easy.

Budd was making toast when the phone rang. She spread butter and picked up the phone with the practiced skill of a teenager. "Hello," she said.

Caroline laid the paper on the table and sipped coffee. Budd was strangely silent. Caroline looked up from sipping her coffee and saw eyes white and wide with fear.

"What?" Caroline said. Budd threw the phone down on the table, abandoned the toast and ran out of the room.

"What?" Caroline screamed after her. She picked up the phone. "Hello?" Her throat was tight and dry, her eyes squeezed together as a dark voice confronted her.

"Such an emotional young woman. I'd sure like to get to know her better."

"Stay away from my daughter, you pervert," Caroline yelled into the phone. "You stay away from her." Then she slammed the phone down on the table and ran after Budd.

Chapter 17

Caroline went upstairs, stomping as she took each step. When she reached the top of the stairs, she paused outside Budd's room. She could hear Budd sobbing. Caroline took a deep breath, cooled herself off and stepped into the room. Budd was sitting on the floor on the far side of her bed curled up with her arms over her head. She was shaking. Caroline knelt down beside her and stretched her arm out to stroke Budd's head. Budd pulled away into an even tighter ball.

"You're okay, Budd, everything is okay." Caroline's voice was soft. "Your dad and I won't let him hurt you."

Budd slowly lifted her head; her dark blue eyes were red and swollen from tears. "Mom, that voice . . . that horrible voice said he wanted to get to know me. He said he wanted . . . .he wanted to . . . oh, I can't even say what he wants to do."

Caroline leaned forward and pulled Budd to her. She rocked Budd back and forth, stroking her hair and saying, "Shhhh, you don't have to tell me, honey . . .I'm sorry, I'm so sorry. Budd, I love you. Your dad and I'll protect you." Budd sobbed and tears rolled down Caroline's cheeks, too.

Caroline's anger burned inside her. This lowlife had gone too far. He had ratcheted everything up several notches. If he was willing to take this step, was he willing to go beyond phone calls? Caroline decided she couldn't take that chance. She didn't want Budd out of her sight today until she and Charles could talk. "Do you have any tests today?"

"No, not today, Mom. I have a paper due in Political Science." Budd's sobs had been replaced by sniffling and deep gulps.

"What if we drop your paper off at school and you come into the shop with me today. I'll talk to your teacher," Caroline said. "I could use the help."

"I don't know, Mom, I don't want to go anywhere. Please, I want to stay in my room."

"Honey, I have to go to the shop and I'd feel better if you were with me. I don't want to leave you alone."

"Oh, God, do you think he would come here?" Budd's eyes widened and the tears came faster again.

"No, honey, no. You're just so upset I don't want to leave you alone." A seventeen-year-old shouldn't have to deal with this. They sat in silence for several minutes.

"I don't want to go to school today. I just can't, Mom. I'd like to go to the shop. . . . if that's okay with you."

"I'll be happy to have you with me. Go wash your face; we'll go downstairs, have some toast, gather our things and see what the day holds."

Caroline called Charles as Budd freshened up. She told him about the phone call and her plan for the day. His voice was measured. "I can't believe this is happening. If he has our home phone number, he probably knows the address. We need to talk to Will."

Caroline's breath caught. She hadn't thought that this creep would know where they lived. "Budd is so upset I don't want to scare her even more. We're going to have to really think about how we can shield her from this."

"Why don't I come and take her out to lunch today, that way I can see how she's doing and maybe reassure her that we'll take care of her."

"That sounds great," Caroline said. "She's coming down now, so I'll talk to you later. I love you, Charles."

"I love you too."

"Ready for that toast now?" Caroline asked as Budd came into the kitchen.

"I guess so."

Budd took a few bites of her toast and Caroline had a fourth cup of coffee. They gathered their things and headed for the high school. Caroline talked to Budd's political science teacher and dropped off her paper. Budd would have to check with some friends to get all the assignments for today.

Caroline and Budd got to the quilt shop about ten minutes after 10:00. Nan had opened the shop and was already helping two new guild members. After the ladies left, Caroline introduced Nan to Budd. Thankfully, Nan didn't ask any questions.

Caroline led Budd to a cutting table and told her which fabrics to cut for the table-runner kits. Nan helped and within no time the girls seemed like old friends.

⌘

Annie woke Monday morning anxious to run her errands. The first would be to the Bureau of Vital Statistics. She'd had a fitful night's sleep. The thought that her marriage to Walter could be a scam kept her awake a good part of the night.

Annie turned as Walter came into the kitchen. "Good morning, how are you feeling today?"

"I'm fine. I was wondering what your schedule is like today. I have an appointment to get my car checked. I need you to follow me to the dealer's so I don't have to sit and wait there," Walter said.

"Oh . . . I just had some errands to run."

"Well, I'll go with you and then you can drive me back to pick up my car," Walter said.

"Uh . . . all right," Annie said, hiding her frustration. Her research would have to wait a little longer.

Walter had a quick cup of coffee and Annie had a light breakfast, a very light breakfast. Her appetite had gone missing since her conversation with Olyria on Saturday and the possibility that she wasn't married.

Annie followed Walter to the dealer and then they headed to Always in Stitches. She manufactured errands as she went. She couldn't very well take Walter with her to investigate their marriage certificate. She decided to start with the quilt shop; after all, she did need fabric for that Ohio Star quilt she wanted to make. Walter could just sit and wait.

⌘

The bell on the shop door rang as Annie and Walter walked in; they smiled and called hello. Annie walked over to Caroline. Walter glanced around and watched the two young girls working at the cutting table. He studied them intently.

"Well, good morning. What are you up to today?" Caroline asked.

"I wanted to get fabric for my first quilt," Annie said.

"I can help you with that." Caroline turned towards Walter and smiled. "Walter how are you feeling?"

Walter cleared his throat. "I'm just fine. Don't worry about me. Just wait on Annie so we can run our other errands."

"I'll try to make this as quick as possible," Caroline turned back to Annie. Annie glared at Walter.

When Annie and Caroline walked through the shop looking at fabric, Walter studied the girls. Budd looked up and Walter smiled. Budd shuddered.

The bell on the door rang again. Caroline turned and felt instantly relieved. "Hi, Hon," Caroline said. "Is it lunchtime already?"

"Yup. How's everything going?" Charles asked.

"Good . . . better. Charles, this is Walter Wilkins and his wife, Annie," Caroline said.

Charles shook Walter's hand. "Nice to meet you two," Charles said. Walter nodded.

"Well, how about lunch, Budd?" Charles asked.

Walter turned to look at Budd and smiled again as she walked back toward Charles. "You have a beautiful daughter, Mr. Clarkson."

"Thanks. I'm sorry but I'm on a tight schedule. It was nice to meet you," Charles said. He studied Walter intently before they turned and started for the back door. Charles would be suspect of any man that might have contact with his family. "We'll see you later, Caroline."

Charles and Budd walked down to Traugott Bakery. Charles had a taste for one of their Mettwurst sandwiches made from pork sausage smoked to perfection; and their Black Forest cake was the best. Budd ordered just a salad.

Charles watched Budd as he took his first bite of his sandwich. "You need to eat."

"I know, dad. I just don't feel very hungry."

"Do you want to talk about it?"

"No . . . .not really. I just want to forget about it."

Charles placed his hand over hers. "We won't let anything

happen to you Budd. Everything is going to be okay."

"I know, dad, it was just so horrible." Her eyes started to water. "I'll be okay."

Somehow the Mettwurst sandwich Charles had always enjoyed didn't quite do it for him today. The Black Forrest cake would have to wait for another day.

By the time they got back to Always in Stitches, Walter and Annie were gone and Caroline and Nan were busy cutting fat quarters for the sale.

"Did you have a nice lunch?" Caroline asked, trying to judge the look on Charles' face.

Budd smiled, nodded and gave her dad a hug; "It's always nice to have lunch with dad."

Charles squeezed her a little tighter, kissed the top of her head then lifted her chin, "You keep your chin up. I love you Budd."

Budd went up to help Nan again and Charles gave Caroline a hug. "She's going to be okay but we need to keep an eye on her."

"I called Will while you were out. He said to be cautious. He said he'd put some notes in the file and that we should screen our calls at home through an answering machine. He said that typically crank callers are seeking attention. When we react in shock or anger we're 'making their day'. He was somewhat concerned that this mystery man has stepped up the calls by making them to our home."

"I'll get an answering machine on my way home. I hate those things but I'll do anything to help Budd," Charles said.

"Thanks, Hon. See you later." Caroline hugged Charles good-bye.

"Hey, good lookin', what ya got cookin'?" Goldie said. She patted Charles' arm as they did a dance in the shop door trying to step out of each other's way.

Charles looked at her brightly colored skirt and blouse and smiled. "Hey, Goldie. You're looking good."

"If you weren't already taken I might try marriage for a fifth time."

"You be good now," Charles winked, "I've got to run. Take care."

Goldie entered the shop and sighed. "You have a great husband, Caroline."

"Hey, girl, good to see you. Charles is pretty great. How can I help you?"

"I came in to get some fabric for that apron and I thought I might make a small charity quilt."

"Sounds good to me. Oh, Goldie, this is my younger daughter, Budd."

"Nice to meet you, Budd. You have your father's eyes and your mother's smile. It's a dynamite combination."

Budd just smiled, embarrassed, and looked down.

"Hey, Nan, how's prince charming?" Goldie asked.

"Oh, I forgot, you had another date yesterday. Didn't you go to the zoo?" Caroline asked.

Nan's face was beaming but she was uncomfortable talking about Stan. She didn't want to jinx what looked like a promising relationship. He was perfect. "Oh, we had a good time," she said trying to downplay the date. Her eyes gave her away.

"Come on, girl, you're smitten with him," Goldie said. After four marriages, Goldie was an expert.

The phone rang and Caroline froze. Budd jumped, as she was standing right in front of the handset. Caroline hesitated a moment before she answered it. The harassing calls had made the phone an enemy. Budd backed away and let Caroline pick it up. A smile washed over Caroline's face as she heard her older daughter's voice. Goldie, Nan and Budd turned away and Caroline walked behind the counter to have more privacy.

"How's everything going? Anything new?"

"No, Mom, I still don't have an answer. I'm so confused. I've tried four different pregnancy tests and get different answers. I'm feeling good, though."

"That's great honey. Have you told Tommy yet?"

"No. Not yet. He's been moody as he's dealing with a lot right now. I wanted to wait until I knew for sure."

Caroline could understand Jamie's feelings; after all, she waited to tell Charles about the strange phone calls and she delayed telling him about Jamie moving in with Tommy. Caroline also knew the strain that can be placed on a relationship by holding things in. "Don't wait too long, Jamie. Tommy's an adult. He's made some adult decisions and he should be able to accept the consequences regardless of timing."

"I know, Mom. I'll tell him," Jamie said. "Oh, I also wanted to tell you how much I enjoy working at Electric Quilt. I never realized there were so many different patterns and the things you can do with this program is amazing. You can digitally create a quilt, select a block, change the colors and size, add whatever borders you want and see what the finished quilt will look like before you ever take one stitch. I'm helping to create some of the traditional quilt blocks for the block library for the newest version. I'm having so much fun and the money is really helping," Jamie said.

"I'm so glad you like it, but how's your schoolwork coming, Jamie? You're getting to the end of the semester and you have to be sure to keep your grades up," Caroline said.

"I'm keeping up, Mom. I'm tired sometimes at night but it feels good. I'm going to have to go now, Mom, but I'll keep you posted.

And, Mom, thanks for being there."

"No problem, honey. I love you."

Caroline went to help Goldie look for fabric and as she did, she passed by the baby fabric. She glanced at the fabric, secretly fingering it as she passed. She wouldn't be too sad if there was to be a baby in the family. She felt like the family was falling apart, and a baby might pull them all back together again.

Goldie chose a black-and-gold sunflower print for her apron. It was bright and busy, typical of her choices. Once Goldie paid and left the shop, the afternoon got very quiet. By 5:00 Caroline was ready to go home. It was nice to have Budd to share the ride. She seemed more interested in quilting after spending the afternoon in the shop.

When they arrived home, Caroline and Budd could hear Charles talking to someone. They found him sitting at his desk talking into the phone with a puzzled look on his face. He was recording a message for the new answering machine. He looked up when they walked into the room.

"Listen to this and tell me what you think. I've recorded it four times," Charles said. He punched the button and played the recording.

"Hello, you've reached the Clarkson residence. We are unable to come to the phone right now. Please leave a brief message and we'll return your call as soon as possible." Charles' voice sounded formal, somewhat stiff, but it would do the trick.

"Sounds good to me," Caroline said.

Charles looked at Budd and said, "From now on we're going to let the answering machine pick up the calls before we answer."

Budd barely smiled. "That sounds good, dad. Can I use the phone now? I need to check on my homework assignments for tomorrow."

"Sure, go ahead," Charles said. Caroline sighed and sat down. It was good to be home.

⌘

Tuesday had rolled around again, and as the Guild members started to arrive, the weight on Caroline's shoulders lifted. The group had grown the last couple of meetings as more and more people became aware of the Guild. Caroline always liked a big party – the more the merrier.

As the group was getting settled for the meeting, Olyria came in. "Hi y'all; sorry I'm a little late." Everyone flocked around her, giving her hugs and asking how she was doing. Olyria winced, but her heart was warmed with their concern.

"I'm doing fine," Olyria said. "Just a little tired."

"When do you start your treatment?" Agnes McDaniel asked.

"Not for a couple of weeks. They want to give the incision a chance to heal before they start radiation. I go to the doctor later this week."

"We're glad you felt good enough to come today. I was about to call the meeting to order," Aggie said. "Jeanine, can you give us a treasurer's report?"

Jeanine distributed a sheet showing the total dues collected and the cost of the fabric for the Quilts of Valor. "Even with the expense of the fabric, the net funds are $320."

"Thanks, Jeanine. Now for the Quilts of Valor . . ." Aggie said.

"I have the top all assembled," Jeanine said. "Now we need someone to quilt it." Jeanine held it up for all to see. The earth tones were rich and blended well.

Sheryll Douglas offered to quilt the top and said she would need a couple of weeks.

Olyria asked how many members had started their aprons.

Everyone held their project up. They were in various stages of completion. For the next program everyone agreed to bring in their very first quilt to share. There were suggestions for other special projects.

"What about Secret Sis or Secret . . .?" Tina DeStocki asked as she looked around for Michael. "Where's Michael?"

"I don't know," Caroline said. "He was in the other day and is still clearly upset about Stella."

"Hmmm, well if you all want to start a Secret Sis type program, I'll provide a questionnaire for us to fill out so your Secret Sis will know something about what you like. We may have to come up with a different name so Michael doesn't feel uncomfortable," Olyria said.

After the meeting the ladies lingered a while, enjoying Linda Hutton's famous Toffee Bit Triangle cookies she had brought for refreshments. Caroline loved the musical chatter of women talking.

"Olyria, I'm so glad you came today. If there's anything you need, let me know," Annie said.

"How are you doing on your research?" Olyria asked.

Annie looked around to be sure none of the other women were nearby before answering. "I searched everywhere at home for the marriage certificate and couldn't find it. I haven't had a chance to get to the Bureau of Vital Statistics yet. I don't want to even think about the possibility of not being legally married to Walter, but I have to know."

"I know everything will work out. Just you wait and see," Olyria said.

"Well, gotta run," Annie looked at her watch. "See you next week."

Annie had wanted to get a copy of her marriage certificate this morning but there wasn't enough time before the meeting. Looking at her watch, she knew if she went now she would run into rush-hour traffic and get home too late. Walter would wonder where she had been. So she got in her car and drove home.

Annie called Walter's name as she walked through the house. She found him in the den sitting in his chair with his head back. His face looked ashen. "Walter, how are you feeling?"

"Fine . . . fine, why do you keep asking?" Annie had difficulty understanding him. His speech was different, like his tongue was too big for his mouth. Walter fell asleep and Annie doubted her own perception. Maybe Walter was just tired. She let him sleep. It gave her time to cut and sew a sample square for her Ohio Star quilt. The afternoon passed pleasantly and productively for Annie. She checked on Walter a time or two and he continued to nap. Annie thought this was just as well. She didn't trust herself to have a conversation with him just now. Annie finished a square and went to the kitchen to start dinner.

When the food was ready, Annie woke Walter. He was very listless and picked at his food. He did manage to gulp down a glass of red wine and to pour himself a second glass. Annie kept her head down and her eyes on her plate. She looked up only when Walter clamped his hand over his mouth to cover it. His eyes were wide as he bolted from the table and ran to the half bath. Annie got up and followed him. Walter was kneeling on the floor over the toilet. All the food and wine he just consumed was retching out of him.

When nothing was left, Annie helped Walter to his chair in the living room. He didn't appreciate her efforts and jerked his arm away from her when she tried helping him sit. "I'm only trying to help," Annie said.

"What makes you think I need your help?" Walter's voice was

mean and the whites of his eye looked grey.

"You're sick, Walter. You just threw up your dinner. Please let me help."

"Maybe the fish was bad." He narrowed his eyes and glared at Annie. "Did you do something to the food?

Annie stepped back, shocked at the accusation. "I ate it, too. Do you think I'm trying to poison us both?"

Walter shook his head. "I don't know, but something isn't right and I think you're behind it." His eyes narrowed to slits and Annie could see he was thinking hard about something, preparing to speak. "I know you've been going through my private papers," he said. He struggled to his feet and stood shakily. Annie put out a hand to steady him and he knocked it away. "What were you searching for?"

Annie didn't think, she didn't hesitate at all. She just blurted out, "Well, our marriage certificate seems to be missing."

Walter threw his head back and guffawed. "Good luck with that."

And, of course, with his words, Annie believed their marriage wasn't legal. She turned to run from the room but Walter caught her arm. She twirled and pushed him away. "You miserable old woman," he yelled. His face went red with fury and he grabbed for her again but missed. Annie stepped out of the way and Walter fell forward onto the floor. He cracked his head on the edge of the coffee table and it made a horrible, hollow noise. Annie turned and started to run out of the room again, but as she reached the door she looked back over her shoulder. Walter hadn't moved. There was blood coming from his forehead where it had struck the table.

"Walter?" she said from the doorway. Still he didn't move. "Walter," she shouted, and still he didn't move. The blood flow from his head had increased and she went back to him and looked at him cautiously from three different angles. Her stomach jumped and she ran to the phone and dialed 911.

"What is your emergency?" a voice on the other end of the line said.

"Walter," she said. "My husband. He's fallen and . . . I think he's dead.

Chapter 18

Annie could hear the siren as the squad approached. She had seen no sign of life from Walter by the time the EMT's burst through the door. She was kneeling beside him, holding his hand and patting it. A burly young man in a blue shirt took her shoulders and helped her to her feet. He moved her toward the couch and out of the way.

"What happened," another man holding a clipboard asked, while a third connected wires to Walter for an EKG.

"It wasn't my fault," Annie said. "He fell. We were having an argument and he tried to grab me but I jerked away from him and he fell."

Her face was strained and pale. She had her arms wrapped around her stomach and was trying to shrink into the smallest possible space on the end of the couch. "It wasn't my fault," she whimpered. "Is he dead?"

The man with the clipboard raised his eyebrows. "You were having a fight?"

"More of an argument," Annie said, "but Walter wasn't feeling well after dinner. He vomited and then he accused me of poisoning him." Two of the men exchanged a glance. Annie saw the glance. "That's ridiculous," she said. "I ate the very same dinner he did."

tightened her arms around herself.

"What's his name?" the man with the clipboard asked.

"Walter," Annie said. "Walter Wilkins."

"And he's your husband?

Annie hesitated long enough that the man with the clipboard
looked up from the paper he was filling out. "Yes," she said. "He's
my husband." Not that it mattered if he was dead. "How is he?"

The man on his knees on the floor beside Walter said," He's
not dead but his heartbeat is thready and irregular and we can't
stop the bleeding. We're going to have to transport him." The third
EMT went out the door and in moments was back with a stretcher.
The man on the floor unhooked the EKG machine and tore off the
paper strip with the record of Walter's heartbeat on it. He handed
the strip to the man with the clipboard. It took all three of the men
to lift Walter onto the gurney and strap him down. Blood was still
flowing from his forehead and one of the EMT's slapped a gauze
pad over the wound and pressed hard trying to stop the bleeding
and then the other two wheeled him out the front door.

"Is he going to be okay?" Annie asked.

"We don't know," clipboard man said. "The doctors will give
you all the information they can when they've had a chance to
evaluate him."

Annie nodded.

"Do you want to ride with us to the hospital or do you want to
drive yourself?"

Annie's hand went to her throat. "I'm too upset to drive. I better
go with you."

Clipboard man nodded, took Annie's elbow and steered her to
the ambulance.

Annie sensed the urgency of the situation when she climbed into the passenger seat of the emergency vehicle. The driver backed out of the Wilkins's drive and flipped on the siren. The other two EMT's worked over Walter in the rear. She could see they were replacing the gauze pads at an alarming rate. Annie hadn't had time to hook her seatbelt and she did so quickly as the driver zoomed out of the residential neighborhood and onto a main route to the freeway. He slowed at intersections and accelerated on the straight-aways, the siren blasting. Cars pulled to the curb or just stopped in the middle of the street. It was a hair-raising ride and Annie closed her eyes when it looked like a close call was coming up.

She could hear the EMT's in the back of the truck talking to staff members in the hospital emergency room. Tears squeezed out the corners of her eyes when she opened them and erupted over the rims when they were closed. *Walter might actually die.*

They slammed to a stop at the emergency room door, and the two men in the back hopped out and hustled Walter through the doors and into a medical cubicle. Annie was shown to a seat in the waiting room.

"Wait here," an orderly said. "Someone will be with you soon."

Annie nodded numbly and sank into an orange, molded plastic chair. Alex Trebek was blaring answers to Jeopardy questions from a television hung up on the wall and a three-year-old child was whining to his mother three chairs over from Annie.

She felt so alone and frightened.

Annie sat for twenty minutes with no contact with anyone. Alex Trebek had yielded to Vanna White and Pat Sajak on the television and the child was still whining. She asked and was given directions to a phone hanging on the wall. She was so befuddled she dialed three wrong numbers before she connected with Olyria.

"It's Annie," she said. "I'm at the hospital with Walter. He fell and cracked his head in the living room. The bleeding won't stop."

"What?" Olyria said. "He fell?"

"Yes, and the bleeding won't stop. I haven't talked to the doctor yet but I'm scared. He might die, Olyria, and I feel like it's all my fault."

"Whatever happens, it's not your fault," Olyria said. "Is someone there with you?"

Annie looked around. "The waiting room is full," she said. "The EMT's went into the back with Walter."

"That isn't what I meant. I'll throw on some clothes and be there as soon as I can." Annie nodded and dropped the phone into its cradle. Olyria was still speaking when she did it. When she turned around a nurse was waiting. "You can come see your husband, now." Annie followed her through the double doors, past several draped cubicles and finally into the cubicle where Walter lay with his head elevated and his face as pale as the pillow he lay on.

"The doctor will be in to see you shortly," the nurse said.

There were several blood-soaked gauze pads in the trash receptacle and Walter was unconscious. Annie hurried to his side and grasped his hand. "Is he going to be okay?" she asked the nurse in a pleading voice.

The nurse shrugged. "The doctor will tell you what we know so far." She turned and left, pulling the curtain closed to give Annie and Walter privacy. She could get no response from Walter and settled for standing beside him with his hand in hers.

The doctor, when she arrived, looked like she was fifteen years old. Her hair was pulled back into a ponytail and her eyes were an arresting shade of green. "I'm Dr. Hardin." She stuck her hand out and shook Annie's. "Is Mr. Wilkins taking blood thinners for any reason?" she asked.

"Blood thinners?" Annie said. "Well, no, not that I know of."

"His INR is elevated to a troubling level. It's an eight and we've administered Vitamin K to bring it down. The head injury isn't serious, but he's hemorrhaging inside his cranium and we're going to have to do surgery to relieve the pressure on his brain. We'd like the INR to be at least half of what it is now before we begin the surgery."

"What's INR?" Annie asked.

"The INR is an *I*nternational *N*ormalized *R*atio that tells us how thin his blood is and how fast it will clot. We're going to have to notify the police, Mrs. Wilkins. The EMT's reported that you and Mr. Wilkins were having a fight when this event occurred. It's classified as domestic violence and the police have to be called."

Annie's eyes were glazed and she stared at the clock that was clicking loudly over the hospital bed where Walter was lying. "I'd never hurt Walter," she said to the doctor without moving her eyes.

"We're doing the best we can," the doctor told Annie.

Olyria arrived shortly afterwards and stayed with Annie into the wee hours of the morning, when Annie insisted she go home and get some rest. Olyria agreed but promised to be back first thing in the morning.

⌘

Michael was standing at the back door to the quilt shop Wednesday morning when Caroline arrived. He had Stella's carrier tucked beneath his arm and was dressed for work. He had on a pair of black chef's pants and a white chef's coat with the name of his restaurant embroidered on the front. It was a snappy-looking outfit. The carrier was covered so Caroline couldn't see inside, but she could hear scratching.

"What do you have Michael? Maybe a new puppy?"

Michael grimaced and ran long, artistic fingers through his hair. "I couldn't replace Stella until her death is avenged," he said. "I'm not sure I can even do it then."

"Hmmm," Caroline said. She stuck the key in the lock and it turned easily. She was grateful to Schultz for this. She pushed the door open and stepped aside so Michael could go into the shop ahead of her.

He put the carrier on the counter and waited while Caroline flipped light switches and unlocked the inside door of the shop. She got the change out of the safe, turned on the computer and began counting money into the cash drawer. "So what is it?"

"Is Schultz here this morning?" Michael asked.

Caroline raised her eyebrows and put a hand on her hip. "Well, I really don't know." She cocked her hip and bent her head to the side. "I just arrived as you very well know."

Michael laughed. "You've got me there. I thought maybe he had a schedule of some sort."

"Not really. He comes at odd hours and we never know when he will show up. What are you up to, Michael?"

"I have a little surprise for him and I want to give it to him in person." He was smiling but the light didn't make it to his eyes.

"I saw Goldie's car in the parking lot. I can call her and ask if she's seen him."

"Would you?"

Caroline studied Michael for a moment, then she picked up the phone and pecked out a number. "Have you seen Schultz this morning?" she said after a moment. "No, I don't have a problem. Michael is here. He wants to talk to him."

Caroline didn't speak for a moment. "Okay thanks," she said.

"Ask him to come over when he gets a moment." She clicked off the phone and set it on the counter. Goldie says he's working on loose floorboards in the upstairs hall. She'll let him know you're here."

"Good," Michael said. He laid a hand protectively on the carrier, jarring it slightly. Scratching sounds came from inside and a chill went up Caroline's spine.

She had the money counted into the cash drawer and the quilt unfurled on the front step by the time Schultz arrived. He blustered and harrumphed when he saw Michael but approached the two of them standing at the counter. "What do you want?" he said in a gruff voice after he had nodded a greeting to Caroline.

"Did you get the letter from my attorney," Michael asked.

"I did and your threats don't frighten me. There is no rat poison in this building. There just isn't. We have checked everything." Schultz sighed, his shoulders slumped. "I'm sorry about your little dog. I really am but I had nothing to do with her death and neither did anyone else in the building."

"I was afraid you'd say that." Michael put an arm around Caroline's shoulder and pulled her to him. "I want you to understand this has nothing to do with you. But it's something I have to do and I hope Stella is up there watching somewhere." He looked up at the ceiling of the quilt shop and then he jerked the cover off Stella's box and opened the door in a simultaneous motion. The box was full of squirming rats, tails entwined, with pointed ears and little black, beady eyes. They were white lab rats, not the brown street rats, and they poured out onto the counter in a tangled mess. Ten. . .maybe twenty of them. Caroline screamed. Schultz tried stomping the ones that jumped off the counter onto the floor. They went everywhere, scurrying here and there, climbing the bolts of fabric that had been left on the floor and then jumping back onto the floor. They squealed and they screeched as they ran for cover. Carolyn screamed at Michael, "Have you lost your mind? This is my quilt shop!" She pulled back her fist and hit Michael with a roundhouse punch.

"Now you have rats," Michael said. He leaned against the counter and rubbed his arm where Caroline had hit him. "Now we'll see if there's rat poison in this place."

The door opened at that moment and Goldie walked in. "Was someone screaming?" Her eyes widened as she saw Caroline with her hand pressed against her mouth, Schultz still stomping the floor with his boots and Michael standing beside the open cage with a self-satisfied smile on his face. She was about to smile herself at the foolishness of the scene when a rat leaped off a bolt of fabric onto her sunflower-print gauze apron and climbed right up to her waist. The moment she saw the rat, she screamed even louder than Caroline had screamed and fainted dead away.

Caroline ran to her with Michael close behind. "Now, look what you've done," Caroline yelled at Michael. "You've gone too far." They bent down on either side of Goldie; and Michael took her hand and patted it, trying to restore her to consciousness.

Goldie's eyes flickered and then popped open. "Rats," she said. "Are there rats loose in here?"

"It's okay," Caroline said. She patted Goldie on the shoulder, trying to calm her down. Schultz stomped past the three of them, and when he was in the hallway he turned and pointed a grizzled finger at Michael. "You are a crazy man," he said. "And you will be hearing from my attorney within the week." He turned on his heel and stomped up the hallway and out of sight.

Michael burst into screams of laughter. It was almost hysterical sounding. "I showed him. I showed him. He can't go around killing other people's pets and getting away with it."

"A law suit would have been a much more civilized solution, Michael." A shudder went up Caroline's spine and she helped Goldie to her feet.

"My lawyer informs me that in the State of Ohio, nobody can bring suit on behalf of an animal. I had no choice but to take matters into my own hands."

"I'm going to have to ask you to leave, Michael. This is just too much. Friend or no friend, I can't put up with this. You are going to have to let me cool off before you come back."

"Those really were rats?" Goldie said. She still had a glazed look on her face and was holding her elbow where it had banged against the floor when she fell. Another fun-filled day had begun.

⌘

It was noon by the time things settled down. Schultz had trapped several of the rats and disposed of them, but who knew how many might be left. Michael had gone to work and promised both Caroline and Goldie a free dinner at his home to make up for his prank. Caroline was still furious with him and hadn't said yes to his invitation.

Stan Darling had been in with a fabric delivery. He asked if Nan was working and showed disappointment that she wasn't.

"Jack asked about Nan when I spoke with him last evening. He's never done that before." His face softened as he spoke and showed a warm smile.

"Nan has a way with children. We love to have her here when they come into the shop."

"I can see why. She and Jack certainly formed a bond in a short time." He spoke in a tender tone and Caroline believed something serious might be going on. She wondered how serious it was for Nan.

After everyone left, the shop was quiet. Caroline had been cutting fat quarters again, still preparing for the sale. The phone rang, piercing the calm that had started to settle. Caroline hesitated; it could be the pervert, and she didn't want to deal with that on top of everything else that had happened. She had to answer, so she reached out and grabbed the headpiece.

"Hello. Always in Stitches," she said.

"Caroline?" It was Olyria. Caroline breathed a sigh of relief.

"Yes."

"I'm on my way to the hospital. Annie called last night and said Walter fell at home and was bleeding into his skull. I spent a couple of hours with her last night and am on my way back to the hospital right now. This morning the doctor says the pressure is increasing and he may not make it. The police are coming in to talk to Annie and she's sure they suspect her of trying to kill him."

"What?" Caroline said.

"You heard me. Seems like they were having an argument when he fell and hit his head. Then Annie said some things that made the EMT's suspicious and now they think she's been poisoning him."

"Poisoning him?"

"The doctors have told Annie the only hope is to do surgery to try to relieve the pressure in Walter's skull."

"When are they doing the surgery?"

"I think as soon as they can get him into the operating room. They wanted to give his blood time to normalize but it isn't happening, so they are going ahead with the surgery. I'm staying with Annie. She has nobody else."

"Do you feel up to that?" Caroline asked.

"I'm okay and she has been such a help to me, I can't possibly ignore her when she needs me."

"Of course not, but please let me know what's happening."

"I will. I've got to go now, but I'll call later to let you know how the surgery went."

"Thanks," Caroline said, but by that time Olyria had hung up and in a second the dial tone was buzzing in Caroline's ear.

Caroline shook her head. What a day she'd had but nothing as bad as poor Annie, and why in the world would the police suspect Annie of killing Walter? Annie didn't have a mean bone in her body.

She'd gone back to cutting fat quarters when the bell on the internal door jingled. The yoga master walked in with an expectant look on his face. He looked around the shop and then walked to Caroline at the cutting table.

"Can I help you?" she asked.

"I was looking for Walter Wilkins," the man said. "He's late for his class and I thought he might have been held up in here with his wife."

Caroline's hand went out to rest on the yoga master's arm. "Oh, David, I'm so sorry. I've just had a call. Walter is in the hospital. He's had a fall and needs surgery."

She looked into his eyes. "They aren't sure he's going to make it."

David pulled his arm away from Caroline. He rubbed the spot where she had touched him. His eyes twitched from side to side. "So sorry to hear that," he said. "He's gotten to be one of my best students." His voice was flat and he licked his lips to moisten them.

"If I hear anything else, I'll let you know."

"Yes, that would be nice." He turned and left the shop without another word.

"Odd," Caroline said to the empty shop, and she bent back to the task of measuring the fat quarters and slicing them off with the rotary cutter. While she worked, she imagined she could hear the skritch-scratch of rat paws running along the wooden floor of the granary.

Chapter 19

Wednesday morning the time dragged. Annie got up from the couch and walked to the window looking out over the hospital parking lot. She paced back and forth from the window to the couch in the small family waiting room. Walter can't die; he just can't die. She had waited so long before she found someone who made her feel like a woman, someone who put a flame inside her. Then, again, there was the other side of marriage, the unexpected side of hurt and pain. What would she do if her husband died? Her husband! Ha! If he was her husband. What a mess her life was. Walter was more of a stranger now than when they married last year.

Finally Olyria arrived. "Thanks so much for coming back in." Olyria stepped out of the elevator and was hugging Annie in seconds. "I can't believe this is happening . . . I can't believe this is happening," Annie sobbed. "They believe I had something to do with this. Can you imagine . . . they think I would hurt Walter?"

Olyria guided Annie back into the family waiting area where they sat side by side on the couch. "I know better. You can't even kill a spider. We'll get this all straightened out."

"What am I going to do if he dies?" Annie's voice was weak. "They took him into surgery over an hour ago. The doctor said he was in critical condition."

"Annie, don't even think about that now. Tell me what happened. How did Walter get hurt?"

Annie told Olyria how she and Walter had argued. How Walter grabbed her arm and she pulled away. How she heard that awful sound of his head hitting the coffee table. She put her face in her hands.

"Annie, everything will . . ." Olyria said as a police officer knocked on the open door.

"Mrs. Wilkins? I'm Officer Dover. I need to ask you a few questions."

Annie looked up and nodded.

"Will you excuse us, please?" Officer Dover said to Olyria.

"I'll go down and get us some coffee. You're going to be okay." She squeezed Annie's hand and left, closing the door behind her.

"Mrs. Wilkins, can you tell me how your husband got hurt?" the policeman asked.

Annie closed her eyes and tried to focus. Then in a calm, measured tone she told the officer what had happened the night before. She was aware that every word she said and how she said it was important.

"The Paramedic paperwork indicates that Walter accused you of poisoning him before he fell and hit his head?" Officer Dover said.

"That's ridiculous. I ate the same food as he did. I would never do anything to hurt Walter," Annie said, trying to keep her voice even.

"What did you prepare for dinner last night?"

"Well, I made broiled tilapia with sautéed onions, rice and a salad. I told you we both ate the same thing."

"What did Walter have to drink?" the officer asked.

"Walter had two vodka martinis before dinner and one with dinner. Walter liked his vodka and wine." Annie's eyes started to tear.

"What did Walter usually do during the day?"

"Walter practiced yoga," Annie said. The officer looked up from his pad with a curious smile. "Yes, he really loves yoga. It gave him a sense of well-being and appreciation of life. He also loves to golf."

"Did he golf or go to yoga in the last couple of days?"

"He went to yoga, but he wasn't feeling well. He slept after he came home and seemed to be groggy."

"Thanks, Ma'am, I appreciate your time. We may have some additional questions for you. Hope everything turns out okay." Office Dover tipped his hat and left Annie sitting staring at the elevator.

When Olyria returned, tears were streaming from Annie's eyes. Olyria's heart ached. How could she help her friend? She put the coffee down; sat next to Annie, wrapped her arms around her and rocked her back and forth.

Olyria and Annie sat waiting for the doctors, sipping the coffee till it was cold and stale. "What is taking so long? This can't be good." Annie said. She was exhausted.

Annie heard footsteps in the hall, and when the doctor turned into the waiting room, Annie stood up. Her eyes . . . the look in her eyes. "Mrs. Wilkins, I'm sorry to say. . ."

"No . . . No. . . . this can't be happening. Please, God, no." Annie fell to her knees.

Olyria knelt down beside her. "Shhhhh, Annie, shhhh, everything is going to be okay."

"What happened? Why couldn't you stop the bleeding?" Annie sobbed.

"Walter's blood was just too thin. It wouldn't clot. We tried transfusions but it was too late. He'd lost too much blood. It had everything to do with his INR, which I told you about before. We're doing a complete toxicology test on his blood now. We expect it to confirm our preliminary findings of rat poisoning. Walter's body is being transferred to the Coroner's office for autopsy. We'll have more answers in a day or two. I'm sorry, Mrs. Wilkins, we did all that we could."

Annie nodded and the doctor left the two women sitting on the floor.

"Are you okay?" Olyria asked.

After a long silence, Annie said in a soft voice, "I don't know what to do."

"Why don't I take you home. Why don't you come down to the main lobby and I'll get the car and pull it around."

Annie nodded. Olyria helped her up and left her sitting in a chair close to the main lobby door. Olyria fumbled for her cell phone as she walked to get her car. She called the quilt shop. "Caroline? This is Olyria."

"Olyria what's happening? How is Walter doing?"

The words caught in Olyria's throat, she swallowed and then said, "He didn't make it?"

"What? What happened?"

"They're going to do an autopsy and a complete toxicology report on him. Confirmed facts could take a couple of days. The police talked to Annie. I think she might be in for a rough ride."

⌘

Thursday morning Caroline arrived early at Always in Stitches. She had a new item on her morning-shop-opening to-do list - - check for dead rats in the rattraps. She could just imagine if a customer stumbled upon a dead rodent. Michael hadn't been back in and that suited Caroline just fine. Friend or no friend, releasing the rats had been a very dirty trick. As she locked the main doors to the shop last night, Caroline thought she heard scratching. She fully expected to find a rat in a trap. Armed with a broom and a trash can lined with a big garbage bag, Caroline checked the traps on all three levels of her shop. All were empty.

Caroline hung the quilt on the front railing and walked back into the shop. It was just seconds later that she heard screaming. Caroline ran through the shop and out the back door. She followed the noise down to Jasmine's tea room. Caroline ran through the door and saw Jasmine standing up on a chair. "Help me, help me . . . there's a big white mouse . . . aaaaah! Help me, please someone help me!" Jasmine screeched. She was pointing down to a tail that was partially sticking out from one of her tables.

Caroline noticed that the animal didn't move with all the screaming. "Where's your broom, Jasmine?" she asked. "And a wastebasket."

"Through that door, just to the right of the stove," Jasmine said, pointing, her hand shaking.

Caroline used measured steps when she walked past the rat to get the broom and wastebasket. When she returned, Caroline laid the basket on its side and started to sweep the rat into the basket. It wasn't in a trap.

"Oh my God, it's a mouse on steroids."

"Jasmine, it's not a mouse. It's a rat. A dead rat."

"Oh sugar, a raaaa . . . . ." Jasmine said as her knees started to give way.

Caroline rushed over to prevent Jasmine from falling and helped her sit. "Wait until I get a hold of Schultz. He better figure out how they're getting in," Jasmine said, her voice much weaker.

"Jasmine, there aren't any structural problems where they are getting in. They were a prank on Schultz yesterday."

"A prank? Who would pull such a prank?" Jasmine asked.

Caroline told Jasmine the whole bizarre story of Michael's little visit yesterday morning.

"I'm going to give Michael a piece of my mind. He can't go around doing this to other people."

"You're right," Caroline said as she tied the top of the trash bag shut. She tried handing the bag to Jasmine. "Now all you have to do is put it out in the dumpster." Jasmine looked up at Caroline with a pleading look in her eyes. "All right, I'll do it. I've got to get back upstairs. See you later," Caroline said over her shoulder as she left the tea room.

"Caroline, you're the best. Thanks."

Caroline walked up the stairs, holding the tied bag out away from her as she concentrated on her mission. "What treasures ya got there," Schultz barked, startling Caroline; and the bag flew up.

"It's a dead rat from down in Jasmine's tea room," Caroline said, grabbing the bag again. "I checked all my traps this morning but this is the only dead one we found today and it wasn't caught in a trap."

"Humph, that man thinks he can do anything and get away with it," Schultz growled, his blue eyes dark with anger. "He hasn't heard the last of this."

⌘

Thursday morning, Olyria and Aggie McDaniel drove to Annie's house. Annie answered the door, her eyes all red and bloodshot. Olyria had a sack of groceries with some staples in it. Annie hugged the two women and they walked to the kitchen. Agnes put on a pot of coffee. While the coffee was brewing, they made a list of things that had to be done. Call friends and relatives, go to the Social Security Administration, and order flowers. Annie gave Aggie her phone book and checked off the phone numbers to call.

The doorbell rang and Olyria yelled she would get it. When Olyria answered the door her face grew dark. "Mrs. Wilkins?" the officer said.

"No, I'm her friend, Olyria."

"May we speak to Mrs. Wilkins?"

"Yes, please step inside," Olyria said, then left for the kitchen. "Annie, there are a couple of police officers here who would like to talk to you."

Annie froze; her breath caught in her chest, and then she walked into the living room. "Hello, I'm Annie Wilkins, may I help you?"

"Mrs. Wilkins, we have a search warrant," the officer said as he showed her the paper. "We'd like to look through your husband's belongings. The warrant lists the things we're looking for." He handed the paper to Annie and she just glanced at it.

Annie showed them to their bedroom and paced while they pawed through Walter's things. She watched them bag prescription bottles, hair dye, Walter's lotions and creams, cleaning products and vitamins from the bedroom and master bath. Then they asked to see the kitchen. "The kitchen!" Annie said. "Why do you want to see the kitchen?"

"We're looking for possible toxins," a cop said.

They took two hours to go through all the kitchen cabinets. Aggie gave them coffee and made a fresh pot. Finally, after taking two boxes filled with food, cleaning supplies, a dirty martini glass, they said they might have a few more questions before the case was closed. Annie nodded and led them to the door, then watched them carry the boxes out to their van.

Annie got as far as the first chair, grabbed her stomach and collapsed in the chair. "They think I hurt Walter, oh God, they really think I hurt Walter," Annie cried. "I can't breathe."

Agnes knelt down next to the chair. "You have to calm down. Take a deep breath and hold it . . . .now let it out. Let's do it again . . . . . that's good." Agnes turned and looked at Olyria.

Olyria knew this wasn't good, that her friend was potentially in serious trouble. She picked up the phone and dialed.

⌘

Thursday afternoon was quiet at Always in Stitches. Jasmine brought a tray with tea and scones to thank Caroline for her heroism with the rat.

The phone rang while Caroline savored the scone. She braced herself for the horrible raspy voice and picked it up. She listened and then said with a smile. "Olyria, how are you today?"

"I think Annie's in big trouble. The police were here with a search warrant. Perhaps we should call Will."

Caroline sat back down, holding the phone in one hand and her forehead in her other hand. "Poor Annie. How could anyone believe she could hurt anyone? I'll call Will now and see what he suggests."

"Thanks, Caroline."

"Olyria, please give her my love. I'll let you know what I find out." Caroline hung the phone up and shared Olyria's report with Jasmine. Jasmine thought a dead rat was nothing, compared to what Annie was going through.

Caroline called Will Douglas and gave him all the details of the situation. "What should Annie do, Will?"

"J.T. and I are on this case and I really can't discuss it with you, but I can tell you she needs a lawyer." Will rattled off three names and phone numbers. Caroline scribbled the information down on a sales check.

"Thanks, Will."

"Olyria is sure she's going to be arrested soon. The police showed up with a search warrant."

"I really can't discuss the investigation, but please stay in touch. Let me know if you learn anything that could help us solve this. How is Annie holding up?"

"I haven't really talked to her. I'm getting all my information from Olyria, who is with her. She has to be frantic."

"I suppose so," Will said. "I'll ask Sheryll if she can stop by and visit. I know anything that can keep Annie distracted is a good thing."

"Annie hadn't been married too long, had she?"

"Just a year. She and Walter were practically still on their honeymoon."

"Hmmm. I can tell you the spouse is the first, best suspect in any murder."

"Annie wouldn't hurt a flea," Caroline said

"I know. I know. Friends and neighbors never suspect a thing."

That wasn't what Caroline wanted to hear but she supposed it was true. "Anything else I should know?"

"Not that I can think of," Will said. "Just hang in there and be ready to do what Annie needs done. Call me again if you have more questions, but remember I can't share details of our investigation."

"Thanks, Will. I really appreciate your help." Caroline's mouth was dry and she felt a terrible sense of dread for herself, for Jamie, for Budd and now for Annie.

Chapter 20

Friday morning the air felt heavy, like it might storm as the day heated up. Caroline had a sense of foreboding and she wondered how Annie had passed the night. She couldn't imagine being a murder suspect, and she figured Annie had never imagined it either.

Olyria was waiting for her at the back door of Always in Stitches wearing jeans and a tee shirt instead of one of her usual flamboyant outfits. There were dark circles under her eyes and her shoulders sagged.

"How's Annie?" Caroline asked as she shifted her armload of stuff and slid the key into the lock. It turned easily and she blessed Schultz once again for fixing it.

"Not good. She hardly slept a wink."

Caroline dropped her load on the counter. She stopped and studied Olyria. "And how are you?"

"Oh, . . . a little tired maybe." She shrugged to show it didn't matter.

"Have the police been back to Annie's?"

"No, but they were pressing her yesterday during the questioning. Said Walter accused her of poisoning him and he is full of Warfarin, which is rat poison, after all. The same stuff that killed Stella if we are to believe Michael and his coroner friend. They've sent Walter's body to the coroner's office, and plans for the funeral are held up till his body is released."

Caroline shook her head. "I know Annie wouldn't kill anyone, especially Walter."

"That's what I have to talk to you about," Olyria said. "There's been some stuff going on between them."

Caroline was opening the safe and stopped in mid opening. "Stuff? What sort of stuff?"

"Annie had bruises . . . and questions about Walter and . . . men in general . . . and marriage and what was okay and what was not okay."

Caroline brought the cash to the cash register and stuck it inside without counting it. "What sort of questions?"

Olyria licked her lips. "It's sort of hard to talk about this," she said. "I think I told you I went out with Walter before he met Annie. He had an unsavory side that I learned about."

Caroline froze. She stared into Olyria's face and didn't say a word. It was a command to go on.

"He took advantage of women. He borrowed money and then left them to lick their wounds. I had several things go missing when we went out. I couldn't prove anything but didn't I tell you I 'lost' my grandmother's diamond brooch and was pretty sure $75 was missing from my wallet."

"Why didn't you warn Annie?"

"I hardly knew her till she started coming into your shop and I couldn't be positive Walter took things from me. Besides, they were already married when they came back from that cruise and . . . I couldn't just blurt out what I knew, so I suggested she sort of spy on him."

"Spy on him?"

"You know, look through his personal papers and see what she could find out."

"Well?" Caroline had crossed her arms across her chest and leaned back against the counter. Her stomach rolled.

Olyria didn't speak.

"Well, what did she find out?"

"Don't get upset, Caroline. It could be a whole lot worse."

"Just tell me."

Olyria pulled herself up and leaned toward Caroline. It was an assertive move. "Walter was married at least once before. He had two sons and one of them died as a child. Annie couldn't find any sign of the second son. His first wife died at a young age and the boy just disappeared."

"What else?"

Olyria eyed the pile of stuff Caroline had dropped on the counter. She looked everywhere but into Caroline's eyes. "Annie learned she and Walter might not really be married."

"What?" Caroline slammed a fist on the counter. "How could that be?"

"Maybe the marriage was never recorded. Maybe the ship's captain didn't follow through." Olyria shrugged. "At any rate Annie couldn't find any official record of the marriage."

Caroline's chin dropped to her chest. "What a mess."

Olyria shifted from foot to foot. "You know what the cops are going to call this?"

Caroline said. "Motive!"

"I'm afraid so. We need to find the missing son. We need to look for the woman who may have been a second wife. We need to keep Annie out of jail and we need to find out how Walter got the rat poison in his system."

"Is that all?" Caroline said.

"It's all I can think of right now. There's a connection between

Stella and Walter. How could they both die of rat poisoning?" Olyria's brow wrinkled. "That's the piece that really has me puzzled."

"Maybe I should call Michael. I'm still furious with him but he's convinced Stella got the rat poison while she was here in the shop. Walter was here in the shop. That could be the only connection between the dog and the man. Oh, god. What if it turns out to be something that happened here?"

"I thought of that," Olyria said.

⌘

Caroline finally got the quilt hung out on the railing and the shop lights on, and Olyria left the shop. Caroline couldn't get Annie and Walter off her mind. She cut fat quarters and folded them in slow motion. The sale was tomorrow and the shop was unusually quiet today. Caroline figured all her customers were waiting for the sale.

She ate a banana for lunch and had just tossed the peel into the trash when the phone rang. She hesitated, unable to answer the phone without a moment of dread. She picked it up and said "Hello."

It was Jamie. "Good news, Mom. I got my period. I am so relieved and so is Tommy. I thought he was going to lose it for the entire last week. He was so mad at me; I couldn't believe he would be so self-centered; it made me so mad like I did it all by myself just to spite him. I even thought about moving out. But I know he's excited about graduating and moving on with his life. I wish I was graduating, too."

"Oh, Honey, I thought you weren't going to tell Tommy until you knew for sure."

"I couldn't keep it from him. But then I was sorry after the fact."

The conversation went on with Jamie expressing relief, new hope for the future uninterrupted by a baby, and her disappointment with Tommy. Caroline was happy and sad all mixed together. She hoped she had made all the right sounds for Jamie, whatever those were; but inside she felt the loss. Babies were so sweet, so unassuming, and so simple. She could use something easy right now. She told Jamie she loved her, it was fine to move back with her girlfriends and she was sure dad would pick up the tab for the rest of the semester.

"I think I'd like to keep my job at the Electric Quilt. I really like the quilters and the creativity involved. I might even stay up here for the summer."

"Oh, Honey, I could use you here."

And without responding to Caroline's job offer, Jamie said, "I love you, too, Mom. I'll talk to you later." The buzz of a dead line was all that was left of Jamie, her excitement, her relief and her plans for the future. Plans that were not going to include her mother except on holidays and other special occasions. Caroline felt empty, rejected, hollow. It was all going too fast for her, and somewhere in the silence of the shop she heard the skritch-scratch of little rat toes running across the hardwood floor.

⌘

Only a couple of customers came into the shop. They picked up small items and left immediately. Caroline finally called Michael, but his phone was turned off so she could only leave a message. It was mid-afternoon before he called back. By this time Caroline could hear thunder echoing across the sky as the storm she'd been expecting materialized.

She looked out the window while they talked. Dark clouds hung low and scudded across the sky just above the rooftops. It could be a bad storm. "Michael, I haven't forgiven you for the rats yet, but tell me why you're so sure Stella was poisoned here."

"The only other place she was loose was at home and I know she wasn't poisoned at home."

"Didn't you take her out?"

"Of course I took her out but she was never out of my sight. I always stayed outside with her so she didn't wander off. Also, I clean up after her immediately."

"What did Adrian say about the poison?"

"I don't know what you want to know."

"Did he tell you just what it was or did he just say rat poison?" Caroline hesitated. "Did he know what sort of rat poison?"

"It's called an anticoagulant rodenticide," Michael said. "He said it's a blood thinner and used in prescriptions for human beings. Actually, it has a very interesting history."

"So Stella could have found a pill someone dropped on the floor of the shop?"

"I suppose so. The effect generally takes a few days to occur. Stella died in three days, which is about typical. Often there are no symptoms, but what happens is the animal bleeds to death from injury or just silently and internally from the effect of the blood thinner." Michael's voice broke as he spoke.

"I'm so sorry, Michael, but Annie's husband, Walter, has died and police believe he was poisoned with Warfarin, a rat poison."

"I knew it," Michael shouted. "I knew Stella got it at the granary. Schultz is responsible for this."

"I don't know what Schultz would have to do with it." Caroline could see Schultz leaning into the wind and hurrying across the parking area as she spoke his name.

"Could there be a stash left in the building from the days it was a grain elevator?"

"I suppose anything is possible, but the building sat empty for ten years and it seems unlikely rat poison would be left here all that time. Besides, how would Walter get hold of it?"

"I don't know but it works just as well on humans as it does on rats or dogs. There's a theory that it was used to poison Joseph Stalin back in the golden days of killing."

"Really? Who told you that?"

"Adrian, of course. He has a vast store of useless information about death and dying. It's an occupational hazard."

Thunder clapped overhead. It was loud and fast, lightning tight on its heels. Large raindrops started to ping against the window. A shudder passed up Caroline's spine. "It appears Walter Wilkins and Stella died of the same thing. The police think Annie did it and of course she had absolutely no means or motive to kill poor little Stella. Walter has been sent to the coroner's office for autopsy, since there is some question about how he died. Could you ask Adrian about it?"

"Sure, I'll check with him but I'd bet Annie wouldn't even kill a rat." He laughed and it was a good sound.

⌘

It was almost closing time. The rain had stopped and the sky had cleared miraculously as only happens after a spring storm. Sheryll and Will Douglas came in the back door.

"I've been to see Annie," Sheryll said. She ran to Caroline and hugged her hard. "It's just terrible, the mess she's in."

Will nodded behind her and Caroline looked from one of them to the other. "I took a casserole for Annie's supper and Olyria was there. Poor Annie is beside herself."

"Have the police released Walter's body yet?" Caroline asked.

"The chief said it would probably be later tonight. There doesn't seem to be much question that he was poisoned. That's all they need the body for."

"Olyria said she would stay with Annie tonight, and Will ran her home so she could pick up a few things. The rain was bad on that side of town."

"It was pretty bad here, too," Caroline said. She turned to Will. "Do you think she's going to be arrested?"

Will shrugged. Sheryll made a fist and slapped it into her other hand. "Annie didn't do it," she said.

"Will they wait till after the funeral?" Caroline asked.

"Hard to tell," Will said. "Depends on what kind of case develops."

"Did you find out what they found when they searched the house?"

"Medications, and I guess there were some old papers; and they did turn up the fact that Walter had a record of some sort."

"Walter had a record?" Caroline said. "What sort of record?"

"I'm not certain," Will said. "It's public information that he was arrested but never served any time that we could uncover."

"What does that mean?" Caroline asked.

"It means he was arrested but never convicted of anything."

"Did you tell Annie?" Caroline asked.

"I really couldn't," Will said. "That's official knowledge and I can't give it to a suspect." He grinned as he said it. "I told you I can't talk about the case."

Walter had a record? Well, that was an interesting development, wasn't it? Caroline thought about it after Will and Sheryll left the shop. She locked the doors and closed things down for the day.

Walter had a record.

⌘

She went down the back stairs into Jasmine's tea room. "I need a bag of scones to take to Annie," she said when Jasmine strolled toward her. There were two tables of ladies having tea. One group wore red hats and furry boas. They were laughing.

Jasmine stepped behind the baked goods display case. "I have only six left," she said. "Apricot."

"My favorite." Jasmine folded a box and began putting scones inside.

"Don't want to speak ill of the dead, but he always gave me the creeps." Jasmine said.

"I'm learning he was a pretty creepy guy, but he was Annie's husband and she loved him." Caroline took out her wallet and laid a ten on the counter.

"Take them," Jasmine said. "In another two hours they'll be day-old baked goods and I'd like Annie and Olyria to have them."

Caroline pushed the ten towards her and Jasmine pushed it back. "Really, I'd like to donate them to the cause. Losing a husband can take the starch out of you."

Caroline walked away from the counter and out the door. Jasmine picked the ten up and stuck it into her bra instead of the cash register.

It was a ten-minute drive to Annie's house. On the way Caroline called Charles to tell him she wouldn't be home for supper. The sun was shining after the rain and the evening was warm. Caroline had to pull around a Channel 10 News van to get into Annie's driveway. She grabbed the bag of scones and hotfooted it to the front door with a reporter running after her, brandishing a microphone and yelling, "Wait, wait! Are you a friend or family member?"

Olyria met her at the door and let her into the house. Annie was standing in the hallway looking shrunken and sad. "You're a sight for sore eyes," Caroline said. She handed Olyria the bag of scones and hugged Annie to her like a child. Tears broke out and they wet one another's shoulders. "I'm so sorry to hear about Walter," Caroline said.

"Thank you," Annie cried. "I was just really learning to be married. It's so sad. I miss him already."

"Have you called a lawyer yet," Caroline asked. She put an arm around Annie's shoulder and led her toward the couch in the living room.

"Not yet. I can't believe I really need one. Surely the police will figure out that I could never hurt anyone, especially Walter."

Caroline hugged Annie again before she sat down. "What happens doesn't always make sense. Will Douglas gave me this list of criminal defense attorneys. He said they all have excellent reputations. I think you should call one of them so they can prepare you for what may be coming."

"Yeah," Olyria said. "Like those news ghouls out on the lawn."

The phone rang at that moment and Olyria went to pick it up. "Hello."

"Yes, she's here. Who's calling please?" Olyria frowned then said, "Just a minute."

"It's Sergeant Dover," she said, and handed the phone to Annie.

"This is Annie Wilkins." Annie nodded and switched the phone to her other ear. "Yes, well, okay. Thank you very much."

She handed the phone back to Olyria who hung it up. "They've released Walter's body," she said. "He told me to call the funeral home and notify them to pick it up." With that she burst into tears again and collapsed onto the couch.

Chapter 21

Saturday morning the sky was still overcast and the scent of rain hung in the air. Jeanine Burke picked up coffee and bagels, then drove to pick up Annie and Olyria. She ran the gauntlet of news media parked in front of the house. A mysterious death in a small town like Buckeye Grove was big news; and since Annie had been named a person of interest, there wasn't a moment's peace for the neighborhood.

Jeanine ran to the back door and slipped inside when Annie opened it. "Oh, Annie, I'm so sorry about Walter," Jeanine said. She wrapped her arms around Annie who looked dazed. Annie had cried so many tears since Walter died; she felt she didn't have any left.

"Thanks, Jeanine," Annie said. "And thanks for going with us to make the funeral arrangements. I need to gather up Walter's things so we can get this funeral home visit over with." Annie left the kitchen and got Walter's clothes while Jeanine and Olyria visited over coffee. Annie's eyes were red, and she had a small bundle under her arm when she returned to the kitchen. The women made their getaway in Annie's car that was in the garage. With Olyria behind the wheel, they inched their way down the drive to avoid running spectators down. All three women in the car were somber and silent. They drove to Schneider's Funeral Home, which was across the street from Always in Stitches.

Annie felt wooden, like a puppet. She shouldn't be arranging Walter's funeral now. Nothing was the way it should be. Nevertheless, there was no place to go but forward. A nice-looking, middle-aged man greeted them as they entered the funeral home. Annie stiffened. "Hello, I'm Mr. Hayes, how may I help you?"

"I'm Annie Wilkins, my husband Walter passed away and I . . ." Tears gathered in the corners of her eyes.

"I'm sorry for your loss, Mrs. Wilkins. Please, why don't you have a seat? I'll get my papers and join you momentarily." Mr. Hayes motioned the three women to a room on his right. It looked like a beautiful living room and Annie, Olyria and Jeanine sat on a sofa.

Mr. Hayes returned, sat down in a wing back chair and opened his folder. "Now, how may I help you?"

"The coroner called and said my husband's body is ready to be released."

Mr. Hayes nodded and took down the answers to all the biographical questions in his folder. They discussed the type of service Annie wanted and the music she preferred. He recommended Pastor Mueller to perform the actual service. "We work with him frequently and he does a good job with a non-denominational service."

"Mrs. Wilkins, do you have cemetery plots?" Mr. Hayes asked.

"Well . . . no, we don't have plots," Annie said in a flat tone. She was holding Olyria's hand and squeezed it.

Mr. Hayes showed Annie a map of their cemetery. Several plots were available. "Do you want to reserve one or two plots?"

The question took her by surprise. Would she want to be buried next to Walter if it turned out they weren't married? After a moment Annie said, "Two."

"Mrs. Wilkins, how did your husband die?" Mr. Hayes asked.

Annie swallowed hard. "The doctor said he was poisoned." Annie paused. "Do we have to put that in the obituary?"

"No . . . No." Mr. Hayes cleared his throat.

"Thank you," Annie said.

"Here, let me read a rough draft of the obituary and you can tell me what else you would like to add." What did she actually know about Walter? She didn't even know if they were married. No matter what he wrote she wouldn't be able to add much.

> *Walter Wilkins, age 62, entered into death suddenly in Buckeye Grove, Ohio. Walter leaves a wife, Annie Wilkins. Friends may call Monday, from 10:30 am until time of services at 11:30 am at Schneider's Funeral Home, 555 Broadway, Buckeye Grove. The Reverend James Mueller, officiating.*
>
> *www.schneidersfuneralhome.com to send online condolences to the family.*

"Mrs. Wilkins, one of the last things we need to do is select the casket. I have a book you can look through or we can go to the showroom," Mr. Hayes said.

"I'd like to look in the showroom." Mr. Hayes got up and Annie, Olyria and Jeanine followed. Annie felt they were going down to purgatory. She never imagined that picking out a coffin would be so hard, and who knew they were so expensive? She felt that the amount of money she spent on the casket would reflect how much she thought of Walter. She loved Walter very much in spite of the way he treated her, but financially she didn't know what the future would hold. She had been careful with her finances before her marriage, but Walter had made quite a dent in her savings since they'd married. If she and Walter weren't legally married, she'd have no inheritance from him. She shook her head to clear these thoughts. How could she be thinking about money at a time like this?

Annie walked through the showroom, and all too eager for this to end, decided on a moderately priced bronze-looking metal casket.

"That's a nice selection, Mrs. Wilkins. We can go back up and finish just a little more paperwork." Annie and her friends followed Mr. Hayes back to the sitting room.

"I'd like the casket to be closed," Annie said. She swallowed hard, "Walter fell before he went to the hospital. His face will be bruised."

"That's not a problem, Mrs. Wilkins. Can you give me names of six people to serve as pallbearers?"

Annie didn't respond. Did she even have six names to give him?

Olyria spoke up to help her out. "I bet Michael Lomand would be willing, as well as Charles Clarkson."

"I could ask my husband, Jeff, if he would help," Jeanine Burke said.

"That makes three. I need three more," Annie said.

"Maybe David would be willing to be a pallbearer. Walter enjoyed his yoga classes so much," Olyria said. "We can stop by the shop after we leave here and ask."

"You can give me the final list of names on Monday before the services and if we are short a couple I can have some of our men help," Mr. Hayes said to Annie. "I also need to know how many copies of the death certificate you'll need?"

"I have no idea," Annie said.

"You'll need a copy for each pension or IRA account, insurance policies, bank and brokerage accounts, and the probate court," Mr. Hayes said.

If she and Walter weren't married how would she walk through this financial minefield? "I" . . . I had no idea."

"Well, why don't I request fifteen? If you need additional copies, we can always get them for you." Annie nodded. "Well, I think that does it for now. Pastor Mueller will probably contact you either this afternoon or tomorrow to finalize the service." Mr. Hayes stood and shook Annie's hand. "I'm sorry, Mrs. Wilkins. We'll see that everything goes smoothly for you."

Annie gave a half smile and nodded. "Thank you for your help."

Olyria, Jeanine and Annie walked out of the funeral home. Annie took in a deep breath of the clean spring air. It was good to be alive, even if poor Walter was dead. "Let's walk across the street to Always in Stitches. If David is free, we can get one more thing taken care of," Olyria said. Annie agreed.

There were thirty customers shopping, five employees in the shop. Stan Darling walked in just behind them. Olyria remembered Caroline was having her fat quarter sale today. They were about half way to the back of the shop when someone recognized Annie. "Aren't you that lady who was on the news last night?" someone asked. "Yeah, that's her," another said.

The back door of the shop opened and a Channel 10 news crew came through with cameras rolling. Maybe they had followed the women from Annie's house. When everyone saw the TV cameras, pandemonium broke out. "Mrs. Wilkins, Mrs. Wilkins, we'd like to ask you a few questions," the reporter called out as she pushed her way past the check-out counter. Rounds of fabric surrounded them. "Keep the camera rolling, Sid."

Customers flocked around Annie, perhaps to get a better look or maybe to see themselves on the evening news. Caroline shouted, "Nan, call Schultz; and we may need to call the police if we can't get this under control." Nan quickly did as she was told. She feared a riot would break out.

Stan Darling forced his way back to Annie and Olyria and put himself between them and the camera. Sheryll Douglas, Tina DeStocki, Goldie and Jasmine were among the customers. They made a protective circle around Annie, Olyria and Jeanine.

"What's going on in here?" Schultz's voice boomed through the store as he came in the front door; David was right on his heels. Schultz was chomping furiously on his gum and taking one serious step after another.

"What's all the ruckus? How can I teach calm and inner peace with all this noise?" David bellowed.

David and Schultz pushed their way through the crowd, back to the news crew. Several of the women stood shoulder-to-shoulder with them as they told the reporter she'd had to leave. Everyone's attention turned to Schultz and David to observe the confrontation with the news crew.

"Stan, run interference for us. I have an idea," Olryia said. "Sheryll, Tina, Jeanine, Jasmine and Goldie surround us. Help us out the front door so we can get down the stairs to the tea shop. We need some breathing room while we think what our next move will be."

The women made a slow break for it with Stan's help. The bell on the door jingled as they left the shop.

The reporter looked past Schultz and yelled, "They're getting away!" The news team tried to push to the front door, but customers blocked the way. "Get out of my way, I have a job to do," the reporter shouted.

Jasmine's hands shook as she unlocked the tearoom door; she had decided to open an hour later today so she could take advantage of the fat quarter sale. By the time the news crew burst out the front door of the quilt shop, Annie, Olyria, Jeanine and their gang of friends were safely locked inside the tearoom. Annie sat trembling at a table in the corner away from the door. The other ladies gathered around her.

"I'll make us some tea," Jasmine said, not knowing what else to do. In just a few minutes Jasmine brought a tray of tea and scones to the table.

"I have to talk to David today. Monday will be too late." Annie was absently stirring her tea.

"It's been almost a half hour," Jasmine said. "I'll call Caroline and see if the coast is clear." Five minutes later she was back. "Caroline said the news crew left. Only the fat quarter customers are left."

"I better get over to David's," Annie said. "Then would you mind taking me home, Olyria?"

JT Hooks was coming down the stairs toward them as they crossed the hall to the yoga studio. "Oh, JT, I forgot you started yoga," Annie said. She did her best to be cordial in spite of her bereavement.

"Hi, Mrs. Wilkins. Sorry to hear about Walter." JT was looking down at his feet instead of at Annie.

"Please call me Annie. We've just been to Schneider's to arrange Walter's service. The service will be on Monday," Annie was holding back tears again.

JT could see the pain on Annie's face. He barely knew Walter, and he and Will were investigating Walter's death. He made a mental note of the time, as he thought what better way to observe the crowd of characters that Walter knew. A crowd that may include some suspects? "This must be hard on you, Mrs. Wilkins . . . I mean Annie. I'm sorry for your loss."

Annie smiled, "Thanks, I appreciate your concern." They entered the yoga studio where David was filling pill gel capsules with a white powdery substance.

"Hello, David, I'm Walter's wife, Annie."

"Hello," he said. "I was shocked to hear about Walter."

"Walter really enjoyed his yoga class and the time he spent here with you," Annie cleared her throat.

David wet a cloth and wiped the counter where he had been working. White powder drifted to the floor. "Custom vitamins," he said. "JT is thinking of trying some. Right JT?" JT nodded, and David moved the filled bottles to the back of the counter.

Annie smiled and looked from one man to the other. Then she addressed David. "I was wondering if you'd be willing to say a few words at Walter's funeral and be a pallbearer."

David hesitated. "Are you sure you want me? I barely knew Walter, except for the bond we had around yoga."

"I'd really appreciate it and the circumstances . . . well let's say the circumstances are far from normal."

David wondered what he could say about Walter, but Annie's eyes begged and he gave in. "Well, . . . ah, . . . I guess I could say a few words."

Annie was clearly relieved. "Thank you so much; I appreciate your help. Well, I won't keep you any longer. I'll see you Monday morning. Calling hours are from 10:30 until 11:30. The service starts at 11:30. Thanks again."

When Olyria, Jeanine and Annie left the yoga shop, JT turned to David. "How well did you know Walter?" JT asked.

"How well can you ever know anyone?" David answered. "He's

been coming to lessons for several months now."

"How did he get along with the rest of the group?" JT asked.

"He got along okay. He liked to preen for the ladies, always putting on the charm. It all seemed harmless except when one of the lady's husbands punched him in the face because he didn't like the way he looked at his wife."

JT raised an eyebrow and scowled.

⌘

Sunday morning Annie drove to the airport to pick up her parents, John and Eleanor James, who'd flown in from Maryland. Annie was shocked to see how much her father had aged. Her mother's smile was wan.

"Walter was such a dear man and he loved you so much," Eleanor said. She hugged Annie close. "How could this have happened?"

"I don't know, Mom, all of it is so unexpected." Tears welled up in her eyes. "And the police see me as a suspect."

Eleanor stopped dead in the walkway. "You didn't have anything to do with it, did you?"

"How can you even suggest such a thing?" Annie said. "Of course, I didn't. Walter fell and the bleeding wouldn't stop. It was a complete accident."

"Of course it was," Eleanor said. "What was I thinking?"

Annie put their luggage in the trunk and helped her father into the front seat of the car. On the short trip home her father asked three times when the funeral was going to be. Annie blinked back tears and patted her father's hand and tried to smile. Not only had she lost Walter, but she was also slowly losing her father to the recesses of his mind.

When they got home Annie got her dad settled in the living room and went to make some tea. Her mother followed her into the kitchen.

"Dad seems worse," Annie said.

"He's not too bad in familiar surroundings; but as you can see, he gets confused when he's in unfamiliar settings. That's why we'll leave soon after the service. I hope you understand."

Annie turned and hugged her Mom. "I'm so worried about you two. I'll try and come up more often now that . . . I'm alone again."

"We'd be happy to have you; come whenever you can, and please forgive me for what I said earlier. I have no idea what I was thinking."

Annie served the tea in the living room while they waited for Pastor Mueller. "He called late yesterday afternoon and said he'd stop by today at 2:00." He arrived right on time. Annie set her cup down, tugged at her shirt and then wiped her hands down her slacks.

"Hello, Pastor Mueller," Annie said as she opened the door. "Please come in."

"Hello, Mrs. Wilkins. Sorry for the circumstances of our meeting," the Pastor said.

"I'd like you to meet my parents. John and Eleanor James. Please have a seat. Would you like something to drink? Coffee, tea, ice water?"

"No, thanks. I'm fine."

Annie sat nervously holding a handkerchief in her hand. Her mother was beside her on the couch, patting her leg to help calm her.

"Mrs. Wilkins, what can you tell me about Walter?" Pastor Mueller asked.

Annie wondered which Walter he was asking about. The sweet, loving Walter, the one who swept her off her feet; or the angry Walter, the one who was such a puzzle?

When Annie hesitated Pastor Mueller asked, "What was Walter like?"

Annie cleared her throat. "He could be so charming. We met and married on a cruise just over a year ago."

"He loved Annie so much," her mother said. "He just swept her right off her feet."

"Did he have any hobbies?" the Pastor asked.

"He liked to play golf and he started yoga the first of the year," Annie said. What else could she tell him? Walter had told her so little about himself. She had to say something and so she told the truth. "There isn't much else I can tell you. I'm embarrassed to say I didn't know Walter that well."

"I'll keep my comments generic," Pastor Mueller said. "It's surprising how often this happens. You are not the first." The Pastor stood, patted Annie's shoulder and shook hands with her father. "I'll be going," he said. "I'll see you tomorrow."

"One more thing," Annie said. "I've asked a young man to say a few words at the funeral . . . David Williams, he's . . . he *was* Walter's yoga master."

"I'll make a note of that Mrs. Wilkins. See you tomorrow." Then the minister left.

Annie and her parents were visiting in the living room when the doorbell rang only minutes later. Perhaps Pastor Mueller forgot something. She went to the door and when she opened it, Olyria stepped inside talking a mile a minute. "Olyria, Olyria slow down. I can't understand you," Annie said.

Olyria turned and shook her head. "Annie, I think I found Walter's son."

Chapter 22

"Walter had a son?" Annie's mother said after Annie had introduced Olyria.

"Yes," Olyria said. "And I've been up all night searching people finders on the Internet. The boy lived with an Amish family in northern Ohio back in the 80's. That's where the trail went cold."

Annie's father woke up. "You found the boy?" he said. "I've been praying for that for years. Where is he?" Olyria was still talking over the old man in her excitement about her new information.

"Dad, you're confused," Annie said. "It's Walter's son that Olyria thinks she's found."

"Not your son?" John's brow wrinkled as he looked at Annie.

Olyria stopped talking. "You have a son, too?" she said to Annie.

Annie's mother had pushed a fist into her mouth as if that would stop her husband from talking. She walked to the side of his chair and put an arm on his shoulder. "Come on, John, you need to lie down and rest for a while." Then she ushered him out of the room and up the hall to the bedroom.

Olyria sunk into a chair across from the one where Annie had been sitting.

"So what I saw in your palm was true?" she asked.

"It was years ago. I was so young, a sophomore in college, and I couldn't keep him. I just couldn't and I had no interest in marrying his father. I was playing with the sexual revolution and couldn't follow through. I had the baby – a boy – and gave him up for adoption. My dad has always regretted it. He would have loved to have had a grandson . . ."

Annie's words drifted off before she said, "I'd still rather nobody knew."

"Your secret is safe with me," Olyria said. "But I need a drink. Do you have any Scotch?"

Annie got into Walter's liquor cabinet and poured Olyria a Scotch. Olyria slugged it back like a trail-dry cowboy in a B western. She wiped her mouth with the back of her hand. "Life just keeps getting more and more interesting," she said.

⌘

Monday was another cloudy morning. "A good day for a funeral," Caroline said when she swooped into the kitchen. She had been on a high ever since she totaled the numbers for the fat quarter sale. The biggest and most interesting weekend since the quilt shop opened. She poured herself a cup of steaming coffee and sat at the table with Charles.

"I'm surprised to see you so cheerful about it," Charles said.

Caroline frowned. "I'm not happy about the funeral, Charles. I feel terrible for Annie and who could imagine? Poor Walter." Caroline sipped her coffee. It was hot so she stirred. "Don't forget you're serving as a pallbearer."

"How could I forget? The service is at 11:30? Right?"

"Yes, I thought I'd go over a few minutes early, but I'm not planning on spending a lot of time. Nan is coming in to cover the shop for me. She has a dentist appointment and I'll have to get back as soon as possible."

"Hmmm," Charles said.

"I know, it's not the most ideal situation but it's the best I could do on short notice, and poor Annie will have Olyria looking after her." Caroline stirred her coffee some more and put toast in the toaster for Budd who magically entered the kitchen.

"How do you do that, Mom? It's spooky."

"Eyes in the back of my head," Caroline said as she turned and smiled at her daughter.

The toast popped up and Budd began to butter it while her mom poured her a glass of juice. "I can hear your feet on the stairs," Caroline said. "I know every single sound of this house and I've heard you come down those steps over five thousand days in a row."

"That many?" Budd said.

"I did the math," Caroline said.

Budd hurried through her toast and juice, Charles kissed Caroline on the cheek and left for work. Caroline began to clear the table and the phone rang. She hesitated before picking it up. "Good morning."

"Mom?" It was Jamie and she was crying again.

"What is it, honey?"

"Tommy and I had a fight . . . a really big fight this time. He left in the middle of the night and I'm packing up my stuff to move back with the girls. I feel terrible."

"I'm sure you do, honey. But it's good that you're going back with your friends. A little space might be the best thing for you and for Tommy right now." Caroline couldn't help but think how happy Charles was going to be to hear this news.

"I'm really not ready to face the girls yet. It's so embarrassing after I moved over here so sure it was the right thing to do."

"You were scared, honey, and had just lived through a horrible experience. Anybody would understand why you'd want to be someplace you felt safe."

"There is no safe place, Mom." Jamie burst into tears again and, sobbing, asked, "Could you come and help me, Mom?"

"I wish I could, Jamie. I really do, but my friend Annie is burying her husband today and the shop is open. I had to get Nan to come in to help while I go to the funeral and Annie may be arrested before the day is out. I need to be here for her."

Jamie sighed on the other end of the line. "I guess it was a lot to expect."

"You're living a grown-up life now, Jamie. Living with men and in charge of your own decisions. You can depend on your dad and me, just not today, to help you move. That is something you can do for yourself."

"I guess you're right."

"You have good friends and you still have a spot you're paying for in their house. As soon as you feel like it, call them and I bet they'll come and help you move your stuff. I'm sure they will."

"I know you're right, Mom." They said good-bye. Cutting the cord was never easy. Caroline hoped she had done the right thing. Not that it really mattered. She had no choice today.

⌘

The shop key still worked. Caroline performed the opening rituals and tried restoring some order to the shop, which was a mess from the fat quarter sale over the weekend. The camera crew incident on Saturday when Annie entered the shop hadn't hurt sales, as Caroline feared. Customers bought more than just the fat quarters while they were in the shop. Bolts of fabric were piled everywhere. She began putting them away and was still at it when

Nan came in at ten thirty.

"Sure was a big weekend," Nan said.

"I'm beginning to see a bit of order restored," Caroline said. "I think half the fabric was in piles on the floor when I came in."

Nan laughed just as Stan entered with two huge cardboard boxes on his dolly. Nan patted her hair and so did Caroline. "Good morning, ladies," he said. The wattage of his smile increased as he turned it on Nan. "I was looking for you Saturday. It was a zoo in here."

"I was probably on the phone in the office trying to call Schultz and the police," Nan said.

"I couldn't stay long. I tried to help Olyria and Annie by keeping the news crew away. After I checked the parking lot to be sure they were gone, I left because I didn't see you." They stood through an awkward silence. "My son was over unexpectedly. I thought you might like to spend some more time with the two of us."

"Why didn't you just call?"

Stan's face turned red. "I lost your number," he said. "Could you give it to me again?"

Caroline rolled her eyes. Nan wrote her phone number out on the back of a sales slip and handed it to Stan. "Thanks," he said and rolled the empty dolly back toward the front door. He stopped halfway. "I almost forgot." He came back and stuck the electronic signature machine into Nan's hand. She bent her head and signed. He went back to his dolly and rolled it out the front door.

"How could he lose my number?"

"How could he forget to get your signature?" Caroline said. "Clearly you have the young man flummoxed."

"Do you think so?"

"I think so."

Sheryll Douglas and Tina DeStocki walked in the back door at that moment. "We parked in your lot," Sheryll said. "There's quite a mob scene in the funeral home parking lot. News trucks and tons of cars."

"That's fine," Caroline said. "I'm glad you're here, actually. I'll walk over with you. I'm sort of dreading it."

"We've only seen Walter here around the shop with Annie, but I do feel for her, losing her husband so soon after finding him."

"It's never easy to lose a loved one," Tina said.

Sheryll checked her watch. "We'd better get going or we may not get a seat."

Caroline grabbed her purse from the back room. Tina started toward the front door with Sheryll. At that moment the phone rang. "You got that, Nan?" Caroline asked. Nan nodded and Caroline hurried toward the door.

"It's the phone company," Nan called after her. "The investigation bureau."

All three women stopped. "I better take this," Caroline said. "You two go ahead, but save me a seat." She waved them on.

Sheryll and Tina left the shop and Caroline hurried back and grabbed the phone. "This is Caroline Clarkson."

"Hi, Mrs. Clarkson. This is John McConnell with the phone company. We have the results of your call investigation. We'll mail you a written report, but it's our policy to get results to patrons as soon as possible when the police are involved."

"Yes, thank you," Caroline said. "Who's been making the calls?"

"We can't be certain on all of them but the majority came from a phone registered to Annie and Walter Wilkins. The rest came from various pay phones on the southwest edge of Buckeye Grove."

"Walter?" Caroline said. "Oh my god. Walter?"

⌘

When Caroline made her way into the room where Walter's funeral was to take place, it was standing room only. Sheryll and Tina had saved her a seat near the back of the room. It was in the middle of a row and she had to climb over three people, one of whom she recognized from the evening news. "Excuse me, excuse me," she said as she stepped on toes and stumbled into her saved place.

Annie was standing by the head of Walter's casket and Mr. Hayes from Schneider's took her by the elbow and escorted her to a seat that was waiting for her in the front row. Her parents were on either side of the empty chair. Olyria and her mother were also in the front row with Annie and her parents. The pallbearers, including Charles, were standing on either end of the casket at the front of the room. The piped-in organ music stopped, as the minister stepped to the podium to begin the service.

Caroline clenched her fist and said, "God help me but I'm glad he's dead."

"What?" Sheryll said. She leaned her head toward Caroline expecting her to repeat her comment. Caroline shook her head and tears of relief began to flow. She wouldn't have to worry about Budd being hurt anymore. She wouldn't have to be fearful of answering the phone every time it rang. She dug a tissue out of her purse and dabbed her eyes. Sheryll put a sympathetic arm around her shoulder.

In the front of the room, Pastor Mueller had already exhorted the crowd to faith and confidence in a better place that awaited them all. It was a standard funeral message with very little that was personal. A clue he had probably never met Walter while he was living. He said a prayer and offered the podium to David Williams. The yoga master walked to the microphone. He straightened his shoulders and began to read from the book of Psalms:

> *"Come near and rescue me, O Lord:*
> *Redeem me because of my foes.*
> *You know how I am scorned*
> *Disgraced and shamed*
> *All my enemies are before you.*
> *May the table set before them become a snare;*
> *May it become retribution and a trap."*

The minister looked at the yoga master with eyes that rolled back in amazement at the scripture choice for a funeral. David went on – "In the family of man, there are fathers and sons, there are mothers and daughters. They should not do harm to one another. I did not know Walter Wilkins well, but I knew him well enough to know he had a troubled heart. He was not opposed to harming others if it suited his purposes." David looked over at Annie. "He was an avid and apt student of yoga. I wish he could have embraced the philosophy for his life."

With that, David nodded to the audience, turned and nodded toward Walter's coffin. His shoulders slumped perhaps from relief that his portion of the service was over or perhaps from grief over the loss of Walter. Then he returned to his position flanking the coffin. Annie was sobbing into her hankie and her father had a soothing arm around her shoulders. Someone in the control room turned the organ music back up and the pallbearers prepared to move the casket to the hearse.

Olyria left Annie in the embrace of her father and hurried to David. Another woman had beaten her to him. She was a tall woman in a plain coat that swept almost to the floor. Her grey hair was pulled to the back of her neck in a bun. There were wisps of hair straggling out of the bun. She was speaking angrily and Olyria stopped to listen.

"Did you have a part in this?" the woman asked. She pushed her face towards David. "Did you?"

David smiled and did not retreat. "We have serious business here getting the deceased into the ground," he said to the woman. "It's way past due." He turned his back on the woman and stepped away. When he did, Olyria put a hand on his arm to stop him.

"What did you mean by that message?" she hissed. "What were you trying to prove?"

He shrugged. "Annie asked me to speak. That's what I had to say."

"Well, it was totally inappropriate." Olyria was still trying to keep her voice down, but not so vigorously.

Charles tapped her shoulder. "We're ready to move the casket."

Olyria saw that she was holding up the funeral and that the other angry lady was still standing behind her. She stepped aside and let Walter's casket and the pallbearers pass. The audience was clacking chairs; and the low grumble of sympathetic, but shocked, conversations filled the hall.

"How did you know Walter Wilkins?" Olyria asked the plain woman. The woman just looked at her before she turned and walked away.

The newsman next to Caroline hurried to the hearse and had his cameraman get a shot of the casket going into the back. Caroline didn't move. She wasn't ready yet to speak to Annie. She was afraid she would let her relief and anger at Walter show. Charles would have to represent the family for the rest of the funeral. "I have to get back to the shop," she said to Sheryll and Tina.

"We're going to visit a bit and then we'll be back to get our car."

Caroline headed back to the shop and Sheryll and Tina headed toward Aggie, Olyria and her mother.

⌘

"Not one customer while you were gone," Nan said, when Caroline entered Always in Stitches.

"All my customers were at the funeral." Nan hurried out the door in order to try to salvage her time with the dentist.

After about an hour Caroline picked up the phone and dialed Charles. "Is the grave-side service over?

"Yes, I'm in my car on the way back to work."

"It was Walter."

"I know it was Walter."

"No! The phone company called. It was Walter making the calls," Caroline said.

"Walter Wilkins?"

"Yes. And he's dead so we don't have to worry about him hurting Budd. I'm so relieved, Charles."

"I never thought I'd see the day you'd rejoice at somebody's death."

"I didn't either, but I'm glad he's gone. Glad he's gone."

Chapter 23

Annie was exhausted and numb by the time she and her parents got home from the funeral. Her father sat down in the recliner and was asleep in moments.

"Would you like some tea, Mom?" Annie asked as she went into the kitchen, hoping her Mom would say yes.

"I'd love a cup, dear." Eleanor followed her daughter into the kitchen.

"I can't believe how my life has changed in just one week," she said, reaching for the teacups.

"I know, Annie, sometimes life takes unexpected turns."

Annie set the tea, sugar and cups on the table, still waiting for the water to boil then sat down next to her Mom. "We've hardly had a minute to talk since you arrived. How's dad really doing, Mom? I'm so worried about you." Annie retrieved the teakettle and poured the boiling water into the cups.

Eleanor looked down at her hands, trying to hide her eyes. "He's doing all right, dear. Don't worry."

"I can't help but worry about the two of you, Mom."

"You have enough to worry about, dear . . . I'm concerned about you. You waited so long to find happiness and then for it to be cut so short." Eleanor swallowed hard.

Annie hadn't told her parents about Walter's mood swings. She hadn't told them about his controlling nature. She hadn't told them about his rough ways. She was too embarrassed. Annie stirred her tea and straightened her shoulders. "I'll be fine, Mom. I've been alone before; I'll just have to adjust to being alone again."

Eleanor took hold of Annie's hand. "You're a strong woman, Annie, but you're still my little girl."

Annie and her mom spent the rest of the afternoon enjoying each other's company. Eleanor caught Annie up on all the local news of McConnelsburg, Maryland.

When it was time for dinner, Annie set out the various dishes her friends had brought over the last couple of days - tuna noodle, lasagna and meatloaf. Everyone filled their plates and Annie warmed them in the microwave. After dinner Annie helped her mom pack for the trip home the next day. She spent a restless night and dreamed of Walter and how happy they had been after they were married, if they were married. Morning took a long time to arrive.

⌘

In the morning Annie pulled up in front of the terminal and helped her parents out of the car. A skycap came over to help with the luggage. "I know how hard it was on you to come, but I really appreciated it, Mom," Annie said. "You have a safe flight and I'll talk to you soon."

Eleanor cupped Annie's face in her hands. "You take care of yourself, dear. Come to visit us any time you want to get away."

"I will Mom, as soon as I can." Annie hugged her parents then stood and watched them walk through the automatic doors into the airport.

Annie drove home on autopilot. She pulled into the garage and put her arms on the steering wheel and laid her head down on her arms. She sat for a few minutes dreading going into the empty house. Finally, she could put it off no longer. Annie wandered from room to room, not sure what to do first. She sat down on her favorite chair in the den to think. The silence was overwhelming, yet the clock ticking on the mantel sounded like Big Ben. The house felt like it was closing in around her. She had to get out; she couldn't just sit and do nothing. She hadn't planned on going to the Guild meeting this morning, but the thought of being with friends was comforting.

⌘

Caroline was looking forward to getting back to a normal routine after the last several days. No rats had been spotted in the shop since the incident in Jasmine's tearoom. The shock that Walter was behind all those horrible calls still hadn't worn off. Attending the funeral yesterday, seeing Walter's casket, knowing there would never be another harassing call and that Budd was safe gave Caroline a little peace. Yet her heart ached for Annie.

As the ladies started to arrive for the Guild meeting, Caroline could hear pieces of conversation regarding the funeral yesterday. Caroline was pleased at how many of the Guild members attended Walter's funeral in support of Annie.

"Sorry I'm a little late," Nan said as she came through the back door.

"No problem, everyone is just getting settled. If you could straighten up all the fabric bolts and fat quarter bins, I'll talk to you after the meeting," Caroline said.

Caroline went upstairs and joined the group. Michael slipped in beside her just a moment later. He was carrying his dog carrier. Caroline leaned over toward Michael and whispered, "Michael, you better not have any more pranks up your sleeve."

Michael smiled and wiggled his eyebrows. "I'm beyond that, Caroline. Stella is resting in peace now."

Agnes McDaniel raised the gavel and held it in midair as Michael opened the carrier. Goldie screamed, "You better not have more rats in there, Michael."

"No, no, no. I just wanted to introduce you to Della." He pulled out a tiny puffball version of Stella. Della had a white curly coat and black eyes just like Stella, but she was still a puppy. Della barked softly and wagged her tail - - eager to play with all of Michael's friends.

"Oh, she's so cute, Michael."

"She looks just like Stella."

"How did you find her?"

"She's Stella's niece. I went to the breeder that purchased Stella's sister. Isn't she adorable?" Michael beamed.

Agnes looked at Michael and the dog over the top of her glasses. He got the message, and Della went back into the carrier.

Agnes tapped the gavel on the table. "The meeting will come to order. Sheryll, will you read the minutes from the last meeting?"

Sheryll Douglas stood and began reading. She stopped when the guild members began to stand. Sheryll turned and saw Annie coming to the top of the stairs. The entire Guild got up and went over to Annie.

"Oh, Annie, I'm surprised you came," said Tina DeStocki.

Linda said, "We didn't think you'd come."

Michael wrapped his arms around her and said, "We're here for you, Annie."

Annie stood quietly; tears filled her eyes. "I just had to get out of that house. I felt like it was swallowing me whole. After I took my parents to the airport it seemed so big and empty."

"Well, we're glad you came. We'll be here for you whenever you need us, Annie," Caroline said. She wrapped her in a big embrace.

Everyone settled back in their chairs, eyes still fixed on Annie. Annie said to Agnes, "I'm sorry I disrupted the meeting."

"Oh, Annie, don't worry about that. How are you doing?"

"Things have changed so quickly and I'm not over last Thursday when the police executed their search warrant. Living with Walter has been such a puzzle. I didn't even know my husband. How could it have come to this?"

There were curious looks now. "Honey, you were married only a year. It takes a lifetime to really know someone," Goldie said.

"It was so hard to make funeral arrangements, to provide information for the obituary. I knew very little about Walter's past. I think he had family, but he never talked about them. I think he was previously married; he may even have had a son. Olyria's helping me do research. She has some leads that we need to check out, but I'm having trouble staying focused," Annie said.

"We'll help you anyway we can, Annie," Aggie said. "For now, why don't we skip the formal reports and do something fun. Let's get to the First/Worst Quilts." Agnes thought that might get Annie's mind off her problems. "Okay, who wants to be first?"

Linda Hutton stood up. "I'll go first; that way, everyone will feel better about their own." Linda held up a baby-size Rail Fence quilt. It was done in blues and greens. "I made this for my son, Max. As you can see, it's not quite square," Linda said with a half smile.

Goldie stood up and unfurled a Duck Tracks quilt. She'd chosen green-and-gold mini-prints. "I made this after my divorce from my second husband, Frank. I figured he walked like a duck and I was making tracks leaving him." Everyone laughed.

Jeanine Burke stood up next. "This is an Ohio Star quilt I made fourteen years ago. You can see that some of my points are cut off and my seams don't meet. I tell friends that's because I made an Ohio Star quilt in California. As a Californian I saw things a little differently."

One by one the rest of the group stood up and showed off their quilts. It gave them all consolation knowing that others had the same problems they had when they started. Annie just sat and observed, numb to everything.

Agnes turned the meeting over to Olyria. "We talked about a Secret Sis type program. Has anyone thought of another term for it?"

"How about Secret Charm because our friends are like charms that we treasure?" Sheryll Douglas asked. Everyone liked Sheryll's suggestion.

"Okay, Secret Charm it is. Here is a form to fill out so that your Secret Charm will know something about what types of things you like. You can take it home, fill it out, and then bring it to the next meeting. Does anyone have any . . ." Olyria stopped. There were police officers climbing the stairs.

"Mrs. Wilkins, we need you to come with us," one of the officers said.

"What!!!! Why?" Annie said. She stood and grabbed her purse.

"Put your hands behind your back," the taller officer said.

"You're going to handcuff her?" Caroline said.

"Standard procedure," the other officer said. Olyria shoved an elbow into the cop. "Do you want to be next?" he asked.

Annie had tears in her eyes as she handed her purse to Olyria and put her hands behind her back. The taller cop snapped the handcuffs into place and the officers led Annie by the elbows toward the stairs, down to the main floor of the shop.

As they walked away the group heard, "Mrs. Wilkins, you are under arrest for the murder of Walter Wilkins. You have the right to remain silent. Anything you say can be used against you in a court of law. You have a right to an attorney. If you can't afford one, one will be provided to you."

"Don't worry, Annie, we'll spring you," Goldie yelled after them. The officer in charge turned his head toward the women and raised his right eyebrow.

The entire Guild sat stunned as they watched Annie walk away in police custody. Then everyone started to talk at once.

"Hold on, hold on," Olyria said. "Something is just not right here. We all know Annie would never hurt a fly." Several of the women shared statements of support for Annie and questioned things that happened at Walter's funeral.

"What was all that nonsense the yoga master said at the funeral?" Jeanine said. "If he didn't know Walter, why would he say something about Walter hurting people if it suited his purpose?"

Caroline sat quietly. She didn't want to share the side of Walter that she knew. How could she tell the Guild that Walter was behind some unseemly phone calls and possibly even threatening Budd, before she had a chance to break the news to Annie? She wouldn't do that to her friend. Caroline dreaded the idea of telling Annie but knew she would have to face this issue as soon as possible.

"Yeah, and who was that strange old woman that came? I watched her as she paid her last respects. She stood up at the casket and kissed her hand then laid it on the casket and patted it. I heard her whisper something about forgiving Walter," Aggie said.

"Who ever thought that in a town as quiet as Buckeye Grove we would have such a mess and that Annie would be in the middle of it. It's just beyond belief," Tina DeStocki said.

"Olyria, how can we help Annie? What can we do?" Jeanine asked.

"Well, for one thing, she's going to need a lawyer. Caroline, do you still have that list?" Olyria said.

"I think the carbon copy of the sales slip is in my purse. I gave Annie the original. I hope she has it with her," Caroline said. She went to retrieve her purse from the office.

"I think we should go down to the station and let everyone know Annie has friends, especially if the news crews are there. Maybe we can make enough noise to bring attention to this injustice. What do you think?" Olyria asked.

"I'd do anything for Annie. You know it could be one of us next time," Aggie said. "What do you say gals . . ." she noticed Michael and amended that to "ah, guys and gals?"

"Oh, Michael, we could probably use your help with some Internet research," Olyria said.

"Count me in," chimed Michael.

"Here's the list of the lawyers," Caroline said, waving a slip of paper.

"Great, meeting adjourned," Aggie said.

"I'll meet you at the police station," Olyria said. "I have something to do first." She stood and went straight down to the yoga studio.

It was just before 1:00. Soothing music was playing. When Olyria entered, David was putting away his vitamins and supplements. Olyria spoke his name and David jumped, startled, and turned around glaring at her. David wasn't expecting anyone. He'd cancelled all his yoga sessions for the afternoon.

"What are you doing here?" he asked Olyria.

"I have just a few questions for you, David," Olyria said, standing straight with shoulders back, right up in front of him.

"Well?"

"I thought you said you didn't know Walter, yet you said some very unusual things at the funeral."

"I didn't know him that well."

"What prompted you to make those remarks?"

David dumped the rest of the vitamins and supplements into a cardboard box. "I thought long and hard about what to say. Walter was the kind of man who would get what he wanted no matter what it took. I watched him schmooze with the ladies in the class all the while he was married. Did you know one of their husbands even took a poke at him?"

"Really," said Olyria. "Is that what the stuff about harming others if it suited him was about?" Olyria studied his eyes as she waited for an answer.

"No. I saw him mistreating his wife. One day he forgot some of his supplements" David lifted a bottle of Ginseng and then threw it back in the box. "I ran after him. By the time I got to the back door, I saw Walter rough handling Annie. Her face was contorted in pain. I've seen men like that before. The women in their lives are treated like throw-away souls."

Olyria nodded. She had seen the bruises on Annie's arm. There was something, however, in David's eyes that told her there was more to this story. She studied him intently with so many more questions swirling around in her mind; she decided to think this through before she proceeded.

"Oh, David, one more question." Olyria couldn't help herself; she had to have his answer. "Who was the woman you were talking to just before Walter was put in the hearse?"

"With the media attention Walter's death has received, who knows where these people come from and who they are," David said.

"She seemed to know both you and Walter. We need to turn her name in to the police who have just arrested Annie for Walter's death. They think she poisoned him," Olyria said.

"Annie? Well, if she did kill him, she did the community a favor."

Olyria opened her mouth to speak but then thought better of it. "I'm headed to the police station to see how I can help Annie."

Chapter 24

The women were assembled outside the Buckeye Grove Police Station, which was located three blocks from Always in Stitches. Tina and Sheryll arrived in time to see the two cops escort Annie into the back entrance with her hands still handcuffed behind her back. There was a cop on either side.

"Annie, Annie," Sheryll called out and waved. Annie turned to look at her, stumbled and fell to the ground. The cops grabbed her by the upper arms and pulled her back to her feet. Her knees were skinned and a rivulet of blood ran down one shin.

The policemen hurried Annie into the back door of the police station.

The police station was just across the street from the library and it was toddlers' story hour. Mothers escorting children craned their necks to see what was going on as the rest of the guild women arrived and assembled in a small knot on the sidewalk in front of the building.

Michael was there with Della in her cage. He handled it carefully as he set it down next to a small tree near where he was standing. Then he began a chant, "Set Annie free. Set Annie free." The quilting guild picked up the chant and cars honked and people waved as they drove past. A carload of high school kids, Annie had taught several of them, pulled to a screeching stop in front of the police station and jumped out of the car. They joined the chant with fists raised in the air.

The knot of people had grown to a small mob by the time the news crews arrived. The chief of police, George Evans, chose this moment to come outside and try to disperse the crowd. Olyria arrived from her chat with the yoga master and made her way to the chief's side.

"Can I see Annie?" she asked.

"Not yet. We had to call the paramedics to look after her skinned knees and then she has to be processed."

"How long does that take?" Olyria asked.

"Could be an hour, could be two," the Chief said.

"I have a list of lawyers for her to choose from. You have to let her see a lawyer."

"I can take the list in for you," the Chief said.

"How do I know you'll give it to her?"

"I'm telling you," he said. Olyria clenched her fists and stuck her face into the chief's face. "Watch yourself, little lady. Just watch yourself."

Olyria turned to the crowd behind her. "He won't let me go inside the building to see Annie. He's being unfair because we're women."

Michael started a new chant. "Chief Evans is unfair to women! Chief Evans is unfair to women!" The crowd picked up the new chant and the camera recorded it all. Even a couple of mothers with toddlers in arms joined in, and little Della started to whine and bark from her carrier.

Olyria turned back to the Chief, crossed her arms over her chest. "Well?"

"All right," the Chief said. He took Olyria's arm and started to lead her through the front door of the police station. She jerked her arm away and walked in ahead of him. The chanting was still audible even after the door was closed. "Didn't I see Sheryll Douglas in that crowd?" the Chief asked Olyria. She just shrugged and fingered the list of lawyers she had pulled out of her pocket.

He stopped at the dispatcher's station and said, "Get Will Douglas into my office immediately." The dispatcher, a pretty, young, blonde woman, said "Yes, sir."

The Chief led Olyria into his office and left the door open. Will Douglas arrived as the Chief took a seat behind his desk. "You know this woman?" He waved his hand toward Olyria.

Will nodded. "How are you today, Olyria?"

"Did you hear the crowd out front?" the Chief asked.

Will nodded again.

"Your wife is one of the instigators." The Chief scowled at Will from under his thick brows. "Go out there and make her stop."

"It might *not* be that easy, Chief."

"You bet your sweet a . . . butt it won't be that easy," Olyria said.

The Chief wiped his brow. "Just do it. I don't care how hard it is; and on your way drop Miss . . . Olyria off in the waiting area so she can see Annie Wilkins when her processing is finished."

"Yes, sir," Will said. "But . . . sir, I can't just order my wife around and expect her to obey. She has a mind of her own."

"I don't care how you do it, Douglas. Just get the crowd out of the street or I'll bring in the SWAT team."

Will shook his head and then led Olyria out of the Chief's office. "The SWAT team?" Olyria said. "Is he serious? I didn't even know Buckeye Grove had a SWAT team."

"I'm sure he wasn't serious," Will said. He dropped Olyria off in the waiting area, which was littered with newspapers and pop cans. She brushed off a chair with the paper in her hand before she sat down. "I have only an hour," she said. "Then I have to leave for my first cancer treatment."

"I'll check with the arresting officers and see how they're moving along." Will stepped through a door he needed a key to unlock and was back in just a few minutes. "They should be finished in half an hour," he told Olyria.

"Good," she said and leaned back into the chair.

Will took a deep breath and headed for the front door of the building. He could hear the chanting before he opened the door. Michael was on the sidewalk leading the group. He held little Della in his arms; her curly white ears bounced every time he chanted "Chief Evans is unfair".

Will stepped out the door. "Sheryll, could I speak to you?" He shouted to be heard over the chanting.

Sheryll looked from side to side and both Tina and Aggie urged her forward.

Will leaned in close and spoke to Sheryll, cupping his hands over her ear. She stepped back, looking at him, shocked. She shook her head from side to side. He put his mouth close to her ear and spoke again. She frowned but this time she nodded.

Sheryll motioned to Michael to stop the chanting, which he did.

"Annie is being processed and will be another half hour or so. If we break it up out here, they'll get a judge to do her arraignment this afternoon and she won't have to spend the night in jail if she can make bail. We may as well go home and figure out another way to support Annie, who I know is innocent." Sheryll looked at Will with a forehead-crinkling frown. "Even if the police don't."

"Will they release her if we leave?" Michael shouted.

"Maybe, maybe not," Sheryll said. "She can call an attorney

as soon as she's processed but under no condition will she be arraigned today unless we disperse."

"Can they do that?" Tina asked.

"I think so," Sheryll said. The crowd grumbled amongst themselves but began to drift away.

"We love Annie," some of the high schoolers yelled; and the young mothers began to drift across the street and into the library.

Tina, Aggie and Michael headed back toward Always in Stitches. Michael had Della back in her little cage and was carrying it protectively under his arm.

"It will be at least a couple more hours," Will said.

"We can wait," Sheryll said. She tossed her head and walked away from Will and toward the other guild members. It was going to be a really long evening at home. He could see the writing on the wall.

⌘

The Guild members returned to Always in Stitches and filled Caroline in on the rally at the police station. "I never thought they'd actually arrest Annie," Caroline said. "This is getting serious."

Michael set Della's little carrier on the check-out counter. She curled into a corner and closed her eyes.

"Olyria is going to give Annie the list of lawyers and she could be out by this afternoon," Sheryll said. "But you're right, it is getting serious."

"Michael, could we talk to Adrian about what's happening? Maybe he can give us some tips on how to help Annie," Caroline asked.

"Certainly," Michael said, "Come to the house. I'll cook you dinner, but I don't know how much help Adrian will be. He has the autopsy information on Walter and on Stella, but he's not a cop."

"He's a medical detective," Caroline said. "Seems like that's what we need."

"Okay," Michael said.

"Can Goldie come, too?"

"I'll check with Adrian, you check with Goldie. I have to work tonight because I've had the morning off for the guild meeting, but we can try for tomorrow night."

"I'll talk to Goldie and let you know," Caroline said.

Della whined in her cage. "I think the baby needs to go out and I have to get to work, so I'll talk to you later today," Michael said.

He picked Della's carrier up and tucked it under his arm. He said good-bye to all the ladies and left through the back door.

"I have to go, too," Sheryll said. She and Tina followed Michael out.

Aggie and Caroline were left alone in the shop. "Olyria has a treatment this afternoon," Aggie said. "She said she'd have to leave the jail in half an hour. Annie will probably take longer by the time she's arraigned, gets hold of a lawyer and he comes to spring her."

Caroline nodded.

"If Annie needs anything, have her call me," Aggie said. "I'll stay home so you can reach me."

"No cell phone?"

"Not me." Aggie said and left the shop

⌘

Caroline called Goldie, who was not home, and left a message asking if she was free for dinner on Wednesday evening. It was five hours after all the commotion of the Guild meeting with not a single sale, when Annie came in the front door of the shop.

"Oh, honey. Are you all right?" Caroline said. She hurried to the front door and put her arms around Annie and hugged her hard.

Annie sighed. "I'm okay, if you don't count the part about being arrested for the murder of my husband and the fact that I've skinned both my knees. I had to charge my bail."

"You can charge bail?" Caroline said.

"The judge set bail at $100,000 which means I had to come up with ten thousand. Thank goodness I have a fifteen thousand dollar limit on my credit card and only a two thousand dollar balance due."

The phone rang. Caroline reached out and picked it up. "Always in Stitches. May I help you?"

"Sure has been a lot of action the last few days. I waited to call." It was the raspy voice of the sinister caller. "How's your little girl?"

"You're dead," Caroline said after a sharp intake of breath.

"Hardly," the voice on the other end said. "I have my eyes on you and on the rest of your family. I heard your other daughter broke up with her boyfriend, for instance."

Caroline slammed the phone onto the counter, then threw it to the floor.

"Caroline?" Annie's voice was frightened. "What is it?"

Caroline's face was pale. Sweat beaded on her forehead and her eyes were clenched shut.

"It's Walter," Caroline said.

"Walter?"

"Oh, Annie. I've been getting threatening phone calls here in the shop and at home. We had the phone company investigate the calls and they were traced to Walter's phone. I didn't want to mention it to you with Walter's death and all, but that was the caller."

"Walter misplaced his cell phone. He hasn't been able to find it for the past month. We both thought it would surely show up.

Probably had fallen behind the couch or something." Annie wrung her hands. "Somebody must have stolen it."

"I'll have Charles call the phone company and check on this last call. See what information they have."

"I'm so sorry," Annie said.

"It isn't your fault," Caroline said. "Or Walter's either, it seems."

The women hugged and stayed that way for a long, long time before Annie left to return to her empty house.

⌘

It was ten minutes to closing time when Olyria came through the back door. "I'm trying to find Annie," she said.

"She's out of jail, was here for a bit and has gone on home."

"What a day. What a day," Olyria said.

"How was your treatment?"

Olyria shrugged. "I got meds to keep me from being sick to my stomach. They say I won't really get much of a reaction until the second or third day."

"So, you feel okay?"

"So far," Olyria said. "I guess I might as well feel okay. I have to do this five days a week for a total of six weeks, and it beats most of the alternatives."

Caroline patted Olyria's shoulder. "I know you can do it."

"It might beat being a murder suspect."

Caroline laughed. "I'd rather skip them both."

Caroline started closing down the register and Olyria locked the front door and turned off the lights to help out. When the shop was closed down for the day, Olyria said, "I'm headed to Annie's. Do you want to come along?"

"I'm beat," Caroline said. "I had a good visit with Annie this afternoon and I have some things I have to discuss with Charles this evening, so I'd better go home."

"Okay," Olyria said and the women parted company in the parking lot.

⌘

Annie peeked around the curtain on the back door before she opened it to Olyria.

"How was your treatment?" Annie asked.

"It's over for now." Olyria shook her head as if to shake out pesky thoughts. "What are your plans?"

"I want to box up Walter's stuff. I got boxes at the grocery store on my way home. Ten people stopped me before I got out of there. It was awful, Olyria. They think I killed Walter." Tears filled her eyes.

"They don't know you," Olyria said. "All your friends know better."

"I haven't told anyone else, but even my own mother had her doubts."

"You're kidding," Olyria said. "Is there some way I can help clean out Walter's things?"

"Yes, I'd love to have your help. I also have to try finding Walter's phone." She told Olyria about the harassing phone calls to Always in Stitches coming from Walter's phone.

"Who could have stolen his phone?"

"Someone at the golf course, I suppose. Or if he dropped it or lost it someplace out on the street, anybody could have it."

They started in the closet. "Check all the pockets," Olyria said. They began folding Walter's clothes and boxing them. Annie tossed four nice pairs of shoes on top of the first box and taped it shut.

"I can smell Walter in the clothes," she said.

"It's very sad," Olyria said.

When they got to the dresser drawer with the pouch Annie had found only three weeks earlier, they took the pouch to the bed and sat down. "You open it," Annie said to Olyria.

Olyria took the leather pouch and unzipped it. She took out each piece of paper individually and unfolded them one by one. Nothing had changed but Annie noticed the life insurance policy had a cash value to some stranger and now Walter was dead. The beneficiary on the policy was named Claudia Wilkins.

"I wonder if we can find Claudia," Annie said.

"Or she may come out of the woodwork now that she has some money coming to her."

"How would she know?"

"If she's in the area she could have seen it on the news . . . or read Walter's obituary in the newspaper."

"I suppose you're right"

Olyria was down to the college grade sheets when a small brown envelope fell out of the folds. It landed in her lap. Olyria opened the envelope and slid the contents into her hand. There was a lumpy paper folded up tightly. Olyria gently opened the paper and a key fell out. The women's eyes met. "I wonder what this fits," she said.

"I didn't see this before. Is there a name on it?"

Olyria turned the key from side to side. "It says Master Pro on it. That doesn't tell us much."

"What about the paper it was wrapped in?" Annie asked.

Olyria opened the paper up completely and studied it. "It's a contract from Storage Unlimited. Have you ever heard of that?"

"No," Annie said. The women sat in silence, thoughts churning through their minds.

Chapter 25

Annie jumped up and grabbed the yellow pages; laid it on the bed, frantically flipping through the pages to the storage section. "Oh, you just passed it," Olyria said. "Go back a page."

"There it is," Annie said. "It's on the other side of Route 71 by Home Depot."

"Doesn't Michael live over that way at Pillar Point?" Olyria asked.

"I'll be right back." Annie ran to the spare bedroom and grabbed the directory for the Guild. She returned a minute later. "Yeah, Michael's just off Buckeye Parkway."

"Let's call Michael. I have a plan," Olyria said.

Annie's heart was pounding when she handed Olyria the phone. Olyria dialed. "Hello, Michael, this is Olyria, Annie and I want to stop by and talk to you for just a minute tonight. Is it too late?"

"So they sprung Annie, that's great. I had to work tonight and just got home. Have you had dinner yet?"

"Annie's holding up pretty well, all things considered, and neither one of us has thought much about dinner." Olyria closed her eyes and hugged her stomach. The thought of food right now was not appealing.

"Come on over, I'll make some tea and fix some nibbles."

"Thanks, Michael, we'll be there in about twenty minutes."

"What are you thinking?" Annie asked.

"Where are all the photos that were in the drawer?" She turned from side to side looking for them. "Michael's good with computers and I think he can help us."

Annie grabbed her Morton & Bassett Spice Company canvas tote and filled it with the documents and pictures they'd found in Walter's dresser drawer. They were out the door in just five minutes.

"What are you planning?" Annie asked.

"Well, Michael is a master on the computer. He knows the ins and outs of the Internet and he has a digital camera."

"And the digital camera will help, how?"

"Michael has a photo-editing program to enhance any pictures from his digital camera. Perhaps he can play with the photos from Walter's dresser and show us what the people in these photos would look like now."

Annie turned her head toward Olyria. "How will it help us to know what they look like today when we don't know who they are?"

"One step at a time, Annie. We have to do something to help you and this is just one small thing." Olyria turned to Annie and smiled. "Besides, maybe Michael can help us track these people down."

It was almost 9:30 by the time they parked in front of Michael's house; and Annie was starting to feel a little more in control, a little more hopeful. Michael answered the door with a big smile and a tight hug for Annie. "I'm so glad to see you're out of jail. Please come in." He waved his hand toward the chairs in the living room. There were trays of snacks on the coffee table with teacups, a creamer and sugar bowl. "Have a seat. I'll just get the tea."

Michael returned before Olyria and Annie had settled into their chairs. He poured the tea. "Please help yourself to something to eat," he said.

Michael tossed a bacon-wrapped walnut into his mouth. "Now what can I do for you?" Annie and Olyria explained the project. Michael looked through the photos while Della barked at his feet until he picked her up. He tucked her in his arm, then picked up the school photo and studied it.

"We thought maybe you could do an age progression on the pictures with one of your fancy programs and give us an idea of what they would look like now," Olyria said.

"I can try. I just saw a tutorial online that shows how to do an age progression in Photoshop. I haven't done it before but I'll give it a try. I can't promise anything."

"It might be harder on the boy." Michael rubbed his chin. "I'll give it my best try and we'll see what happens." He tossed another fancy walnut into his mouth and then fed one to Della.

"Could you help us track these people down?" Olyria asked.

"Ahhh, now that's something I can probably help you with. I have some friends who are expert genealogists. They should be able to help point me in the right direction. I'll just scan these into my computer and let you have the originals back."

Michael went to the computer with Della scampering after him.

Olyria sipped her tea and tried a walnut. Annie sat with her hands clenched in her lap. "You should at least try a cracker."

"I'm not hungry. I can hardly swallow the tea." Olyria could see the exhaustion on Annie's face.

Michael returned with the original documents and photos. "Thank you so much for your help, Michael. You'll never know what it means to me." Annie put the documents in her canvas tote.

"Hey, sweetie, you keep your chin up," Michael said to Annie. "I'll let you know what I find out." He grabbed Della before she trotted out the door.

The women got into their car. Olyria yawned. "It's getting late; let's come back tomorrow to go through the storage facility."

Annie nodded. "I'm not sure I could face what we might find in that locker tonight."

Olyria drove past Storage Unlimited and then headed toward Annie's home. The house was dark when they pulled into the driveway.

"I hate the thought of going into that empty house," Annie said. She took in a deep breath. "I know I lived there alone for many years but its different now. I expect to hear Walter rustling the newspaper or coming up the stairs or making the floor in the hallway squeak. But all I hear is silence."

Olyria knew what Annie was going through. She'd felt the same thing when her husband, Kyle, died in a car crash. They had just celebrated their twenty-third wedding anniversary. Olyria gently rubbed Annie's forearm. "Things will get better, Annie. It's hard to believe right now but you must hold on to that thought."

"I'm not only mourning the loss of my husband, but I'm mourning the loss of the marriage I always wanted and never had." Annie whispered, tears rolling down her cheeks.

Olyria and Annie sat quietly for a few minutes. "I have a treatment tomorrow morning. I'll pick you up at 1:00 tomorrow afternoon and we'll go through the storage unit. Perhaps Aggie will be able to help. You're not alone, Annie." Annie leaned over, hugged Olyria and then stepped out of the car. Olyria watched her friend go into the dark, empty house.

⌘

When Caroline arrived home that night, Charles was surveying the food in the refrigerator. He closed the fridge door after she walked in. "What's wrong?" he asked.

Caroline dropped her purse on the counter and walked into Charles' embrace. "Charles, this has been the worst day," Caroline sighed. "It was awful watching the police handcuff Annie and take her away in front of all her friends. She's innocent but things don't look good."

"Where are they holding her?" Charles released Caroline, and they sat down.

"She was arraigned shortly after she was booked," Caroline said with a slight smile forming on her face.

"What?" Charles asked.

"Well, the Guild members demonstrated in front of the police station pleading for Annie's release. High school kids passing by stopped and joined. People going into the library came over. From what I heard, the chief was very unhappy, to say the least."

"Really?" Charles said.

"Channel 10 News was there so you might catch a condensed version on the news tonight," Caroline said. "They sent Will out to disperse the crowd."

"Just Will?"

"The Chief figured Will had influence with Sheryll and that the 'mob' would listen to her. A few other officers came out as backup and helped to break up the crowd. They even got rid of the news crew. I don't know what they told them, but the reporter left." Caroline said.

"Is Annie okay?"

"She came back to the shop late this afternoon. She was telling me about her arrest when …" Caroline put her head down and tears started to well up in her eyes.

"Caroline, what happened?"

"I got another phone call," Caroline sobbed. "Charles, the calls weren't from Walter."

"What?" Charles jumped to his feet and immediately started pacing. "What about the information from the phone company? They said it was Walter."

"Annie was there when the call came in. She could see I was upset. I told her that the phone company had been tracing the calls and said they were made by Walter. Obviously, she was shocked. She said Walter lost his cell phone and anyone could be making the calls."

"Budd will have to change her plans for the summer. I'm not letting her go away when there is some lunatic out there making threats against her," Charles growled.

"She'll be disappointed; but I agree, we have no choice." Caroline looked down at her hands. "We'll talk to her after dinner and then I'll call Will just to let him know what is going on."

Dinner was strained. Charles and Caroline were both tense with the new developments, and the thought of breaking their daughter's heart by canceling her summer plans weighed heavily on their minds. As Budd stood to clear the table, Charles and Caroline asked her to sit down again. Budd ran from the kitchen after they explained the situation. Caroline went after her.

⌘

Things were quiet at breakfast. Charles read the paper and Budd sat with her head hung low, nibbling on her toast. Caroline sipped her tea, contemplating the day ahead of her.

Caroline dropped Budd at school. Budd dejectedly got out of the car and slung her backpack over her shoulder. "See you later, Mom," she mumbled.

Caroline sighed and drove on to Always in Stitches. This was a fresh, new day and Caroline was looking forward to an uneventful day at the shop. Wednesdays were normally one of the quietest of the week. After the events of the last couple of days a normal day at the shop would be very welcome.

The shop had been open for only an hour and so far no customers. Caroline was upstairs restoring order to the quilting books. She bent over to pick up a book, when she felt a hand on her back. Caroline jumped, startled, as she hadn't heard the bell on any of the doors. "Mom, I'm so sorry I scared you." Caroline looked up, and to her surprise Jamie was smiling back at her.

"Jamie! What are you doing here?" Caroline gave her a big hug.

"I've finished up my classes and asked for a day off from work before I start full time. I decided to drive down for the day."

"When will you start working full time?" Caroline asked.

"I have a project I'm finishing up at work tomorrow and Friday, and then Monday I start forty hours a week," Jamie said. "I never paid much attention to quilting before this, but it's really a beautiful art form."

"I sure think so," Caroline said. "Have you heard anything from Tommy?" Caroline bit her lip.

"No, and I'm okay with that," Jamie said confidently.

"Good for you. Can you stay for lunch? Nan should be in soon and she can watch the shop while we grab a bite."

"Actually, I made plans to have lunch with Brook. I wanted to stop by and say thanks for all your support. I couldn't have made it through the last few months without you." Jamie hugged Caroline. "I've got to run but I'll call you soon. I love you."

"I love you, too, Jamie," Caroline called as Jamie left; then she returned to organizing the books. She was determined to finish this before lunch. She thought warm thoughts of her girls while she finished. She was going back downstairs when the phone rang. Caroline picked it up. "Always in Stitches, may I help you?"

"You helped me more than you can ever know," the raspy voice said. "Your daughter is a breath of fresh air."

"You stay away from Budd, you hear me. Stay away from her." Caroline's hand gripped the phone; her breath was short and uneven.

"I'm talking about your older daughter. What's her name? Jamie, isn't it?"

Caroline clicked off the phone. She sank to the chair behind the counter, her hands shaking as she rested her head in her hands. She wasn't going to listen to this mad man any more, but how could she stop him. Her stomach churned and she knew there would be no lunch today.

⌘

Olyria rang Annie's doorbell. "You ready?" she asked as Annie opened the door. "Aggie is waiting in the car. I thought we could use all the help we could get."

Annie smiled meekly and shook her head. "As ready as I'll ever be."

When they arrived at Storage Unlimited, the attendant looked at Annie's papers. "I'm Mrs. Wilkins." He nodded and opened the gate. Annie took a deep breath to center herself.

Olyria drove slowly, looking at the unit numbers, and then stopped abruptly. "Here it is," Olyria said. She turned off the car and then looked at Annie. "Okay?"

Annie was curious but she was filled with dread, unsure of what she'd find. The unit was a five-foot by five-foot space with a shrouded type padlock on it that could not be easily cut off. Walter wanted to make sure that whatever was in this unit would be safe.

Annie's hand was shaking as she put the Master Pro key in the lock. It worked perfectly. Olyria helped her pull open the door. Eight boxes were stacked haphazardly inside the unit. They hadn't been disturbed for a while. Cobwebs hung from the boxes and dust had settled on top of them. Olyria brushed a hand across one of them and sneezed at the dust she raised.

"Looks like these haven't been disturbed for a while," Aggie said.

Olyria got a cloth out of the trunk of her car and brushed dust off the boxes.

"Why don't you and Aggie load these up and we'll take them back to your house, Annie? That way we can take our time going through them," Olyria suggested.

Annie nodded and the two of them started filling up Olyria's trunk. It would take more than one trip. They locked the unit back up and took the first load home. One by one they carried boxes into the dining room and set them on the table.

"I'm scared," Annie said.

"Nothing to fear," Olyria said. "I'm betting the answer to a lot of our questions are in these boxes."

"Let's go get the rest of the boxes before we start opening these," Annie said.

"That's prolonging the agony," Olyria said. "I think we should open these and see what's inside before we get the other boxes."

"Okay," Annie sighed and she pulled open the first box. There were many small velvet boxes with beautiful jewelry inside. A sapphire and diamond ring with matching necklace and earrings. A natural pearl pendant, with over seventy freshwater pearls. "This has to be an antique," Annie said as she laid it on the dining room table.

"I think we should catalogue these as we take them out of the boxes," Aggie said. "That way we'll know what we have when we're finished."

"Good idea," Annie said. She went to the kitchen for a pencil and pad of paper and the women began an inventory of Walter's treasure trove.

There was a pair of beautiful antique silver candleholders that must have graced an elegant table. Aggie wrote everything down as Annie unwrapped. Olyria took pictures to support the inventory. When they had recorded each item in the first box, they transferred the contents gently back into the box.

"I hate to think about where Walter got all these things," Annie whispered. Her stomach was churning again.

The next two boxes were more of the same. Olyria opened the fourth box and Annie gasped. "That looks like my Tiffany desk lamp, it's an antique. My grandfather bought it for my grandmother. When Walter moved in, he wanted some of his things around. He said he didn't like the lamp and that he put it in the attic. I bet it's not there."

When they finished the fourth box, the women piled back into Olyria's car and returned to Storage Unlimited for the other four boxes. Again they arranged them on Annie's dining room table. There was more jewelry, more silver and gold, even a magnificent brooch that had once belonged to Olyria's grandmother.

"Annie, I recognize that brooch," Olyria said. "It belonged to me, and I suspected Walter of taking it back when we went out."

"Olyria? You knew about this?"

"I wasn't sure, Annie. Not sure enough to say anything to anyone."

Annie handed the brooch to Olyria. "I'm so sorry," she said.

"You had nothing to do with it and I certainly don't hold you responsible; but I'm awfully glad to have it back, for sentimental reasons."

"I suspect we have a lot of sentimental favorites here," Annie said. Angry tears filled her eyes and she brushed them away with the back of her hand.

The final two boxes were smaller than the others. Aggie lifted them to the table. Annie shook her head; she could do no more. Aggie looked at Olyria and Olyria nodded. Aggie opened the third box and set the items on the table as before. There was a metal lock box and a few more pieces of jewelry. A key was taped to the box, and when they opened it they all gasped in unison.

"I've never seen that much money. How much do you think is there?" Aggie asked.

Annie stood frozen, stunned by what they had found. Olyria started to count, and when all was said and done there was $175,000 sitting smack in front of them. Aggie and Olyria looked up at Annie with wide smiles.

"I'm having trouble taking this all in. I can't imagine where Walter got this kind of cash." Annie whispered. "I'm not sure I'm ready for the last box."

Olyria and Aggie cleared the table and repacked the third box and lifted the last one to the table. But the contents of this box were different. No valuable jewels, no antiques, but a child's pair of cleats, a small baseball cap, a trophy. Annie looked curiously at what lay on the table. She fingered the baseball cap and then picked up the trophy. "Economy Eagles? That sounds familiar." Annie looked at Olyria. "Isn't that the name of the school on the picture we found?"

Olyria nodded. Again tears started to trickle down Annie's face. "He loved his son enough to save these, yet he abandoned him."

Chapter 26

On Wednesday evening, Goldie, Caroline, and Adrian sat down in Michael's dining room with candlelight, wine and a hearty seafood gumbo along with buttermilk biscuits that melted in the mouth. Adrian had arrived in a pinstriped suit, spats and a bowler hat. He was just coming home from work. Della was underfoot and finally took up a spot under the table, hoping for crumbs that might fall her way.

"MMMMmmm," Caroline said. "This is the best soup I ever ate."

"Gumbo isn't really soup," Michael said. "Technically, it's a stew and usually it has okra as an ingredient. I've left out the okra because I don't care for it."

"Whatever," Caroline said. "It's delicious." She scooped another spoonful into her mouth and broke off a piece of biscuit, liberally buttered, as a chaser.

"So," Caroline said. "What can you tell us about the autopsies of Stella and Walter?"

Adrian took a sip of wine before he answered. "They died from the same drug," he said. "It isn't always a poison and actually is a medication in fairly wide use today. It works by thinning the blood and interfering with the clotting factor. The dosage makes all the difference."

"Sort of like aspirin?" Caroline asked.

"Very good," Adrian said. "Sort of like aspirin on steroids. It's used in rat poison which is what I thought might be the source when Stella died. It takes a few days to work in rats." He scooped a spoonful of gumbo into his mouth. "They bleed to death internally."

Goldie put her hand over her mouth and asked to be excused from the table. Michael pointed her towards the bathroom and she made a dash for it.

Adrian licked butter off his finger and took another sip of wine. "Sorry about that," he said. "I forget some people are sensitive to this kind of conversation." He looked at Caroline. "Are you all right?"

"I'm fine," Caroline said, but her face had paled and her spoon rested in the gumbo bowl.

"I doubt Walter accidentally ate rat poison," Adrian said. "So one would have to figure out how they both had access to the same toxic agent."

"It had to be at the quilt shop," Michael said. "That is the only place Stella was out of my sight for a week in either direction."

Caroline shook her head. "Schultz talked to every tenant in the building. Nobody owned up to having any rat poison on the premises. I know I certainly have none."

"I know I don't have any. I hadn't seen any rats, dead or alive, in the building until someone smuggled them in," Goldie said, raising her eyebrows and turning her head towards Michael. She sat back down at the table after her return from the bathroom.

Michael smiled at Goldie, then cleared his throat. "Is it something that could be left over from the granary days of the building?" Michael asked.

"I doubt it," Adrian said. "The building was empty for at least a decade, and I'm sure there were plenty of rats in the building during that time to eat up any stray poison."

Caroline stirred her gumbo in the bowl but didn't take another bite. "What about the medicinal form of the drug? Could it have come from that source?"

"It could, I suppose," Adrian said. "But it would almost have to be a hostile act under those circumstances."

"Murder?" Michael said.

Adrian used a biscuit to sop up the last bits of gumbo sauce from his bowl. He popped it into his mouth. "Yes," he said.

Adrian smiled as Caroline's and Goldie's jaws dropped.

"I have dessert," Michael said. "Beignets to go with the gumbo."

Caroline and Goldie said no thanks in unison and Michael went to the kitchen to get the sweets for Adrian and himself.

⌘

Thursday morning, Caroline was late getting into the shop. A carload of Four women who had traveled from Dayton were waiting at the back door. "Sorry, sorry," Caroline said. She had her arms loaded as usual, but the key was still working well so she didn't fumble as she unlocked the door.

"Thank you dear Schultz," she said. The women swooped into the shop behind her. "I'll have the lights on in a few minutes. Feel free to look around while I get myself organized."

"We plan to hit five shops today, so we don't have too long to spend in one place," one of the women said. There was no mistaking her displeasure at Caroline's lateness.

"I'll try not to hold you up any longer," Caroline said. She hurried through the shop, turning on lights, and hung the quilt on the front railing at breakneck speed. She opened the safe and counted money into the cash register.

The women were full of questions and not shy about asking them as Caroline straightened and tidied the shop. It had been left in a bit of disarray the previous evening as she had hurried to get to Michael's for dinner. The women sniffed their disapproval as Caroline scurried about and tried at the same time to wait on them.

Each one bought fabric, and one of the ladies bought an armload of pattern books that had arrived that week. The women decided to go downstairs and have tea before they went to their next stop, and Caroline felt relieved. They weren't in that much of a rush.

They had just left when Olyria came in. "You busy?" she said, peeking her head into the shop.

"Olyria, I'm so glad to see you." Caroline hurried to the door and took her by the arm. "How's Annie?"

Olyria blinked. "Shaky," she said and wiggled her hand back and forth. "We've been going through Walter's stuff. It's been really hard on her. We found a key and traced it to a storage facility on the edge of town."

Caroline was a rapt listener as Olyria described the loot they had uncovered and the fact that Walter surely must have been stealing from the women he courted over the years. "He had quite a pack of goodies," Olyria said.

"How's Annie taking it?"

"So-so," Olyria said again. "She feels like a fool."

They were standing by the back door into the shop in heavy conversation when a woman came into the building's back hall. Olyria glanced her way and then ducked out of sight, away from the glass panes in Caroline's shop door.

Caroline looked out the door and saw the woman, too. "What?"

she whispered to Olyria.

"The woman from Walter's funeral."

"She could be a reporter," Caroline said. The woman had gone down the stairs toward the yoga studio by this time, and Olyria hurried out the back and looked down the steps. Olyria hurried back to Caroline inside the shop.

"Dressed like that? Not a chance," she said.

"It is a different on-camera look," Caroline said.

"We've got to find out who she is."

"How?"

Olyria thought a minute. "We'll follow her."

"I can't leave the shop."

"You have to. She'll recognize me from the funeral."

"Can you stay here?"

"I can't run the cash register. I'd be worse than nobody. Caroline, we have to do this for Annie."

Caroline thought about it a minute; then she scribbled out two notes, one for each door that said, "Closed for Family Emergency. Back ASAP." She taped one on the front door and one on the back. She grabbed her purse and car keys; then she and Olyria hurried to Caroline's car, where they waited for the plainly dressed woman to come back outside.

It took fifteen minutes; during that time Olyria filled in more of the details of the jewelry and family heirlooms found in the storage facility loot, and Caroline told Olyria about dinner with Michael and Adrian. When the woman walked out, Olyria scrunched down in the passenger seat of Caroline's car and Caroline snapped a picture of the woman with her cell phone. "Got it," she said.

"Take another one," Olyria said and Caroline did. Then she flipped the phone closed and started up the car. The woman got into a modest blue sedan and Caroline followed her out of the parking lot and onto Buckeye Grove's main drag.

"What's the license number?" Olyria whispered.

"She's in another car. She can't hear you."

"Right," Olyria said. "Tell me the license number."

"CAR465," Caroline said and Olyria wrote it on a scrap of paper she had found on the floor of the car.

The woman headed north on I-71 and Caroline stayed behind her as she wove through the mid-morning traffic. "Don't let her see you," Olyria said.

"We're all going the same direction," Caroline said. "If she does see me, she'll just think we're going to town, like she is."

"Just be careful. We don't want to lose her. You should speed up, maybe pass her for a mile or two."

"Think about it, Olyria; if I'm that far in front of her how do I follow her if she gets off? Relax, I'm doing the best I can."

At that very moment the blue car veered between two tractor-trailers and applied her brakes so that she could take the Greenlawn exit. There was no way Caroline could follow.

"Well, you were right, we lost her."

Olyria sat up in the passenger seat and looked around. The two tractor-trailers still kept Caroline in the center lane. "Damn," Olyria said. "You're no Steve McQueen."

Caroline took the next exit she could manage and headed back south towards Buckeye Grove. The letdown of the missed opportunity made it a long ride home.

⌘

Michael slipped away during the morning lull at the restaurant and stopped by Always in Stitches before Caroline and Olyria returned from their wild-goose chase. He found the family emergency note Caroline had taped to the doors. He wouldn't be able to get back to the quilt shop today, and he didn't want to leave his information at the door. It was too sensitive. So . . . he headed down to the tearoom.

There were two tables of red hat ladies having morning tea. Jasmine was flitting around, trying to see to their every need. When she saw Michael, she excused herself and went to him.

"What brings you in this morning?"

"The quilt shop is closed and I have some things for Caroline. Could I leave them with you?"

"Sure," Jasmine said. "Is it a secret?"

"Not really. Olyria and Annie asked me to do an age progression on some photos on my computer. I was up most of the night learning how to do it and I think I got a pretty good result. I wanted to get them into the right hands as soon as possible. I called Olyria's house and her mother said she was at the quilt shop . . . so I brought the stuff here."

"The shop is closed? I heard Caroline come in this morning, a few minutes late but I know she was here."

"There's a sign on the door saying there was a family emergency."

"I sure hope it's nothing serious."

"Me, too," Michael said. "I have to hurry. Can I leave the stuff with you?" Michael held out the envelope and Jasmine took it.

"I'll paste a note to the door and tell Caroline to check with you."

"Sure," Jasmine said. She waved him off, laid the envelope on the counter and returned to the red hats sipping their tea.

⌘

Olyria and Caroline had been gone about an hour. They saw two regular customers leaving the parking lot as they pulled in.

Caroline waved and the women waved back.

"Hope I haven't missed too much business," Caroline said. "Those two will be back, but I'd hate to have missed the ladies from Dayton this morning. You don't get second chances with some people."

"It was for a good cause," Olyria said. "We can find out who the woman is from her license number."

"We could've walked to the parking lot and gotten that."

"I'm sorry," Olyria said. "I guess it was sort of a hair-brained idea. I just want to help Annie so much."

The women walked to the door of the quilt shop and Caroline pulled Michael's note off the door. "Michael was here and we missed him. He left something for us with Jasmine."

"I'll run down and get it. You get back to the shop."

"Yes," Caroline said. "I need to get the shop opened back up."

Caroline unlocked the door and Olyria headed down the stairs to the tearoom. She had the front door unlocked and checked the cash drawer when Olyria came flying back into the shop. "It's the pictures," she said. "Look" and she thrust the pictures into Caroline's hands.

Caroline studied the photos. There were six of them, three progressions for each of the two original photos. She turned them this way and that. "Well, I see something familiar in the boy's eyes but I don't recognize the woman at all."

"Look at the picture you took with your camera," Olyria said. "Just look at it."

Caroline laid the photos on the counter and fished out her phone. She retrieved the photo and looked from it to the age-progressed photos and to the original that Annie had found in Walter's pouch. "The hair is so different," she said. "But . . . it could be. It really could be."

"I think this may be one of Walter's wives, the one who disappeared."

"But why would she be going to see the yoga master?" Caroline asked.

"Good question," Olyria said. "Very good question."

Chapter 27

Olyria looked at her watch as Caroline printed the picture from her cell phone. Olyria grabbed the envelope Michael had dropped off and said, "I've gotta run. I want to drop this off at Annie's before she leaves for downtown. She has an appointment with her lawyer this afternoon."

"Wait, don't leave without this. Here's the picture from this morning." Caroline handed Olyria the freshly printed picture. "Let me know how things work out," Caroline called as Olyria left.

Olyria rushed over to Annie's and arrived just twenty minutes before Annie had to leave. "Hey, Olyria. I wasn't expecting you this morning. I'm just getting ready to leave."

"I know, Annie, I won't keep you long but I have some information I thought you might need before you see your lawyer."

Olyria and Annie sat in the living room. "What's so important?"

"Remember that woman at the funeral, the one that dressed rather plain like she was Amish or Mennonite?"

"I kind of do. Everything was such a blur."

"Well, I overheard part of a conversation she had with David, and she wasn't very happy. Then, this morning, I went to Always

In Stitches and I caught a glimpse of her going down to the yoga studio. Caroline and I followed her when she left. We got her license plate number; and oh, yeah, Caroline took a picture of her with her cell phone. There's something else. Remember we asked Michael if he could do an age progression on the photos you found in Walter's drawer? Well, he dropped them off today." Olyria handed Annie the papers. "Take a close look at all of the pictures and see what you think."

Annie had listened intently as Olyria relayed the events of the morning. "I will." She quickly looked through the pictures from Michael and the papers from Caroline and Olyria's escapade this morning. "These could be important," she said, and then tucked them into her tote. "I have the best of friends." Annie hugged Olyria and then went to her meeting with the lawyer, and Olyria left for a cancer treatment.

⌘

Annie sat nervously in the waiting room of Muller, Hunter and Ackerman Law Firm. They specialized in criminal law. The office was located in the brewery district, not far from the Franklin County Courthouse. Annie never thought in a million years she'd need a criminal lawyer, but here she was anxiously waiting and in dire need of legal services.

She looked around the waiting room and took in the rich burgundy and gold colors. The receptionist's desk was made of a rich cherry wood decorated with a brass container filled with stately bluish-purple silk hydrangeas. The furniture in the waiting area was a couple of large overstuffed chairs in a deep blue and gold. Beautiful paintings hung on the walls. Annie could only imagine what an office of this size would cost to furnish and rent but knew it would be reflected in her bill. She pushed the thoughts of legal fees out of her mind. Right now she had to concentrate on getting the charges dropped.

The receptionist picked up the phone; Annie hadn't even heard it ring. "Mrs. Wilkins, Mr. Hunter can see you now. Please follow me."

Annie stood, clutching her Morton & Bassett Spice Company tote - - praying that the contents would some way help her case. Annie followed the receptionist down the hall to the first office on the right. There was a huge mahogany desk along the windows and a round mahogany table to the right of the door. There were wall-to-ceiling bookshelves lining the walls to the left of the door, filled with volumes of legal books. Two beautiful burgundy leather wing-back chairs were in front of the desk.

"Hello, Mrs. Wilkins, please come in and have a seat," Mr. Hunter said as he motioned to one of the wing-back chairs.

Annie nodded and sat stiffly with a death grip on her tote while her lawyer walked around his desk and sat down.

"We have a lot of work ahead of us," Mr. Hunter said. "Would you like some coffee or tea?"

"Tea, please."

Mr. Hunter buzzed for his secretary to request the tea. "Let's review what happened the night Walter died," he said while they waited.

"Well, Mr. Hunter."

"Please call me Gregory."

"Gregory," she said and then started at the beginning - - telling him about how she got home on Tuesday, May 9th, and Walter didn't look good. How she made dinner and what they ate. How Walter got sick after dinner. Annie's eyes looked down at her hands. "Walter and I hadn't dated that long before we married. He was like two different people. There were times he made me feel like the most beautiful woman in the world." Annie smiled weakly and blushed. Then her face went solemn. "There were times," Annie rubbed her arm, "when he was more authoritarian, almost abusive."

Gregory's secretary came in with a cup of tea for Annie and coffee for him. Gregory thanked his secretary, then nodded at Annie as he wrote some notes. "Please go on."

"After we were married I tried to get to know Walter. He didn't want to talk about his past. I tried to find out on my own. I searched through his belongings and found these." Annie showed Gregory the school pictures and divorce papers. "I started to wonder about our marriage and looked for a copy of our marriage certificate. That's what Walter and I argued about the night he fell." Annie hesitated and drew in a deep breath. "I'm not even sure we were married." Tears started to well up in Annie's eyes and Gregory offered tissue.

"After he died, a friend of mine was helping me sort through Walter's things. We found a key for a storage unit." Annie hesitated while she looked in her tote again. "There were eight boxes in the storage unit. Here is the inventory and some photos of what my friends and I discovered." Annie waited while Gregory looked over the documents.

"Looks like Walter was a busy boy. This jewelry looks valuable and a strong box with $175,000 in it! Do you have any idea where all this came from?" Gregory asked.

Annie shook her head no. "The only thing I can guess is that it is from other women. He knew the captain of the cruise ship quite well and I think he must have been on other cruises. The Captain of the ship is the man who married us, if we were ever married. He never even told me he was previously married."

"The police will want to see this. They may find some clue to where the items came from but it's unlikely. But there may be no records at all. Men regularly fleece vulnerable women, and the women too often don't even report it because of embarrassment and humiliation."

"I can sure understand that," Annie said.

Gregory Hunter smiled. "If we don't find theft reports, the items will come to you as part of Walter's estate."

"If we're legally married," Annie said.

"Yes, of course, that is an issue."

Annie handed Gregory the age progression pictures. "A friend of mine attempted an age progression of Walter's son, using his school picture, and the woman in the first pictures I handed you."

Gregory raised his eyebrows. "That's a help but we'll give the original pictures to the Ohio Department of Criminal Identification and Investigation and see what they can do with them."

"There was an unknown woman at Walter's funeral. She had a conversation with David, the yoga master. This morning she showed up at the yoga studio. My friends followed her. This is a picture of her and her license plate number." Annie handed Gregory the documents. "Something doesn't seem right. We believe she might be one of Walter's former wives, but we're not sure of her connection to David."

"Well, this is a very good start. I suggest you provide copies to the police. It may help in their investigation. You've done a wonderful job of putting together information for your defense, Mrs. Wilkins. I'm impressed."

Annie smiled, satisfied with herself. "When will the Grand Jury be convened?" she asked.

"It all depends on how long it takes the police to finish their investigation. I'll keep you informed," Gregory said. "All your information will help."

"Thanks," Annie said as she stood and shook his hand. "I

appreciate your help."

⌘

At Always in Stitches, Caroline was in high gear from the thrill of the morning's chase. Her mind was whirling, trying to put all the pieces together. Nan and Kathy were working and business had been brisk since she returned from her joy ride with Olyria.

Both Nan and Kathy were helping customers when the bell on the front door rang. Caroline looked up to greet the potential customers and was surprised to see Will Douglas and JT Hooks.

"Well, what brings my favorite detectives here today?" Caroline asked.

"Hey, Caroline, just wanted to see how things were going?" Will said. "Have you had any other phone calls from your strange friend?"

Caroline gave a tentative smile. "Not since the other night when I called you. Annie said she would contact the phone company and cancel the cell phone number. Hopefully that will be the end of it," Caroline said.

Will nodded, thinking to himself that the cell phone wasn't the only phone in the world. "Let me know if you have any more problems."

"What's new with Annie's investigation?" Caroline asked.

"You know I can't discuss any of the evidence of that case with you," Will said.

"We had dinner with the coroner at Michael's and he said the poison that killed Stella and Walter were the same. And I remember Annie telling me Walter was taking vitamin supplements. Annie urged him several times to check with his doctor first. She was concerned that some food supplements can interfere with prescription medications and interact with different foods," Caroline said.

"What was Walter's reaction? Did he go to the doctor?" Will asked.

"No, he was perturbed, he felt Annie was meddling. But Annie was leery about getting the supplements from David without reviewing it with his doctor."

JT's face went blank. "I've been taking supplements from David. Walter told me how good he was feeling. He said they gave him stamina and helped with his balance."

Will's head snapped to the right as he looked at JT. "You've been taking supplements you got from David? How long have you been taking them?"

"About a week and a half," JT said.

"How are you feeling?" Will asked.

JT hesitated slightly then said, "Well, I actually feel pretty good."

"We better get them tested just to be on the safe side," Will said. He turned to Caroline and asked, "Is there anything else you can tell us?"

Caroline hesitated, torn between telling Will about her chase with Olyria after the plain woman this morning. Would she be betraying Annie if she told? "Doesn't seem fair I have to do all the talking here while you guys are totally mum."

Will shrugged. "That's the way it works."

That's all I can think of about the supplements," Caroline said.

"Annie stopped by after her attorney's appointment and gave me a package," Will said. "There were some pictures and a license plate number for someone who might be worth talking to, along with an extensive list of items Walter had in a storage unit." He looked at Caroline intently.

"Olyria noticed a woman we'd never seen before at Walter's funeral. She seemed rather agitated at the end. Then this morning she came to see David," Caroline said.

"David?" JT interrupted.

"Yes, Olyria had just come into the shop and she recognized the woman from the funeral. We followed her," Caroline said weakly.

"Like Starsky and Hutch?" JT asked.

"More like the Keystone Kops. I'm not very good at that sort of thing. We were on I-71 and she slipped away. She managed to get off at the Greenlawn exit and I couldn't get over soon enough to follow her." Caroline said, a bit embarrassed.

"Well, I'm just glad nobody got hurt," Will said.

"Me, too, we just wanted to help Annie. She's innocent, I'm sure of that."

"We checked the license number, and the plates belong to a Claudia Miller who lives in Orient. We're going to check it out," JT said.

"Good," Caroline said. "Olyria and I wondered why she came to see David."

"I wonder, too," Will said as he looked at his watch. "JT and I need to get back to the station." And the two men left the quilt shop.

Caroline was thankful for the normalcy of the rest of the day after its harried start. Nan and Kathy took care of the customers and Caroline was able to get caught up on paperwork. There were fabric and books and thread to order, a new trunk show to coordinate. Caroline was grateful for the tasks as it helped to keep her mind focused.

Nan and Kathy had left for the day and Caroline was closing the shop when the phone rang. Caroline grabbed the phone, hoping it was Olyria with news from Annie. "Always in Stitches, may I help you?"

"Soon, very soon you will help me," the raspy voice growled.

Caroline's hand shook as she cupped it over the mouthpiece. "You leave me alone."

"Well, then, if you don't want to help me, I'm sure Budd or Jamie will."

Caroline slammed the phone down; her face was pale. Would this never end?

Chapter 28

First thing in the morning Will and JT went to question the plain woman in Orient. They had traced her from her auto registration. The house was set back from the road, up a long gravel lane. The dust kicked up as Will drove down the lane. Both men rolled up windows to keep the dust outside the car.

The house needed paint. So did the barn that set back even further behind the house. Something about the place looked familiar to JT. There were a couple of skinny cows and a geriatric horse in the pasture. Their car pulled to a stop in the turnaround and a woman stepped out onto the porch. She put a hand to her forehead to shield her eyes from the morning sun.

Will and JT gave the dust a minute to settle before they opened the doors and stepped out of the car. "Good morning," Will called. He introduced himself and JT while extending his shield. The woman didn't respond.

"Are you Claudia Miller?" Will asked.

The woman dropped her hand from her forehead and nodded her head. "Yes, what do you want?"

"We want to ask you a few questions," JT said.

Claudia turned her gaze on him. "I don't have any answers."

"Let's give it a try and see." Will and JT were on the porch by this time. The plain woman didn't offer them a seat though there were rocking chairs on the porch.

"We saw you at Walter Wilkins' funeral; what's your relationship to him," Will asked.

"Do I have to answer that?"

Will rubbed his chin. "No, but if you decide not to we'll have to take you into the station and question you there."

"That man has been nothing but trouble in my life," she said.

"Walter?" Will asked.

The woman nodded. "Nothing but trouble from the first day I met him."

"When was that?"

"1975."

"Do you want to tell us about it?" JT asked.

Her shoulders drooped and she appeared to have surrendered to the situation. "We might as well sit." She motioned toward the rocking chairs and took one for herself. Will sat in the other and JT leaned against the porch rail.

"I'd like to tape this," JT said. "It will save having to go through it again."

The woman nodded, giving permission. She leaned back in the rocking chair and closed her eyes.

"I was Walter Wilkins's second wife. He had been through hell. He and his first wife had two sons. One of them died when he was four. It was a terrible ordeal for Walter and his wife. In less than a year Walter's wife died. He had nothing to anchor him to the earth but his younger son, who was only two at the time."

"We met at a Parents Without Partners meeting at a Methodist Church." Claudia leaned her head back and laughed. "It was the most common thing and it was the Seventies. We got married and things weren't bad for a year or two. Daniel was a sweet little boy and I grew to love him."

Will and JT exchanged glances. "Daniel?"

"You know him as David. Walter drank too much. He'd fall into fits of despair and get mean." The woman paused for breath.

"Did he hit you and the child?" JT asked.

Claudia nodded. "It went on for years. He'd have a fit of rage and then disappear for days at a time. When he came home, he'd be sorry and for a while I thought he might actually change but it didn't happen. Daniel was twelve and started to want to stand up to Walter. Just a boy but he looked to solve the problems like a man. He took a swing at his father and I thought Walter would kill him. He went crazy, beat him till he was unconscious." Tears filled her eyes. She pulled a hankie from her apron pocket and blew her nose. "Sorry."

"That was the last straw. When Walter stormed out of the house, I cleaned Daniel up and packed a few things. We ran to a Mennonite farm that wasn't far from us. They hid us from Walter when he came looking a week later. Daniel healed physically, but he was never really the same after that beating."

"So you stayed with the Mennonites?

"I did. Daniel left when he was sixteen. For a while he came back to visit but eventually he stopped visiting and we lost touch. I had heard from friends that he was looking for me but I hadn't seen him since he was sixteen."

"And Walter? Did you lose track of Walter, too?" Will asked.

"I haven't seen Walter in twenty years," Claudia said. "Then I saw the news photos of the riot in the quilt shop. And there was Daniel, clear as day."

"I didn't know television was allowed by your religion," JT said.

"Mennonites are different from the Amish. They live in a more modern world," Claudia said. "But I left the Mennonites two years ago. I came here with Abraham who also left the sect. We aren't married in the church but we're making a go of it here. Abraham understands what I have been through and I'm happy for the first time in years. He has three grown children still with the Mennonites and we are able to see them when they have time. It's a life," she said with a shrug. "The best life I've had since I met Walter Wilkins all those years ago."

"Were you surprised to see David, I mean Daniel, on the news?"

"Surprised doesn't really cover it. He hated his father. Praying didn't help. Punishment didn't help. Living with people for whom hatred is the biggest sin didn't help. Daniel hated his father so much he had plastic surgery and changed his name from Daniel Wilkins to David Williams. But his eyes, I could never forget his eyes."

"Do you think he might have been involved in his father's murder?"

Claudia shrugged. "I sure couldn't say he wasn't."

⌘

Caroline felt a little more hopeful for Annie, based on her discussion with Will and JT the previous afternoon. She had spent a restless night and was still freaked out about the harassing phone calls. She went through the paces of opening the shop the next day and then got Annie on the line.

"Annie, have you had a chance to cancel Walter's cell phone?"

"I forgot all about it," Annie said. "I'm so sorry, Caroline. I meant to do it this morning but Olyria and I found a storage unit the other day full of Walter's things and I've been busy with my lawyer and the police. The police are here now going through all the stuff we found."

"I'm so sorry for all this trouble, Annie, but if you could take a minute and cancel Walter's account, I'd sure appreciate it."

"I'll do it right now."

"The caller can find another phone. I know that, but then perhaps the phone company can trace that phone and get a better idea of who is making the calls."

Caroline hung up and just as she did fourteen women came through the back door chattering and laughing. "We're on a minibus tour of quilt shops today," one of the ladies said. "Some of us even have some money left."

Caroline smiled at the women. She'd get a second wind and have the chance to have a good day.

⌘

Will and JT were on their way back to Buckeye Grove when Chief Evans radioed them into his office.

When Will and JT walked into the Chief's office he didn't look happy. "Sanchez just called and the prints on Walter Wilkins' pill bottle matched the prints on JT's. Proof that both came from David Williams. Mr. Wilkins' capsules were liberally laced with coumaden, about ten times the therapeutic dosage. Instructions were to take two tablets a day. According to the coroner's office this would build up to a fatal dose in the body in a week, ten days at the most. All it took was the head injury to produce a fatal bleeding episode." The Chief slammed his fist onto the desktop. "It would have been fatal in another day or two without a fall, according to the coroner."

"What was in JT's capsules?" Will asked.

"Protein powder, vitamin C and sugar," the Chief said. JT let a deep breath out. "It looks like David is our killer. I want you two to go to the yoga studio and pick him up."

"Bring him in for questioning?"

"Arrest him," the Chief said. "Read him his rights and cuff him to bring him in. Bring in any drugs you find in the studio. Have him fingerprinted and photographed first thing, so we have his actual prints on file. We'll want to do that comparison, too." He cleared his throat. "This is Buckeye Grove. We haven't had an unsolved homicide in thirteen years. I don't intend to start now."

⌘

Caroline breathed a sigh of relief as the last of the bus tour ladies left the shop. The driver had had to come in and tell a couple of laggers the bus was ready to leave and they needed to be aboard in five minutes. Sales had been brisk and several of the women promised to come back on their own. Caroline was delighted but pooped. Seemed like this always happened when she was manning the shop alone.

The phone rang and Caroline hesitated just a moment before answering. It was Annie. "I got Walter's cell phone cancelled. You shouldn't be getting any more calls from that number."

"Thanks so much for taking the time to do that, Annie. I know you must have other things on your mind right now."

"It's no trouble. I owe you and the ladies from the quilt shop so much for all your support during this awful ordeal."

"We quilters have to stick together," Caroline said. She had just hung up the phone when the back door burst open and the yoga master ran into the shop. "David? What on earth . . .?"

She didn't get her question out before he grabbed her left arm, twisted it back and then pulled her toward him. He grasped her around the chest in a classic hostage pose, her upper arms pinned to her sides and her knees on the verge of buckling. He held the biggest knife Caroline had ever seen to her throat. She could feel the cold steel, sharp against her skin. It was micro seconds later when Will and JT burst into the shop, their guns drawn, their adrenalin flowing."

"Drop the knife," Will yelled and, of course, David didn't.

"What the . . .?" Caroline said again. And then her training kicked in. She hadn't lived through a bank robbery only to die in the shop of her dreams. She made a 'v' out of her right elbow and rammed it backwards into David's abdomen while using her left hand to push his right hand away. He expelled a puff of wind and bent over at the waist. The knife dropped to the floor; and before Caroline could recover, JT and Will had pinned him to the floor and cuffed his hands behind his back.

Will stood and helped JT haul David to his feet, then he grabbed Caroline's arm. "Are you okay?" he said. "That was crazy. He could have slit your throat. Do you know how lucky you are?"

"I wasn't thinking," Caroline said. "I used to work security in a bank and my instincts kicked in." She smiled at the detectives and said, "Now, you'll have to fill me in on what's happening."

JT's face was stern. "You'll have to come to the station and provide a statement of what just happened here and whether you want to press charges." He bent over and picked up the knife with his handkerchief. . . ."

Chapter 29

Caroline called her sister, Amy, and asked her to watch the shop for a few hours. She told Amy that David had been arrested and she had to go to the police station to answer some questions.

While Caroline waited for Amy, she called Charles. He could hear the tension in her voice. "Are you all right?"

"I'm fine Charles, but David has been arrested and the police have some questions for me. I don't know how long it will take, so I'll call you later."

Amy arrived in fifteen minutes. Still shaking, Caroline gave her a big hug and said, "I've got to go. I'll try and be back before closing but if not please lock up for me."

At the police station Caroline was escorted to Will's empty desk. When he finally arrived he smiled then asked, "Do you mind if I record your statement?" Caroline said "No."

Will started with his questions, "What were you doing just after lunch." Caroline answered all of Will's questions. She told him the whole story about how she was on the phone with Annie when David burst through the door and grabbed her. Caroline suddenly stopped speaking and froze as she watched David being ushered from the holding cell to another area of the station. He sneered at her. She shuddered as he walked by. "Where are they taking him?"

"Caroline, please continue. Tell me what happened next," Will said gently.

Caroline looked at Will, puzzled. "You saw everything that happened after David grabbed me."

"I know, but we need your statement."

Caroline continued to tell Will the rest of the story, and the realization that she might have been killed that afternoon started to really sink in. Caroline fought back the tears, took a deep breath and straightened her shoulders. A quilt shop was no safer than a bank. Maybe Jamie was right; no place was safe any more. "What will happen to David?"

"They're booking him now, that's all I can say."

⌘

It was late afternoon before Will and JT finished the paperwork at the station. They walked over to the yoga studio to see how the forensics team was doing. When they got there, the team had bagged up a lot of bottles of vitamins, powders, and a huge box of empty gel capsules.

"Find anything unusual, boys?" Will asked.

"Yeah, there was a box thrown in his storage area full of cell phones," one of the investigators said.

"Can you get me a list of the phone numbers so we can have the phone company run a check on who he's been calling?" JT asked.

"Sure, once we get this all cataloged we'll get a copy to you. All this stuff," he motioned to the capsules and powders, "will go to the lab. It shouldn't take long to identify what these substances are. We'll get the results to you ASAP," the lead investigator said.

While Will was talking with the investigators, JT started to look around the studio. He had never paid close attention to the pictures hanging on the wall, perhaps because he was nervous and embarrassed during his first few yoga lessons. JT stopped in front of one picture that captured his eye and stared.

"Will, when you have a minute come and tell me what you see," JT said.

Will nodded to the investigator and walked over to JT. He looked at the picture on the wall, "I see a picture of a farm."

"Does it look familiar?" JT asked.

"Well, yeah, it does. Do you think that's a picture of Claudia Miller's farm?"

"Sure looks like it to me," JT said. "Take this picture along with you, boys, we'll need it for our case."

⌘

Friday night Caroline got home before Charles. The phone rang and Caroline stiffened. She waited for the answering machine to kick in and when she heard Will's voice she picked up the phone.

"Caroline, this is Will. How are you doing?"

"I'm doing better."

"Well, I just wanted to let you know that we think we know who's been making the calls to you. We won't know for sure until early next week."

"You do? Who do you think it is?" Caroline asked.

"David. We found a box full of cell phones in the storage area of his studio. We'll work with the phone company to confirm our suspicions."

"David?" Caroline's voice was in a whisper. "Why would he do that?"

"The best we can figure, he connected Walter and Annie with you and the quilt shop and he wanted to hurt everyone connected to Walter." The detective shrugged. " It makes only a bit of sense, but we may not learn the reason, beyond that."

"Thanks, Will, for telling me."

Caroline hung up the phone, then sat down at the table; she put her head on top of her arms. She was silently saying a grateful prayer that life might soon return to normal. Caroline lifted her head as Charles came through the back door. "Oh, Charles, I have so much to tell you."

Caroline went through all the details of David's arrest that afternoon, including how David had grabbed her and held a knife against her throat. Charles' face went white; he stood and started to pace. When Caroline told him how she jabbed her elbow in his stomach and pushed the hand with the knife away, Charles stopped pacing.

"Do you realize how dangerous that was?" Charles said.

"Charles, it's over. I'm all right. They arrested David, so he's behind bars. Will even thinks it might have been David making the phone calls; they'll know for sure early next week."

Charles hugged his wife. "It's been terrible not knowing how I could keep my family safe. I knew I would never give up trying, but I felt so helpless; and here you turn out to be Rambo again."

Caroline laughed. "Rambo-shambo." She kissed Charles and said, "You can't expect to be in four places at one time. Life happens."

⌘

Caroline let Nan and Janet Moeller run the shop over the weekend. She needed a few days off with her family. Budd was relieved to hear the threatening phone calls were over and that the caller was in jail. She was happy to resume her plans for summer work.

Otherwise, the weekend passed uneventfully, just the way Caroline wanted it. On Monday morning there was still yellow police tape across the door to the yoga studio. It sent chills down

Caroline's spine. She closed her eyes, took a deep breath and then opened the shop. The key turned without a hitch.

Nan came in with a thousand questions. Caroline answered all that she could, but some would never be answered.

⌘

The following day JT and Will informed Annie that David Williams had been arrested for Walter's murder and that all charges against her had been dropped.

"Why would David kill Walter?"

"Walter was his father. Walter was abusive to his second wife, Claudia, and when David got old enough he tried to fight back. After a particularly vicious beating, Claudia took David and fled. Time doesn't heal some things."

"We didn't find any stolen property reports on the jewelry and heirlooms in Walter's storage unit. They will go into his estate and you will inherit them," JT said.

"If Walter and I were truly married," Annie said. "I'm not sure I want any part of stolen property. I'd be haunted by the women he stole from."

"It has to go somewhere," Will said.

"What about what Walter stole from you," JT said.

"What Walter took from me can never be replaced." Annie's eyes looked distant and started to water.

"You were married. That's how David found Walter in the first place. He saw the marriage license on-line and followed Walter to Buckeye Grove as part of his plan to get even with his father. He hacked the system and removed the information out of spite. That's why you couldn't find it when you looked." JT took Annie's hand in his. Will patted her shoulder.

"David told you this?" Annie's eyes were wide.

"He did. It's all recorded in his statement and signed by him.

He said Claudia was the only mother he'd known and it was good to see her again after all this time. So, maybe something good has come out of all this. But, David . . . he'll be going away for a long time. Twenty years or more."

A weight had been lifted off Annie's shoulders. JT could see the muscles in her face relax. "I could drop the jewelry off tomorrow if you'd like."

"I guess that would be okay."

"Glad to help." JT smiled and the detectives started for the door.

"JT, I have one more question." Annie asked. "Do you have Claudia Miller's phone number?"

For the first time in a long time there was a hint of a smile on Annie's face.

⌘

Tuesday morning. Caroline was too busy getting ready for the Guild meeting to think about anything else. The table and chairs were all set up and ready. Sheryll Douglas arrived first. She had agreed to bring some refreshments, so she hurried up the stairs to set everything up before everyone else got there.

It wasn't long before the shop was filled with Caroline's friends and customers. Aggie called the meeting to order and quickly dispensed with the formalities so Annie and Caroline could fill everyone in on David's arrest. A loud cheer went up from the Guild members when they heard Annie had been cleared. Annie gave a little speech. "I appreciate your support, helping me through Walter's funeral and picketing the Police Station." Annie lifted her eyebrow and turned to look at Caroline and Olyria. "Chasing after strangers. But most of all I want to thank you for believing in me, never giving up on me. I am so fortunate to have such good friends."

"Why don't we celebrate with some treats?" Sheryll asked.

"I have an idea, too," Annie said. "I want each of you to buy ten yards of fabric on me. Walter had some money put away that I will inherit and I want to share it with my good friends." A cheer went up among the women and they snacked and shopped and shopped and snacked.

It took longer than usual for the group to break up. When everyone but Annie was gone, she approached Caroline. "That was very generous of you," Caroline said. "And it sure boosted my bottom line for the week."

"I'm glad," Annie said. "I talked to Claudia Miller about taking some of the money and she wants no part of Walter's ill-gotten gains. We decided to give a portion of the money to a battered woman's shelter here in town. Michael has agreed to sell the jewelry and heirlooms for me on eBay."

"What a good idea," Caroline said.

Annie blushed. Caroline's approval was embarrassing her. "There is one more thing," she said. She studied her hands before she spoke. "I want to set up a quilters' foundation with the money here at Always in Stitches. Each year I want the guild to fund a project that will allow quilting to make a difference in someone's life, the way it has in mine." Tears rolled down her cheeks. "I don't know what I'd have done without these women this year."

Caroline put an arm around Annie and the women stood among the bolts of fabric and the quilts for a long, long time before they closed down the shop and left for the day.